KNIGHTS, WITCHES, AND THE VANISHED CITY

A CALEC OF THE WOODS MYSTERY THRILLER - BOOK 4

R.M. SCHULTZ

SKY SEA AND SWORD PUBLISHING

DEDICATION

This one is for Matt.

And, as always, to those who still dare to read and tread the worlds of imagination.

1

Jaremonde paced along but ducked before continuing under the Blackened Bridge, the only route to Stake Square—the fabled area where a century ago the people of Valtera burned a witch.

The Rogue River murmured as it tumbled past Jaremonde, just beyond the edge of the walk. Its sleek body darkened under the bridge, appearing thicker and more akin to tar than water.

"We're going *under* the bridge, constable?" Rimmell, a late adolescent boy, tall and gangly, asked from behind. The sunlight seemed cold and distant where it lurked over his shoulder, the sky a matting of gray clouds that rode west on some heavenly wind. The lad appeared to have just woken from a nap, his eyelids hanging low, his voice groggy. "The square is above us."

Jaremonde dragged his first and middle fingers along his substantial mustache as he pursed his lips. "The echoes the witness described would've much more likely come from under the bridge than an open square."

Rimmell crept along behind him. "What do you think is causing it?"

"The deaths?" Jaremonde asked.

Rimmell nodded, his sandy hair flopping about his shoulders.

He tries hard but is too inexperienced and doesn't think enough. Hopefully someday he'll find his brains and rise to the task.

"If I knew that, we might have a better idea on what the curse actually is." Jaremonde patted his paunch as he scrutinized the dim walk beneath the bridge. No blood or drag marks. No signs of a confrontation or violence of any kind. But at this scene, he was expecting the aftermath of such an event.

"I can only picture a bunch of worms or little bugs of some kind burrowing into the victim. Or out of them. Given the size of the wounds."

Images of larvae crawling out of a person's skin made Jaremonde's stomach knot and cramp. He stopped and coughed, and the sound rattled around under the bridge and hollered back at him.

Insects burrowing out of a person? Where does this lad get his ideas?

"It just seems like something a witch would do for a curse." Rimmell's footfalls thudded on the path and echoed off of something ahead.

"Well, you're not here to think the same way as I do." Jaremonde lit a torch, and its red flames rose like unfurling wings. Light cast itself around the underside of the bridge, and the walls of volcanic rock hurled fiery reflections back at them. "I'm to teach you how to think about these things, but you wouldn't be much use if you only came up with the same ideas as me."

Rimmell nodded. He was handsome for a young man, although he needed to fill out, and if he ever had a choice to make between even two simple things, he always chose the worst option. Maybe someday he would be useful to Valtera, but not anytime in the next few years. And maybe, someday, he could become a man good enough for Jaremonde's daughter, Desi. God knew there weren't enough eligible suitors in Valtera.

Jaremonde crept farther under the bridge. The daylight slipping in from the far side of the short but wide bridge seemed as if it were on the other side of a cavern.

Something pale lay ahead.

Jaremonde hurried, jogging now, his chest starting to heave

for air. A human foot protruded from some alcove under the Stake Square side of the bridge. Jaremonde's heart trundled, and a sharp pain lit across the left side of his chest. He ignored the sensation, as it was not uncommon over the past few months, and he positioned himself so that he stood away from the protruding foot but could peer down the alcove. It ran at least twenty paces into the banks of city, the bridge its roof.

And there it was—a body.

A young woman's. Strewn across the slick surface of the blackened stones. Twisted. A hundred small holes gaping in her skin. Many small punctures the size of quill tips covered her hands and bare feet, and fewer but larger punctures continued up her arms and legs, corresponding to holes in her tunic and leggings. Each puncture was rimmed in red, and her body resided in a pool of blood, which was congealed and stiff like cooling wax.

A ring of blackened skin, like a rash, ran around the woman's wrist. The same as always. The scorch mark of the curse.

Rimmell gasped from behind Jaremonde's shoulder, and the harsh sound of his breathing stopped.

Whatever did this to the people of Valtera bled them like animals. So many wounds. No one could survive. It seemed to strike no one in particular, and it did so without warning.

It was the cursed witch's revenge on the city and its inhabitants in the decades following her death.

Jaremonde's focus was drawn to the glistening sheet of the rock wall beside him. A crystalline network of frost clung to portions of the wall, but his torch reflected off the deeper black surface. His round face and thick mustache seemed to be watching himself from inside the wall, as if he were buried in another world. The flames danced and cast half his face in light and half in shadow, his eyes buried in pools of darkness. The frost dripped as its skeletal-appearing branches melted away.

What do you think you're supposed to do to break a century-old curse? Jaremonde thought to his reflection. *Transform the city back to its previous wonder?*

Ever since that witch had been burned, a curse lingered over

Valtera. In legend, Valtera's streets and the walls of all its buildings were altered from lustrous green-tinged stone to the black shimmery surface of volcanic glass. A hauntingly beautiful city, but no longer the Emerald City of Valtera as it was once called.

Jaremonde had never known his city to hold as much beauty as it supposedly had with its greenish stones of legend, but the most significant part of the curse wasn't even the transformation of all the structures to the volcanic rock around him. The most significant effect was even more evident to every citizen of Valtera both day and night. So Jaremonde never questioned the validity of the rest of the tale.

The legend said the Emerald City of Valtera had been transformed from its gleaming beauty to darkness and deceit. Not only in the color of its stones. Images of beauty and splendor and kindness and honor had long been forgotten, now remembered only in paintings and in old tales.

And part of the curse was that no man or woman of the city, or even an outsider, would ever be able to break the spell. Stories of victims dying by being bled out through many holes in their skin had been part of the old myths, but those incidences had stopped many decades ago. Not until these past few months had more and more of these types of victims been found.

Rimmell knelt as he reached out for the young woman's body. He stuck out his little finger as if to test if the size of his finger was appropriate for the holes on the victim's arms.

Jaremonde shook his head as his eyelids fell shut like dropping portcullises.

The people of Valtera are doomed for eternity.

2

CALEC BRUSHED PAST THE NEEDLES OF A PINE, AND A RUN OF ICY water slipped under his collar. The slow and steady drip of the melt occurred all around him. He led Wyndstrom—his destrier from his days of knighthood—along as the steed's hooves crunched into the frost coating the underbrush.

A forest of crystal lay around them but was turning to water: frosted branches, rocks helmeted in caps of snow, brush encased in ice and shimmering like jade.

Winter was about to bury its ugly head before the coming of spring. Hopefully not too many more weeks to go. But something about the ice was beautiful. Teasingly beautiful. It was not always kind to live amidst, but it was serene to look at from a position beside a warm fire.

The camp of the people of the woods lay just ahead. Calec slipped under the last branches and entered a clearing where huts resembling hummocks dappled the area. Sunlight spilled over the grasses, and pockets of snow hid in the shadows within the deeper foliage.

Spears of icicles dangled from branches and needles and ringed the edge of the clearing, and their reflected sunlight seemed to blink when drips of water slid down their icy shafts. The fired water in Calec's waterskin seemed hotter now as it rested against his leg.

A deep itch rose somewhere in Calec's gut, a longing for the open road. He'd been living in these woods for nearly two years, and while he accepted them as his home, something called to him. Something primal, unexplainable. Probably something left over from his years as a knight when he'd traveled about. Or from his childhood when he was shuttled from Westingsheer to the woods to live part of his life with his sage father and part with his witch grandparents. Maybe he wasn't meant to live in only one place. Other than on his ventures to assist those in need, since leaving the knighthood, he'd lived all his days in these woods. And he hadn't been summoned elsewhere in several months.

An urge pulled at him and beseeched him to venture out, an ancient desire that tugged at his bones. But there were other more pressing matters weighing on his mind.

Serileen. Her mother.

Traveling any distance other than to Westingsheer would have to wait. And Calec shouldn't talk to Serileen about this new feeling of wishing to roam. She might believe he wasn't happy in the woods, with his choice to live here, or she might worry he wasn't happy with her. He'd have to keep this to himself. For now. Mayhap there was only something wrong with him because of how he was raised or because of how his father ran with the energy of a lunatic on a daily basis, completing study after study so he could shine the light of knowledge into this dark world.

Calec grunted and bit his lip. Those matters could wait.

He led Wyndstrom to the grasses outside the camp and then headed to the fire centered between all the huts. Black smoke wafted like dark feathers from the flames only to be torn away by the wolf wind—the icy wind that blew in winter and came barreling down out of the north.

Calec had just returned from Westingsheer, where he'd spoken with his sister. Their plan of obtaining castle records pertaining to past happenings was underway, but in the last few months, no documents had been delivered to Skoena for her supposed research. It almost seemed that if Calec or Skoena hoped to obtain anything, they'd have to locate and retrieve the documents themselves. But Calec or Serileen couldn't be the one to do it. That would arouse far too much suspicion from those in the castle, and the entire affair would be ended.

Skoena could be trusted with the work of digging through uncatalogued documents in some darkened archive where scrolls and parchments were piled high. But Skoena was already a busy woman.

Calec would have to be patient in confirming King Trithemore Simblade's alibi and his answers to Calec's questions pertaining to the day Serileen's mother was murdered. Calec was always impatient. Especially in matters of grievances and death. But he'd have to move on a bit, at least for now, and there were a few other people he'd like to share words with. Two of them lived alongside him and Serileen here in the woods.

Calec pulled his cloak tighter about him and clutched his heated water to warm his hands. Many witches and druids walked about the area, but Calec's attention was drawn to the druid Foram and the third-ranking priestess, Jirabelle. They moved in the distance and slipped past the smoke on the far side of the fire.

The druid who always supports Serileen and her opinions.

Was it a trick? To get on her good side? Foram, however, seemed to prefer Jirabelle's company, and Jirabelle did not conceal her animosity toward Serileen. Foram and Jirabelle seemed at odds in that regard but otherwise appeared to be good friends.

Calec followed the pair—the druid who wore a brown cloak and the witch in black.

Foram whispered something in Jirabelle's ear, and she laughed.

As Calec approached, Foram glanced in his direction. He said something to Jirabelle, who kept pacing away, but Foram stopped and greeted Calec with a smile.

"Calec, my friend." Foram bowed his head. "What news from Westingsheer?"

Calec studied him: a wild mane of blond hair, a similar

beard, dark eyes, tall and wiry. Calec searched the druid for signs of guilt or suspicion, but his hands didn't shake and nothing could be discerned beneath the joyful mask of his expression. Nor within the deep pits of his eyes.

"Only dealings from my old life," Calec said with a hint of a smile. "You know, speaking with my sister and old friends. Rubbing elbows with the king. That sort of thing."

Foram's smile faltered before it climbed back into position and lifted higher. "You jest."

Calec let a sincere laugh escape his lips. Foram was always such a kind man whenever Calec dealt with him that Calec had a hard time picturing him as a murderer. But with the possibility dangling over Foram's head, Calec would have to put any personal assumptions aside and never allow himself to grow too close to the druid. All the suspects would have to be investigated in a similar manner. No allowances for those who seemed trustful. Then, if Foram was cleared of any wrongdoing, maybe Calec would befriend him. But only then. And until then, Calec often tried to make his responses to Foram unexpected in hopes that Foram would be surprised and let slip anything he potentially knew about Merindal's murder.

"I'm always just so wary of that place," Foram said. "After the events of the winter plague."

Calec peered over the druid's shoulder to keep an eye on Jirabelle, who glanced back at them but was hurrying away into the woods.

"Can I help you with anything?" Foram asked as he followed Calec's line of sight, and his posture stiffened.

"I was hoping to speak with Jirabelle." Calec wasn't sure if he'd wanted to speak to Foram or Jirabelle, but with the way the witch was avoiding him, she piqued his interest. "I wanted to ask her something."

Foram placed a hand on Calec's chest to stop him from following her. The druid shook his head.

"Why does she avoid me?" Calec asked.

"We both know Serileen and Jirabelle are not on the best of terms. Both being just behind the High Priestess of the Mother.

And with Serileen's surprising rise in power just a few years ago. Both are my friends, but Jirabelle worries that you are already poisoned against her. She fears speaking with you alone or creating any more animosity between Serileen and herself. We have enough problems to deal with in this world already."

Calec nodded as if he understood or agreed. "But I must speak with her about something, soon. It pertains to the well-being of the people of the woods. Mayhap *you* can ask her to meet me."

Foram nodded regretfully. "Jirabelle has shared her worries with me over such a meeting, but if you request it, I will ask. I do not know if a priestess will follow the lowly advice of a druid of the woods, but I will try to persuade her."

Calec forced a friendly smile and clapped Foram on the arm. "In all my musings and hunting for magic and killers under this new sky sea, the biggest mystery to me is still the ways of women."

Foram laughed, and his dark eyes became buried under the squint from his rising cheeks. "Too true, my friend. Too true."

"Join me for a drink this eve to celebrate my return. We can discuss our woes."

Foram nodded, but something—perhaps regret—lingered in his expression.

3

CALEC SAT ON A LOG PLACED AROUND THE FIRE IN THE CENTER OF camp. Orange flames licked at the darkening sky. Many druids and witches sat on logs around him, dining on fired nuts and roots or strips of gamey venison. Most were lost in conversation.

Shep, the black dog with the white nose and stripe between his eyes, lay at Calec's feet, content with gnawing on a bone.

Calec patted Shep and sipped dark wine, its earthly liquid clinging to his palate and rolling like a thick wave down his throat. He'd been unable to find Serileen, but that was not uncommon. She had much to do as the second-ranking priestess. Her work for the Mother helped guide the strands of fate and helped all of the Mother's children prosper. So many in the outer world worked against this, and Serileen was rarely not burdened by her tasks. He would see her when she was available and allowed for it.

Foram passed on Calec's left, conversing with other druids and laughing as he chewed on stringy remnants adhered to a deer femur. Foram noticed Calec watching him, and the druid nodded in his direction.

Calec lifted his horn of wine in a salute and to remind Foram of his promise to join him. Foram's smile faded, but he turned back to his companions and spoke to them for several minutes.

Calec waited, as if he were patient.

Foram eventually glanced at him again, tossed the bone into the blazing fire, and stumbled over and sat beside him.

"An earthy wine this evening." Foram drank heavily.

"And as thick as sap." Calec sipped at his.

"You are not with your mate?"

Calec shook his head. "Haven't seen her since my return."

"Ah. Such is the life with a priestess. They are never truly ours or any one man's. It is the way of the Mother. And they always have to perform her work. If you ask me, it is much easier to assist the priestesses, offer protection for our people, and provide for our meals."

"Thank the Mother for that. Although I am not the best at providing from the woods. Still trying to reach your level of proficiency." Calec laughed and smacked Foram on the back. "A childhood in the city has made me less useful for such things."

Foram smiled. "But better at protecting our woods and for diplomatic relations with the people of Duminborne. The people of the woods would not still live here if you'd not joined us. You have earned your place here, brother."

A warmth flowed out of Calec's core. Was this man only trying to manipulate him? Using compliments like he did with Serileen ... Or was he genuine?

"I will not stop trying, but my dealings with Westingsheer and the king are not always fortuitous," Calec said. "And the growing sky sea seems to be bringing too much dark magic along with it."

Foram gazed into the heavens at the largest moon that floated as a waning gibbous against the horizon. Then he seemed to take in the increasing number of smaller moons around the largest and the others that speckled the night sky. The moon with the markings that appeared like a demon's twisted face with scratch marks beneath it drew Calec's attention. Demon's Coin was how they referred to that moon now. Ominous.

"Is it true, then?" Foram asked. "That these returning moons have some power to hold water in the sky?"

Calec nodded. "My father called it gravity. The same force

that pulls us to the earth. The moons hold such power, if it is not a form of ancient magic. Not only can the moons draw the tides of the seas, they can also summon tides to the sky. In greater numbers, these moons can supposedly hold solid bodies of water up there rather than only the mists of clouds."

Foram shook his head. "It is such a wonder. The magic the Mother has bestowed upon this world. And yet people only speak of the darkest forms of magic returning with the coming of the second sky sea."

Calec sat in thought for a moment. "I've seen some of that magic. More than I could ever explain with reason."

"And you have truly discovered wielders of such magic and have imprisoned them?"

Calec nodded. "A couple. But there is at least one other who is free and still draws my interest."

"Oh? And who is this mage and where do they reside?"

"Here. In the woods."

Foram studied Calec.

"Their magic is displayed with the death of a witch every few years." Calec watched for any sign of nervousness or apprehension in Foram. "It struck the former high priestess a couple decades ago."

Foram's head drooped as he studied the ground. This druid had been at the scene of Serileen's mother's murder, or at least he'd been watching from a tree, per what Serileen shared with Calec. Jirabelle, on the other hand, had actually stood beside the high priestess in the sacred circle of trees when that secret meeting with the king was about to occur. But supposedly the king had grown nervous because people caught wind of the meeting, and so he only sent a knight in his stead. Several others showed up as well. The necromancer of their woods, who was angry and claimed the king and the high priestess could not discuss the fate of the woods without him. There was also a master hunter who claimed the woods belonged to the people living in the country of Duminborne. Also, a strange merchant who allegedly only stumbled upon this meeting while seeking to sell items to the people of the woods. But the events around his appearance and disappearance left many questions.

"If what you say about magic is true, then we already have other evils plaguing us," Foram said, breaking Calec's reverie. "If the murders you speak of are not randomly committed by the people of the city out of hate and fear."

Calec sipped at his wine. "And so you know nothing of these matters?"

Foram ran a hand through his beard. "No details. Only that our people are being killed like they've been for all the years since others settled and built the city of Westingsheer."

"You've seen nothing on the days of such incidences?"

Foram looked up into Calec's eyes and didn't blink. "No. I only hear about them after the fact."

"And what did you see that day the high priestess died?" Serileen had seen Foram jump out of a tree and run from the sacred circle just before she found her mother's body. Foram supposedly shouted as if with victory and then yelled something along the lines of never being betrayed again.

"Serileen has asked me about this many, many times already. The last I saw of Merindal, she was speaking with the merchant. Jirabelle was still with her."

"And what were you shouting about when you jumped from the tree and fled the area of the meeting?"

Foram wrinkled his brow. "I hardly remember it now, but I seem to recall thinking the king and his knight had fled and that the woods would be ours forever. I was a naïve adolescent at the time."

A long minute passed between them as Calec studied the druid and waited for the awkward silence to tempt him into saying more.

A woman emerged from the shadows around the fire and appeared in the rim of light. Tall and slender. Dark hair and eyes. The faded blue of a crescent moon tattoo on her forehead. Serileen.

Calec's heart leapt, and Shep's tailed thumped against the ground. Serileen strolled past those lounging around the fire, her eyes settling on Calec's. A deep intensity burned inside hers, and she cast him a smirk. Something deeper bubbled inside Calec. That was the look she could cast his way and make his blood run hot with desire. And it'd been several days since he'd seen her.

But she didn't wander any closer. She meandered over to a table and picked through the fired roots and herbs. Her hand came to rest on her abdomen, and a little bulge seemed apparent there. Something that'd never been there before.

Calec's heart stampeded inside his chest, throbbing against his ribs. Was it true? A pregnancy? Something they'd been attempting for months now. He and Serileen had both decided they shouldn't wait to find the killer of their people before trying for a child. They might never find this person. Or it could take them several years. But the thought of a daughter or son growing inside her and in a few short months crawling around the woods with a killer made Calec's chest heave. During his last venture to Hillsvale, he'd worried about children every day. About his dream of the Horseman watching mothers consume the fresh grave soil of their buried young. His blood seethed, and he realized he was playing with a yellow ribbon, running it between his fingers. A little girl's from Hillsvale.

He would have to try harder to find whatever killer lurked in or around their woods. Work faster. He'd push Skoena, hunt out Jirabelle—

"Calec," Foram said as if he'd been saying it several times. Calec glanced at him. "Jirabelle agreed to meet with you, but she thought you'd probably wish to speak to her alone. And she didn't want that conversation to happen in camp. She'll be out by the Everbrook. Just before dawn."

Calec nodded and glanced back to Serileen, ignoring a warning of suspicion rising in the back of his mind. Maybe he was jumping to conclusions with Serileen's pregnancy. He didn't even know if it was true. Maybe she'd already eaten a large meal and that was all. He forced a slow and calming breath.

"Thank you." Calec stood. "Excuse me, if you will. I must have a word with Serileen."

4

CALEC HEAVED FOR BREATH AND ROLLED OFF OF SERILEEN AND onto his back, his chest bare. He stared at the ceiling of their hut where dark shadows danced against firelight. Shep slept near the doorway.

Serileen turned to him and ran a hand down his chest. "You missed me?"

Calec nodded and swallowed. "You make it hard not to miss you."

She grinned as she pressed her breasts up against his shoulder. "There's something you should know."

Calec's heart seemed to catch in his throat, and it felt as if the cords in his neck constricted around the beating organ. She'd been acting strange ever since Hillsvale. Depressed. But she would never tell him why, and he'd waited patiently, never pushing her or forcing her. When he'd done that in the past, it usually just drove her further away from him in such emotional matters.

"Are you listening?" Serileen asked.

"Of course. I'm only waiting to hear what it is I should know."

"I ... went to visit the necromancer in our woods."

Calec's heart chilled and slid back into his chest.

"I wished to discover what he truly knew about my mother's

murder," Serileen said. "To test his knowledge against something I knew but that he shouldn't have."

"You went without me?" Calec's blood began to seethe with heat. "After you told me to never travel there alone? After Hillsvale?"

Serileen pulled away. "I knew you'd be upset."

"Of course I am. You put your life in danger, our"—well, maybe they didn't have a child yet—"your life. You should have at least asked me to come with you."

"You were in Westingsheer. And I asked another priestess to wait for me."

"I was trying to look into the king's alibi! Your visit could have waited until I returned."

Serileen sighed. "But this necromancer wouldn't have been forthcoming if you were there. I know, after speaking with him prior."

"Who is the necromancer in our woods? Is it the Brenson we met in Landing?"

Serileen fell silent. If Calec's anger ever got the better of him in their conversations, that was how she typically reacted. Not speaking. So then he'd never get anywhere with her.

"And did you learn if he is lying or actually speaking with the dead through flame and some arcane means?" Calec asked.

"It is still debatable. But he definitely knows more than he should."

"He's using you." Calec sat up and started pulling on his leathers. "Using the weakness he's found in you, and he's feeding you false information to entice you into coming back for more. So he can use you further, for whatever purpose or plan he has."

"Are you only worried about him wishing to bed me?"

The rising heat in Calec's chest climbed up his neck. So, if she was pregnant, it might not even be his child. Such was the way of the priestesses. They were encouraged not to limit themselves to one man.

"Or he murdered your mother and knows exactly what happened," Calec said.

"You accepted everything when wishing to be my mate," Serileen said. "You knew it could end at any time, or there could be other men, if the Mother desired it. Priestesses are supposed to procreate and birth strong daughters for future generations."

Calec gritted his teeth and pulled his tunic over his head. He knew it, but he'd thought it would be different. Brenson was a hulking brute of a man, more likened to a barbarian than a necromancer. Dangerous but handsome, and the thought of him made Calec want to crush the man's throat with his bare hands. That man also wielded some form of the dark arts, if not something of pure evil.

"I worry about your safety," Calec said.

"I can take care of myself. And that's why I do not wish to discuss everything with you," Serileen said. "You are my mate, not Brenson."

"So he *is* the one who lives in our woods? Who followed us or found you all the way in Landing? Who you found that night in Hillsvale?"

Serileen shrugged.

"What does he claim to want?" Calec asked.

"He's said he will help me determine who killed my mother by speaking with the dead, as he desires to bed me and get me with child."

"So he wants you and your child for his purposes. And you go to him in the woods without me."

"To discover what really happened to Merindal. To avenge my mother and release her soul from the sky sea."

The anger inside Calec writhed against her attempt to reason with him.

Serileen scooted away and sat against the far wall. "The ancient tales of our people from the time of the first sky sea say that those who are murdered, their souls are harbored in the heavenly waters and are tormented by the Horseman until they are avenged."

"And I'm doing all I can to prove who we should take our vengeance out on." Calec ducked as he approached the doorway.

"Where are you going this late at night?"

"Out to learn what happened to your mother all those years ago."

Calec stepped over Shep, who rose to follow him, but Calec commanded the dog to stay this time. Calec then slipped out into the night and disappeared in its shadows.

5

Desi dipped her pail in the Rogue River as she took in the countryside. Mountains rose in jagged peaks to the north. Cliffs whitened by snow and ice. The plains lay to the south. Snow-laden foothills to the east and west.

It was beautiful here, if not utterly cold today, but she never knew what the surrounding country would look like on any given day. Not as a resident of what some still referred to as the Emerald City of Valtera, although there was nothing emerald to be seen besides the pines in the mountains.

She sighed and brushed her long brown hair behind her ears. There was no escaping this city *or* its people.

Her father, Jaremonde, the constable, tried to keep the people safe, but the curse on Valtera had shifted. People were dying. Supposedly in a way that'd only been described many decades ago. Their changing scenery was no longer the worst of their curse.

"You all right?" Kirstel, her friend, asked from beside her.

Kirstel set one bucket on the black rock walkway and filled another. Her red hair streamed in the wind keening down from the mountains. The gust shoved her dress against her curves and large hips.

"Yes," Desi said. "Just thinking."

"About how to leave Valtera and make a life of your own? Or about those who have been struck dead?"

Desi released a wry laugh. "Same as usual. What I'm typically thinking when I'm quiet. Just wondering what a normal life would be like somewhere else."

"Oh, it wouldn't be much different, Desi. You'd just be filling buckets for your father or mother or husband somewhere else."

"At least maybe I'd find someone worth spending my life with."

"And you don't think Aonor is suitable?"

Desi rolled her eyes. "I'd prefer to never wed and become an old spinster rather than marry him."

"You'd become like the old witch from the manor?" Kirstel's eyes gaped.

Desi laughed, this time with amusement. "Well, without the witch's descendant part."

"But with Aonor you wouldn't have to fetch buckets of water. You'd have others do all the hard work for you. He's the master of collections. Just think of that." Kirstel wiped at her forehead. "It'd beat all the toiling a woman has to do in Valtera these days. And you'd probably be safe inside his estate. I would at least consider becoming his lady if he asked."

"What's the value of personal possessions in the emerald city? It's not even an emerald city. Every stone here's as black as night. It's all a lie."

"He has the final say in who inherits a chateau after the current residents pass on or have a hard turn of luck. If you were with him, you could probably get a bigger share of the food stores as well. Dresses. Almost anything a typical person in a normal city would want."

Desi hefted two buckets and paced away in the direction of her house. Kirstel followed.

"It just doesn't seem like it matters here," Desi said. "Nothing ever changes. People still die."

"Except our surroundings change." Kirstel's breath came in quick gasps from exertion. "I bet people in normal cities wish to escape the boring settings beyond their walls. And I'm sure people die there too. We are blessed ... in a way."

"Blessed because we're cursed?"

Kirstel grunted under her load. "Might as well accept it at some point. Before you get too much older. No man or woman of Valtera or beyond can break the witch's curse. And no one questions that part of the legend."

Desi walked on in silence.

"And what about Rimmell?" Kirstel asked.

"My father's helper?"

"Of course. You think he's dull?"

Desi shook her head. "He seems polite and kind enough. And he wishes to be a constable. Father just says he's a bit ... thick. But he has hope for Rimmell if Rimmell can leave his adolescence behind and learn to think a bit. He's just—"

"Ladies." A tall and pale man stepped into the road before them, removed a feathered cap, and bowed low. Aonor, the master of collections and the scribe of Valtera. Probably three decades older than either Desi or Kirstel. He logged all the important records for the city and, through others, tracked what tasks the Valterians were performing each day while making sure everyone did their part. He coughed softly.

"Hello," Kirstel said. "We were just talking about you."

Desi shot her an evil look, hoping she'd stay quiet.

"Oh, really?" Aonor dusted off some unseen dirt from his stark white tunic laced with gold trim. "I came to have a word with Desi."

Aonor beamed as if the flattery of his attention should be craved and met with overwhelming astonishment and joy. Then he fell into a fit of soft coughing.

Desi smiled politely. "I have work to do, but I am flattered."

"Still no answer for me, then?" Aonor asked. "About my offer?"

Kirstel cast Desi a teasing smirk.

"My father has not accepted any marriage proposals for me at this time," Desi said. "I am flattered, but I am still too young to tie myself down."

"Ah, so you wish to enjoy the courting of many suitors?" Aonor asked. "I understand young women completely. But do not think I will allow any of these other suitors, no matter how much younger, to outdo me. I have my ways."

Aonor winked, and a purse at his hip jingled rather loudly. Then he bowed again. "Do think on it, Desi. You could be a lady —no, *the* lady of the manor. And I will not give up."

Desi forced a polite smile. "I hope you don't, Aonor, but I must decline for the time being."

Aonor nodded and passed by Desi as he departed, disdainfully eyeing the buckets they carried. A sweet floral scent sheeted off him and clung to the air, making Desi stifle a grimace.

After he was gone, Desi hefted her buckets and walked as fast as she could. Kirstel followed.

"Oh, Lady Desi," Kirstel said in a mocking tone and bellowed with laughter. "You could become *my* lady if you'd take my old cock anytime I want you to."

"Stop!" Desi grimaced, and some revulsion turned in her gut. They walked in silence.

Half an hour later, Desi approached her house, the small abode of Jaremonde the constable. Black volcanic glass for walls like everything else in Valtera.

"I'll come find you after supper." Kirstel waved and entered her house next door.

"Desi!" Jaremonde came hurrying up the street, his mustache wrinkling up against one cheek, something he did when anxious. Rimmell and a few other men followed him. "I've been looking all over for you."

Desi dropped the buckets, and water splashed over her ankles. "I just went to the river. What happened?"

"Lanigrad"—Jaremonde gestured to a tall and fit man beside him, maybe a man in his fortieth season or so—"has maps from the citadel. I need assistance with this curse, or all of Valtera will succumb to either death or the fear of it."

"And what do you want me for?" Desi almost gasped. Her

father always shielded her from everything. But maybe the greatest danger now lurked inside Valtera, and she was already there.

"We need someone to visit the emerald city and fall so in love with it they may never want to leave."

6

CALEC HAD SLEPT LITTLE BESIDE THE FIRE AT CAMP, AND NOW HE crept through the woods as quietly as he could, using the light of the many moons to guide him. But for some reason, the light of the smaller Demon's Coin moon seemed the brightest and highlighted his path.

Anger still chewed at his insides like a nest of disturbed ants. He'd speak with Serileen maybe tomorrow or the next day, but he did not want to see her again this night, or morning. Dawn was not too far off. If she'd put her life in jeopardy with the potential murderer of her mother, Calec had every right to be upset with her. Even if she could only learn what she wanted without Calec present. It was just too dangerous. If she didn't want to take Calec, then at least take a few other witches with her. And a druid or three. Not just one witch who was somewhere in the vicinity and would only realize something had happened if Serileen was already dead.

The weltering of a brook sounded in the distance. A nighthawk swooped past. Somewhere, an owl hooted, and something howled.

Would Jirabelle really meet with him out here? Before dawn?

Calec paused. Was he doing exactly what he was angry with Serileen for doing? No. At least this was not as perilous. Jirabelle was one of their own. A suspect, but not nearly as dangerous as a necromancer deep in the woods.

Calec stepped out from the pines into a splash of moonlight. A hard-packed road ran through the woods here, leading up to Jaylen's Pass—the route of many merchants and travelers and their carts to and from Westingsheer. The Everbrook flowed beyond the tree line on the far side of the road.

Shadows stole out of the trees and wrapped around the margins of the road in both directions.

If Jirabelle, or Foram for that matter, or both were involved in the murders of the people of the woods, would they be setting a trap for Calec? Jirabelle might have wanted to get rid of Merindal twenty and one years ago so she could become the high priestess, but at that time, Jirabelle would have only been a young woman. Maybe she'd harbored some lingering adolescent angst or even rage, but Merindal's death did not see Jirabelle into the position of high priestess. Foram, on the other hand, was probably almost a decade younger than Jirabelle. What would his motive be?

Calec passed over the road and into the trees before coming upon the Everbrook—a stream that spoke through its turbulent flow created by many rocks. No one was waiting for him here. Not yet. He turned northeast. He had time to search the area and make sure Jirabelle wasn't preparing some trap. As he hiked along the banks for nearly half a league, he occasionally heard hoofbeats and voices, even shouting, coming from the road. It was atypical but not unheard of for men to travel before dawn, and those men would only be merchants or travelers passing through. The people of the woods never created such commotion on the roadway, and they seldom used that route. The noises also could not be from Jirabelle, if she was alone. And no one yelled for help, and it did not sound like anyone was in danger. Just the noisy passing of people not from the woods.

Calec kept his senses sharp as he moved, feeling for any presence around him or stalking him. Branches and brush cracked in the distance, but he attributed that to animals, as nothing drew closer.

He turned about and followed the brook southwest as sunlight bloomed in the east, retracing his path and continuing farther along in hopes of finding Jirabelle.

Jirabelle is late. Or she's not planning on meeting me. And so she moves up higher on my list of suspects.

Calec continued trekking for another half league before turning around again and returning to where he initially arrived at the Everbrook. Here, he sat. It was the location that any person of the woods would choose as a good spot to meet—directly east of their current camp.

The distant noise of travelers continued.

There are not usually this many travelers in a day, much less continuously for hours.

The sun climbed into the sky as the morning grew late.

The voices amplified, and Calec returned to the roadway, picking his way through the brush without making a sound. While remaining hidden in the tree line beside the road, he paused and glanced about.

Something cracked in the woods to his right near the roadway.

His hand found the hilt of his sword as he turned to face it.

A young woman limped out from the shadows, and forest-filtered sunlight bathed her face. Long brown hair stirred in a soft breath of the wolf wind. A look of fear was etched upon beautiful features.

"Lady?" Calec asked as he stepped out into the road.

She turned to flee.

"Wait," Calec said. "Are you hurt?"

She ran, following the road up toward the pass.

This wasn't Jirabelle or any woman of the woods, given her garb, but she appeared panic-stricken. In need of aid.

Calec paced after the fleeing woman, keeping his steps controlled so he would not frighten her further.

She darted to her right and disappeared into the trees and shadows off to the side of the road.

"Lady, I can help you." Calec kept a hand on his sword hilt as he advanced. "Why are you alone in the woods?"

A woman screamed, but the sound was quickly muffled.

Calec ran for the area where she'd passed into the trees.

In a pool of shadow created by the boughs overhead, a few figures surrounded the woman. These men appeared different from any men Calec had ever seen in his life. Not in size or shape, but they wore tunics of strange cuts and colors—oranges or reds decorated with blue or purple symbols—trousers rather than leggings. And they all wore caps on their heads. One laughed as he stepped up to the woman from behind and wrapped his arms around her.

"Stop!" Calec shouted as he drew his sword and approached.

The men paused as they looked in Calec's direction.

One pulled a jagged dagger from his belt and placed its blade against the woman's throat. He sneered, his crooked teeth flashing in a shaft of sunlight. The woman struggled against the other man's grip.

"Drop your sword." A third man pulled a knife and jabbed it against the woman's side. She screamed, but he covered her mouth. "Drop it, or I will open her belly and let her organs splatter on the ground."

Calec's blood ran hot with frustration and anger. He hesitated.

Should he drop his sword and face three brigands unarmed or let them kill a woman?

"Now!" The man holding the knife to the woman's throat pressed the blade just into her skin.

The woman thrashed, and she released a shriek that was muffled by a hand.

"Don't kill her." Calec crouched and slowly set his sword on the forest floor. "You can let her go and run. I will not follow you. But if you kill her or me, the people of the woods will track you down. All of you. They are witches, and they will do much worse than curse you."

One of the men laughed. "Always wanted to meet a witch."

"You'll wish you hadn't," Calec said.

"Move away from your sword." The man holding his knife to the woman's ribs motioned for Calec to step back toward the road. "Once you get back there a ways, we'll leave the woman and go. But not any sooner. You best be quick. And do *not* follow us."

Calec stepped backward once and then again. The overhanging branches and needles pressed against his left ear. A column of yellow sunlight seeped through the boughs and blinded him for a moment.

"Keep going!" the man said.

Calec took another step.

A rush of air and something else disturbed his sense of the surrounding woods, arising from within the trees behind him. He spun about as something whistled, and a hard object smacked into his head.

His vision flashed white. Then a black curtain dropped over everything.

7

THE FEELING OF A HORSE'S FLANKS MOVED BENEATH CALEC'S chest and waist, and the two-beat clopping of hooves sounded on packed dirt.

A steady, league-eating trot.

But everything was still veiled in darkness; something covered Calec's head and face. Heavy pressure and pain radiated from somewhere along the back of his head.

His hands were bound. So were his feet. He was a captive of some brigands. The horse beneath him reeked of sweat, although the air around him was so cold.

His abductors had likely taken his sword and knife, but what had they done with the young woman? And were they working for Foram or Jirabelle? The timing of their arrival seemed more than coincidental.

Calec worked his hands and wrists against his bonds, as well as his feet, but they were tied well and tight. The cords only bit into his skin.

"He's moving back there," a man said.

Calec froze.

"At least we know your sling and rock didn't crush his skull," another voice said.

"He's a trained knight, and he had a sword and dagger," a

third male voice said. "There was no convincing to be had. I'd rather make his brain into soup then have to fight him."

"We should keep moving. Or we won't make it."

"We're not going to make it anyway. It took too long to find him, and the city is still too far away."

"Then our only hope is to stop and try to reason with him," a woman said.

The horses continued at their jouncing trot.

Muffled whispering followed, or at least the voices became lost in the noise of hoofbeats.

"This is a bad idea," a man said. "We'll all have crows plucking out our eyeballs before the night falls."

The horse Calec was slung over stopped, and its heaving breath rumbled through its nostrils. Someone pulled Calec from its back, and his feet met the ground as he was steadied. A bag was torn from his head.

Calec's vision focused, seeming unaffected by the dull pounding at the back of his skull. The several men he'd encountered stood around him. As well as the woman who'd stumbled out of the trees. She was not their victim; she was one of them.

Daylight was already fading in the west. He'd been out for several hours, given these were the short days of winter in the north. A vast plain of grasses waved under the chill breath of the wolf wind. And long shadows stole out of the grasses like crooked fingers and crept over the land.

"We're in the far country," Calec said. "Beyond Jaylen's Pass."

The strange appearance of these men struck Calec again. The styling of their hair was reminiscent of age-old drawings. And the caps they all wore ... as if they'd stepped out of some artwork in the old books. How people dressed centuries ago. People from a past age. And yet they seemed solid and real.

"Listen to my plea, witch hunter." The young woman stepped up to him and took his bound hands. Her hair swirled in the wind. "My name is Desi. I apologize for what we had to do, but we need your assistance."

Her eyes beseeched him, an unspoken plea aroused by fear or some other similar emotion. Eyes as pale blue as the sky sea or glacial ice. Eyes so deep and filled with emotion they appeared to bare her soul.

"You've a strange way of going about seeking help." Calec pulled his hands back. "And may I ask you what you abducted me for?"

"This was a terrible idea," one of the men said, a man with long hair, narrow across the shoulders but thick of waist. "We're running out of time. Worms will be mining their way through our livers when he's done with us."

"We need your help." Desi grabbed Calec's forearms, her fingers milky and cold. She was young, probably a little too young for Calec to consider her beautiful, but she might be nonetheless. "Our city is in dire need of removing its curse. We"—she waved to indicate all the men around her—"live with this each day. And people are dying again. We cannot stop it. We've all lost someone. The men here, Lanigrad, Climson, and—"

"Did Jirabelle or Foram hire you?" Calec shook her hands off him again.

"Please." A fire of desperation burned in Desi's ice-like eyes. "I do not know of whom you speak. We've only heard rumor of your deeds in Duminborne, and we'd never been so close before. Never close enough to travel there and back in a day."

And why would you need to travel the distance in one day's time? "And so you trick me and ambush me?"

"I told you," the narrow-shouldered man said as he flung his arms out in a gesture of disgust. "We need to gallop the horses the rest of the way. Let's try to make him part of the emerald city before it's too late."

"It's already too late." A tall and svelte man pointed to the last of the reddish twilight splashed across the western sky. "We're nearly out of time, and the city is at least a league away."

"Then we definitely don't have the time to try to convince him." The narrow-shouldered man wrapped his arms around Calec and heaved him up, placing him across the back of a horse.

Calec's head dangled against the steed's sweaty flank.

"But we could kill our horses if we run them any longer," the same man said. "Their hearts will explode inside their chests."

"Damn it. Stop the morbid comments. And that myth isn't true."

"If we had found him quicker then we wouldn't be in this situation."

"We always knew we'd be in this situation."

"Our only chance is to persuade him to find us," Desi said.

Further arguing from the men followed, punctuated by short outbursts from Desi.

Then they fell silent.

Everything remained quiet. Only a ghostly howl from the wolf wind carried on, shuttling an icy chill from the north and knifing through Calec's leathers and cloak.

Calec waited another few minutes. Then he glanced up. Then around. The plains appeared ghostly now under the silvery light of the moons. The men were gone. So was the woman.

He wriggled back down from the horse and landed on his feet, but because his ankles were bound over each other, he lost his balance. He fell onto his backside.

Only he and the one horse stood amid the plains that were brightening under the light of the many moons. The grasses whipped and waved under gusts. Shadowed crags of mountains loomed in the north, the range appearing vengeful and stead-fast, like an army of giants with spiked helms of white snow and ice that brushes the heavens.

An icy grip of fear clutched at Calec's heart. He scooted back and glanced around. Those people still had to be here somewhere.

But the plains lay as empty and sullen as the forbidden lands.

They must be hiding in the grass. But where are their horses?

Over a matter of several minutes, Calec wormed his way through the grasses and over to where they'd been conversing. He didn't see or hear anyone. No one hiding beneath the waving blades of foliage. No holes.

He thrashed through the grass and brush as best he could with his bound hands.

His fingers settled on something hard and cold. His knife. A minute later he found his sword. As if they'd been dropped or discarded where those people stood.

But there were no people or other horses for as far as he could see.

8

Calec cut through the bonds around his ankles with his knife, his hands now free. The cords snapped under pressure and fell into the grass.

Calec clambered to his feet. The bay gelding they'd thrown him over shivered as it dripped with sweat. Its nostrils flared, and its misty breath plumed out into the air. The steed hadn't been cooled down properly, and the wind was so cold. Calec took its reins and led it around, encouraging it to move, although it resisted as its ribs heaved.

"Why only you?" Calec asked as he patted the horse's neck. "Where did the men and the woman go? And their horses?"

The wolf wind tore at Calec's hair and shoved the grasses flat all around him. The gelding's ears swiveled around, listening for danger.

"Why would they leave you?"

"I was too exhausted to keep up with the others," Calec said in a winded voice, speaking for the gelding as he walked it westward. Hopefully Calec could find Jaylen's Pass if he continued in that direction.

"But weren't all the horses just as exhausted as you?"

"Then, perhaps I was left for you."

"But why?" Calec asked.

"So you wouldn't die out here in the far country. So you could ride back."

Calec rubbed at the lump on the back of his skull. Sharp pain lanced across his scalp.

"And why would they care about my wellbeing after hurling a rock at my head and abducting me?" Calec asked. Memories of Desi's blue eyes burning with some need, with entreaty, imploring Calec for aid, bored into his thoughts. "And you have no saddle. I was slung over you, still bound when they left, my sword and knife not given to me. And why would they just leave me here after all the effort of abducting me?"

Calec glanced back at the empty, moonlit plains and shook his head.

"Because they ran out of time and daylight," the horse said. "And they needed to be somewhere and took too long finding you."

"Yes, that's what they claimed, but I was still their captive. Surely, they didn't believe I'd turn into a witch at nightfall or that they'd travel so much faster on their exhausted horses without me in tow."

"Who understands the ways of men?" the horse seemed to say.

"Perhaps it was all a trick. To lure me to some emerald city. But they knew they didn't have time, and then they were all gone. Like ... thieves in the night. But if they left you for me, they might have cared enough to make sure I wasn't stranded out in the far country."

The gelding plodded along beside him, the horse's body steaming over the sweaty regions on his flank and neck.

"You know something, but you won't say it." Calec rubbed those steaming areas down with a gloved hand.

"It is the curse," the horse seemed to reply. "The curse of the emerald city."

They walked on in silence as the wolf wind tormented Calec's hair and the horse's mane and tail. Calec pulled his cloak tightly about him and trudged on. After half an hour, the gelding's breathing steadied, and its sweat dried as white crusts in its hair. Calec climbed onto the horse bareback, and they rode west into the deepening night.

Calec hummed, trying to find the ancient dream track of this land within himself. To guide them home.

9

ULMA TUCKED AWAY A KNITTED SCARF AND HER NEEDLES AND hobbled outside her house into the twilight. She turned and checked her door to make sure it was fully latched and locked so no one would be able to sneak in there and curse her place while she was gone.

The black stones of her house gleamed in the sunlight. When she was a young girl, her mother used to speak of the emerald stones of the city. Of the road to Valtera and the towering falls and the mountains as its backdrop. No living person had seen the emerald city of Valtera in its previous grandeur, but Ulma came close to living during that time period. Closer than any other person in the city.

She turned and stumped away, her wooden shoes clattering on the black street. Walking cleared her mind of a clutter of fog that seemed to gather and grow as she aged. Her knitting kept her mind busy and her hands as agile as could be expected at nearly a century old, but she still enjoyed her walks every morning and evening. It was what kept her alive for so long. And she walked at a pace faster than that of many younger people. A swift gait is how she liked to think of it. As if she had somewhere to be and was in a hurry. It got her heart going and her breath rasping. It made her feel good. Like she still had something to live for.

It was the time she felt most alive ... at least in these days. Telling stories used to be her passion, what others sought her out for, but no one cared for her tales anymore. People got their stories secondhand now from those she'd already told her stories to. The younger storytellers spun the tales in a much shorter time. It seemed to be what even the people of Valtera wanted these days. They also twisted her stories, pumped them full of action and fighting and heroes whose might could not be rivaled. Some turned the facts around, made them more appealing to the younger generations. And so Ulma and what she'd best been known for were long forgotten. Now she walked.

But she still hadn't been feeling like herself for a while now. She often forgot where she put things or what day it was, and time seemed to run away from her. Twilight sometimes leapt across Valtera when she'd thought it was only midday, and she couldn't recall what she'd been doing for the past several hours. It'd all started around the time when the old part of the curse returned—the unexplained deaths of Valtera's inhabitants.

But she would not let that stop her from walking, or she might as well be dead already.

She followed the street and passed through a square where people gathered like knots in her knitting wool. They talked and haggled over breads and smoked rabbit, although the atmosphere about the area was more primed with fear and distrust than ever before.

The scent of the meat also peppered the mountain air and brought a tingle to her mouth. She passed between many people, but no one seemed to notice her, much less said anything to her.

As Ulma exited the square, two people argued in an alleyway to her left. She stopped to get a better look. No matter how loud she walked, no one paid her much attention. Or at least they didn't seem to care that an old lady who'd probably seen more years than anyone else in the city was passing by.

One man gesticulated wildly and shouted at a woman as broad as the man, her jaw just as thick. The woman was the saddle maker, Olinia. Hard not to know her in these parts of

Valtera. And Olinia wasn't having any of the man's complaints. Her voice rose, and she yelled right back in his face, shaking a meaty fist. The man backed away before his gaze flickered over Olinia's shoulder and settled on Ulma.

Their argument raged for several minutes with unintelligible phrases and curses. More than once, the man seemed to notice Ulma, but he kept on arguing.

More minutes passed.

"That old woman's watching us," the man said, probably thinking Ulma was too deaf to hear them. "Just standing there and staring like she does."

Olinia shouted back at the man but didn't bother to turn around. Ulma hurried on her way, her shoes clacking down the street. Across the Narrows Bridge. Up Branber's Hill.

A gust tugged at her thinning hair. The wolf wind was blowing from an angle slightly off from the day before, if her memory served her. Colder too. The chilly nip the wind put on her nose was closer to that of a month or two ago rather than what it'd felt like in the past weeks. And rafts of clouds sailed across the blue overhead. So beautiful. Ever changing. Valtera's scenery, there was nothing like it.

Ulma wondered if anyone else noticed the small things like that: the angle of the wind's origin, the smell of pines carried down from those peaks, the black stones all around them, the cracks riddling the stones. Did anyone else stop and see these things, or were they all still in too much of a hurry to gather food and finish their work before they had to start over again?

Stake Square lay empty across the river, a desolate circle of black stones with only one lone beam standing straight out of them. Where they burned the witch so long ago now.

Sometimes Ulma thought with how cold it was in these plains that fire never seemed like such an evil. The cold and freezing to death seemed more sinister, an ever-present threat that could just sneak up on you out of the dark and silence of the night. Flames could be felt and seen and heard coming. They couldn't take you by surprise or unaware.

Ulma circled back around and headed down the far side of

Branber's Hill. Children ran about the street, chasing each other and screaming.

A smile spread across Ulma's withered lips. Children. Something that always brought warm memories and dispelled current colder ones.

One girl, Kirya, who always noticed her, stopped when she saw Ulma. Kirya was the girl with twin braids in her dark hair.

"Hey, there's the great-grandmother!" Kirya pointed.

The children all screamed and ran up to Ulma.

"Sweeties!" one child shouted.

Ulma dug around in her pockets with a trembling hand. "I'm almost out. Need to head over to the square tomorrow for more."

She doled out a few treats wrapped in brown paper. The children snatched them out of her palm before she could pass any around.

"Hey, I didn't get one." Kirya folded her arms across her chest, and her lower lip stuck out.

"I'm sorry, girl, it's all I have." Ulma patted an empty pocket. "I'll bring you one tomorrow."

"But everyone else got one." Kirya's eyes narrowed.

"I didn't either," a little boy said. "Bad old grandmother."

Ulma gasped. "Now, children. I said I'll bring you more. I always do. How about a story? I have so many of those I will never run out. And I have some good ones you've never heard before."

"I don't want some old woman's foolish stories." Kirya's fists clenched, and her face flushed red. "I want a sweetie."

"Yes, now!" the boy said.

"Well, if that's your attitude, maybe I won't come this way tomorrow at all." Ulma started walking through the throng of children, most of whom were sucking on their sweeties.

"Mean old lady," Kirya said.

Someone shoved Ulma from behind, and her ankle twisted, causing pain as if a knife cut along the inside of it. She stumbled and shouted.

The children screamed and ran. They disappeared down the streets or behind houses in a flash.

Ulma huffed as her ankle throbbed. Some kind of nasty sprain. Any little wrong movement at this age seemed to set her back for weeks. She tried to roll her ankle around, but the pain only worsened.

She gritted her teeth in anger, something she rarely felt these past years, and walked on, clacking down the street. The off-kilter beat of her limping gait for some reason irritated her even more. The sound was different from normal, uneven. So unlike her. Like someone else was now walking in her wooden shoes.

Those foolish children. They'd never done anything like that before. They were never overly respectful of her but never so angry or whiny or disrespectful either. Even resorting to pushing an old woman. They wanted their sweeties, but perhaps she'd finally spoiled them too much. People had told her she'd do that eventually, but she never thought she'd see the day.

Ulma attempted to walk at her normal pace, but her ankle throbbed. So that part of her, too, was curtailed. She could only manage the pace of what would be expected of someone her age. A hobbling shuffle.

At least it wasn't too much farther to her house.

As she passed by a cross street, several young faces peeked out at her from behind corners and crates. At least a couple of them laughed before turning and running the other way.

10

CALEC LED THE BAY GELDING THROUGH THE PINES, THE NEEDLES dragging along the horse's head and back as they walked. The camp's clearing opened ahead, and moonlight from the many moons spilled across the area. A few sentries stood on guard, but most of the people of the woods slept. It was nearing morning the following day; Calec had not ridden the gelding at the pace his abductors had used to travel to the far country, and nights were much longer than days this time of year.

He led the gelding to where Wyndstrom slept standing up in the grass. There, he hobbled the gelding and headed off to find Serileen.

A minute later, he approached Serileen's hut and ducked to peek inside. Shep's tail thudded against the floor of the hut, and the dog released a soft whimper.

A lithe figure lay beneath the pelts on the bed. Calec crept inside and patted Shep, who doused his palm and cheek with a wet tongue. After Shep settled a bit, Calec sat on the edge of the grass mattress and stroked the dog's head, following the path of his stripe.

"So, your anger has subsided." Serileen rolled over and ran a hand along his arm. "And you've decided to return to my bed after all? After being gone for two nights and a day?"

Calec faced her. "I am sorry to wake you. And any anger I felt has long been lost. I was abducted yesterday. That's the primary reason for my prolonged absence."

"Abducted?" Serileen curled into him as if she were still sleeping or didn't comprehend what he'd said.

"Yes. Tricked by some young woman into chasing her. She led me into an ambush where I was knocked unconscious and brought into the far country."

Serileen lifted her head and studied him. "Are you seriously injured?"

"The blow to my head still aches, but other than that I am fine."

"Well, for all that trouble, I hope this young woman you chased after was beautiful."

The facetious and teasing comment struck something inside Calec, and he looked away. "She could have been, but she was very young. Barely a woman. Maybe twenty years if not ten and nine."

"Ah, and so that is why you fell for her ruse. Your greatest weakness. To aid a lady."

Calec sat in silence as visions of Desi's eyes haunted him. Eyes as blue as the sky sea or glacial ice, and like deep wells, as if he could view her soul through them.

Serileen rubbed his back. "It's all right, Calec of the Woods. If you didn't have such a weakness, the people of the woods may not still live here. Or we might not live at all. And how did you escape these abductors with your life?"

Calec quickly explained what'd happened when he'd gone in search of Jirabelle and how his abductors had just left him.

"What do you think they wanted with you?" she asked.

"They mentioned they wanted to bring me to their city, or convince me to find them again, but they'd run out of time."

"That *is* strange." Serileen sat up but didn't speak again for several minutes before saying, "And they did not mention anything suspicious relating to Jirabelle?"

Calec shook his head. "It seems too trusting to think of the abduction only as coincidence, but unless Jirabelle or Foram found and hired strangely dressed people who live far from the woods, they probably had nothing to do with my abduction."

"I will not be able to accompany you on any ventures right now."

Calec's eyes narrowed as he studied her. "I am not going on any ventures."

"But you want to. Or at least you feel you should."

An argumentative retort surfaced in his mind, but he sighed instead. She spoke the truth. "You're partially right. And if you'd have seen how much they needed help, you'd feel the same. But I wish to stay and aid you in searching for the suspects in your mother's murder. That is most important to me. These people only have the power to linger in my mind."

"Then you should go to them, Calec of the Woods. My mother was murdered over two decades ago. There is nothing fresh and new that must be addressed at the moment. And even if you doubt me, I can handle myself."

Calec lay down and stared at the ceiling of the hut. "I place aiding you at the forefront of my duties."

"You no longer have duties, Sir Calec." She smiled and ran her fingers through his hair. "You no longer belong to King Trithemore."

"But—"

"I gather your meaning. And I appreciate your sentiments and concerns, but I've been hunting this killer since the day the murder happened. There will be nothing you can magically turn up in a few days or even weeks."

"I—"

"You must go soon. With every reoccurrence of old magic that sprouts and clings to the lands around us, we all fall into greater danger."

Calec's jaw tensed. "I don't even know where to go."

"*I* know where you can begin your search."

Calec studied her, waiting for further clarification.

"There are old tales that came to us from the far country, in days long past," Serileen said. "Tales that spoke of a city that was cursed."

"Is it an emerald city?"

"Yes, it is. Or *was*."

"All I saw in the plains was more plains. Nothing is out there."

"The plains extend all the way from the northern mountains to the southern hills, and they fill all the lands between Jaylen's Pass and the eastern deserts. The plains are vast."

"And someone knows where this city used to be?"

Serileen shook her head. "It doesn't matter where it used to be. In my understanding, the city is no more. It's been referred to as the vanished city. You will have to find these people and aid them."

"And how do I hope to find them in such vast plains if their city no longer exists?"

"If you've met people from the far country, maybe the city does still exist. Their legend speaks of a glimmering emerald city where they burned a witch alive. The city burned with her. Some claim the fire ran out of control. Others say the witch controlled it and cursed them all. Most believe the city was cast into ruin and only its myth remained. Others say ghosts wander through the grasses of the far country and haunt the plains."

"And so, if I depart, I will wander these plains only hoping to stumble upon some people or their cursed city that may no longer exist? It sounds more akin to a ghost story rather than truth."

Serileen's voice turned tense. "There are also savage clans of nomads living and wandering the plains like barbarians of old. You must be wary, but if anyone knows of the emerald city or of ghosts, it will be those people. It is said they are nomads of the night. That is when they walk the plains."

"Ghosts and a city that was burned but that I may still find. You speak of magic so potent or obscure that I cannot wrap my mind around it."

"We do not need to ponder this any longer at the moment."

She nestled into him and ran a hand along his chest, loosening his tunic and slowly removing the garment. Then she moved to his leggings. "But you must adapt to such magic, Calec of the Woods. And quickly. The old ways, the sky sea, the Horseman, and his moons are returning."

11

Calec dreamt.

Fires raged around the perimeter of the woods. A recurring nightmare consisting of some kind of natural disaster often plagued his dreams, and the sight of that incomprehensible power—whether it be giant waves from the sea, fire, spiraling windstorms that could tear trees from the earth, or earthquakes—paralyzed him. In this nightmare, he could only stand beside a lone tree in the center of a circular clearing and watch as the fires surrounded him and his people. Flames roared as they drew near and consumed trees, lighting up each trunk like an effigy.

People around him screamed and raced about, but his feet would not move, as if his legs were buried in a tar bog. He attempted to run. To find Serileen and save her. To save anyone, but he could only stand like a statue and watch the madness rage around him.

A woman crawled on her hands and knees, arriving from the old woods and slipping into the clearing with Calec. The silhouette of a man with horns of writhing flame and a mask crouched behind a tree nearby, hiding as he sniffed the air. His shadow horse tossed its head, and its red eyes rolled wildly.

The crawling woman kept muttering to herself as she frantically searched about for something. After fighting her way up to a mound of freshly turned soil, she stopped. The grave she'd been searching for.

She scooped up the dirt and lifted it to her face. The man in the mask leered at her from behind the tree, and his horns of flame writhed as smoke spewed from his nostrils.

Calec again attempted to move. To run to the woman. To help her. But all he could do was release a muffled sound of warning.

The woman glanced up in his direction, her gaze locking with his. Her eyes were as blue as the sky sea. As blue as glacial ice. But within their swirling depths he could see her soul. Who she was. Her desires. Her fears. Her desperation. Something inside her called out to him, that subtle voice seeking his soul and rattling around inside it.

Someone shook Calec.

His eyelids unsealed, and sunlight stabbed at his eyes. Late morning or midday sunlight.

"You were whimpering, and you're covered in sweat." Serileen's voice carried to him. At first, her words seemed to be coming from a distant land, but before she finished speaking, she was right beside him.

Calec mopped a pool of sweat from his forehead and rubbed his eyes until circles of color filled his vision.

"I was having a nightmare," he said.

"Like you always do when such occult events are brought to your attention."

Calec sat up. Shep watched him from beside the bed.

"You must go and try to find these people," Serileen said. "To follow the pull of your heart and your need to venture about our world."

Calec pondered the idea. "But you said you could not accompany me."

"You do not need my assistance as much as you believe you do. And I have good reason at the current time."

Calec studied her. "Work for the Mother? It never stopped you before."

Serileen released a long breath as she glanced out the doorway of their hut. "I feel the turmoil roiling inside you. I have turmoil of my own. And ... I've wanted to tell you about it for some time now, but I didn't want to be the one to inject you with that kind of pain."

Calec found himself holding his breath.

"The only reason I do not wish to accompany you is because of what occurred in Hillsvale," she said.

"When you were struck in the head with a rock? Or did something happen during your encounter with the necromancer?"

Serileen fell silent again as the look in her eyes turned faraway, as if she traveled through tunnels of memory. "What I didn't or couldn't tell you before, in Hillsvale, was that I was with child. I lost it. I miscarried after the trauma with the rock and the events there."

Calec's heart shuddered inside its bony cage, and it felt as if something he didn't know even existed, something that lived deep inside himself, was suddenly ripped out of him.

"Wh-what?" he asked.

Serileen nodded, her face pale and downcast.

The hole that Calec suddenly realized resided in his heart weighed more than any other part of him, a great and compressing weight of devastating loss. His mind ran rampant with thoughts that became corrupted by spiraling emotions of shock, anger, and sadness.

Serileen did not like to speak of her deepest and most painful emotions, but this affected him too. He'd said something about not wanting a child after a discovery in Hillsvale, but he'd been under severe duress with the missing children there. Later, he and Serileen had decided to try for that child.

"It was yours, of course." Serileen's eyes grew even more distant and hazy as shadow won a battle over sunlight and bathed her face.

Calec's guts writhed and squirmed. He didn't know if he'd end up shouting at her out of anger for not telling him sooner or if he'd curse the people of Hillsvale or fate itself. Or if he'd start weeping. So he sat in silence, attempting to hold himself together.

"It is my fault," Calec said after a few minutes. He moved to take her hand but stopped short. "I brought you there. I asked King Trithemore if you could join me."

Serileen shook her head and squeezed his hand. "It is *not* your fault. And not all is lost. The only reason I do not wish to travel so soon is that I am once again pregnant."

Calec's gaze flashed up to study her.

A longing for something burned in her eyes now as her gaze shifted over his face. A yearning or need had been partially revealed. "You needed at least a moment to process what I'd just told you, before news of my current state. Miscarriages are common. But we have another chance."

Calec took her hand and caressed it. "A child?"

She nodded, and tears brimmed in her eyes. "But there is something else you should know."

"What?" Calec's heart stilled and teetered on the edge of a cliff.

"Someone predicted that our prior child would not be strong enough to survive in this world. They also hinted that any child by us would find a similar fate."

A jolt of anger spouted from some well in Calec's blood. "Who?"

Serileen's eyes closed.

"It was the necromancer, Brenson, wasn't it?" Calec asked. "It is always that man who haunts the ties between us. That man who tries to sever such bonds. To cast doubt and sow resentment."

Serileen tapped her lips. "It doesn't matter who it was. But I would not risk another child. And surely not so soon. You also have a need to venture itching at you now. A need I agree must be satiated. Not only for yourself, but for the people of the vanished city."

The longing to travel that Calec had recently felt emerged again from a crevice of his soul. He cursed it.

"We have a second chance for a child of ours to grow strong enough to enter this world," Serileen said.

"But when you were struck with a rock, how could a fetus have been strong enough to survive that? It does not mean any child by us will be weak."

"I do not know what it means. I was struck in the head, but I fell. It may have been the fall and only a coincidental prediction from someone who wishes to sow doubt in my mind. *Or* that prophecy, supposedly foretold from the flames, could have been genuine."

"I will stay here and make sure this child survives until birth and beyond."

"If you do so, we will all fall into greater danger. Any child of ours included. The Horseman lives in the sky sea, and his manipulation of our world and its people will torment us all."

"I wish to stay now. How can you ask me to go after everything you've just sprung on me?"

"I am strong and able to care for myself." She pulled his hand to her stomach and placed his palm against her skin. "I am asking you to go for this world *and* for your child. As soon as possible."

12

CALEC RODE HIS NEW GELDING THROUGH THE GRASSES OF THE FAR country a couple days later. He'd made Shep stay behind to keep Serileen company during this venture, although the dog had wanted to come with him. He'd also searched for Jirabelle but could not locate her. She may have been hiding from him.

Calec had been riding through the plains with the gelding he now referred to as Ghost for a day already. There was a greater chance that Ghost might aid him in these lands compared to Wyndstrom, although Calec typically only wished to travel with his destrier from his days as a knight.

The lump on Calec's head was receding and the pain had lessened, but memories of his abduction and Serileen's words concerning dangerous nomad clans, as well as memories of Desi's imploring blue eyes, all spiraled around in his mind. However, even these thoughts were usurped by musings of Serileen's miscarriage and her current pregnancy. Calec would, or at least might, become a father. If the growing child in her womb wasn't harmed. And if this one was strong enough to survive.

His fingers felt along the length of the yellow ribbon he carried in his belt, and a feeling of guilt and loss sank into his gut. He'd never known about the past possibility of a child, and Serileen either thought she couldn't tell him about it, or she hadn't been able to bring herself to speak of it. She was always a distant person when it came to such emotion, but was Calec only telling himself all this to create an excuse? To shirk his involvement in the matter? Mayhap what he'd said to her about not wanting children made her feel like she couldn't tell him. Or maybe it was the necromancer's fault. The one who resembled a barbarian rather than someone who raised and spoke with the dead. If it was anyone's fault, Calec believed it was probably that man's. But either way, Serileen had had to deal with the loss herself. She'd tried to spare Calec even if he didn't want to be spared. And even though she was a strong woman, that fact did not stop Calec from feeling immense sorrow for what she'd endured. A large part of him wished he were in the woods beside her and able to comfort her and see how well or poorly she was dealing with it all.

How would he ever know if a child of theirs was strong enough to survive in the world? Doubt haunted him, as well as its vile friend worry, and they would continue to do so until she gave birth. If she did not miscarry first. Maybe it was better for Calec to try to help the world against whatever evils plagued it rather than sit beside Serileen staring at her stomach in hopes of seeing into her womb and determining how healthy and strong the child was growing.

Hours of thoughts trundled through his head and faded and wore away under the chill gale of the wolf wind and the watching eyes of that army of giant mountains running far to the north. Like shadowed sentinels of the valley.

Calec pulled his hood low and wrapped his cloak tightly about him before rubbing at his eyes. He had to focus on the task at hand. For his sanity and for the people he sought to aid.

Ghost trudged on, his ears flattened against the wind, his winter coat thick like a shaggy pony from the northern lands.

If some ancient city were burned and might never be found, if such myths held any truth, it was likely that Calec was wasting his time. He glanced southward. He couldn't even make out the hills that bordered these plains beyond the leagues of grass that seemed to run into the gray clouds far, far away. How would he ever even find the nomads who wandered these lands?

Daylight faded to night, and Calec halted to clear a spot for a fire before stopping cold and realizing he might be traveling at the wrong time. If such myths about the nomads were true. And he wasn't yet ready for the return of his recurrent dream that'd faded since his last venture to Hillsvale but had returned in full force the other night. Dreams of a woman or women crawling on their hands and knees, scooping up dirt from freshly buried graves. A silhouette of a man in a black mask looming behind them under moonlight. Horns of spiraling flame atop his head. A ring with the insignia of a golden skeleton, a black heart inside its ribs.

"We should push on," Calec said to Ghost. "But not hard during the night."

"I can go on for a while longer," Ghost seemed to say in a casual tone, like a burro who had accepted its journey. "*If* we take sleep in the very early morning and don't start again until evening tomorrow."

Calec climbed back onto Ghost's saddle, a lighter model used by the people of the woods rather than Wyndstrom's heavy war saddle, and they trudged on.

They continued in this manner—sleeping during the day and roaming at night—for two more nights before Calec noticed a pair of eyes glowing in the light of the many moons. Those eyes waited on a hill to his left. They shone yellow and seldom blinked from within their hiding spot in the grasses. Not human.

"I see you, wolf of the plains," Calec said. "Whatever hunger you feel, there is much easier prey out here than me and Ghost."

Calec's hand had instinctively gripped his sword's hilt, but his fear was minimal. Wolves in the plains were much smaller than any timber wolves or dire wolves from the north. And even those larger breeds only attacked travelers when desperate or if the travelers were sick or wounded. This beast was likely much more scared of him than he of it. The people of the city had other names for these smaller wolves, but Calec wished to see the world as a person of the woods.

"I only stop and watch in hopes of you not noticing my presence," Calec said in a voice for the wolf, a bit tricksy and laced with cunning. "And to see if you have any scraps you will leave behind at your fire. The pieces they call bones, which your teeth cannot devour."

"Not this night, wolf of the plains. I have not hunted, and my meats are smoked and dried." He patted a bow strapped to his saddle.

"Then I shall remain here until you are gone." The eyes blinked.

Calec fished out a strip of venison, bit off a large hunk, and tossed the rest into the grass in the direction of the little wolf.

Something sounded over the wind to Calec's right.

He wheeled in the direction as he pulled his sword.

The grasses waved under the light of the moons.

After several minutes, Calec decided it was nothing.

He rode on over a small rise, then descended. At the bottom of the gentle slope, something rose from the grasses before him. Then another and another.

At least half a dozen men wrapped in dark pelts emerged as if sculpted from the night's darkness. Their eyes focused on Calec.

The savages Serileen spoke of.

Calec's hand rested on his sword's hilt, but he left it sheathed. He pulled Ghost to a halt.

"Wolf Tongue," the man before Calec said in a stilted and gravelly tone, as if speaking words foreign to him. "You ride through our plains speaking when there is no one to answer your wasted words. Nothing other than the wolf wind."

"I ... was looking for some—"

"And you ride one of our former horses," the man said. "How came you to own it?"

Calec glanced at Ghost. "He was left to me."

"By whom?"

"Men who claimed ..." Would mentioning a city in these plains sound mad to these people? "They claimed to be from a city somewhere out in this far country."

"There are no cities in the plains, Wolf Tongue." The man waved a muscled arm around.

"Then you've never seen an emerald city?"

The nomads' shared glance was quick but couldn't be hidden.

"I'm hunting for the emerald city," Calec said. "People from such a place came to me for aid and left me this horse."

The one who seemed to be their leader stepped closer. "These people you speak of, were they several men and one young woman?"

Calec nodded.

"They purchased the horse from us not half a fortnight ago," the nomad leader continued. "Said they needed one horse that could be left behind."

"And their city?" Calec asked.

The leader laughed. "You may wander the plains for seasons and never come upon it."

"Then I am on a fool's venture."

"And you wander our lands without permission." Another man stepped forward, brandishing a spear.

"You will follow us," the leader said.

"I hunt the emerald city." Calec shook his head. "And if it is not to be found, I will return to the woods."

"No." The leader stood fast, and his grip tightened on his own spear. "You follow us or you die here. Your presence is not permitted in these lands."

13

CALEC FOLLOWED THE LEADER OF THESE NOMADS THROUGH grasses that waved, the soft undersides of their bellies exposed by the wolf wind. And these bellies threw the light of the moons back at the night. The other nomads surrounded him, and their numbers increased as they moved, as if they appeared out of the grass itself. As if they were ghosts of the plains.

At least a dozen nomads now surrounded him and Ghost—perhaps Calec should have named the gelding something else—and most of these nomads led horses that looked as sleek and fast as swooping eagles. All these people wore what appeared to be bone shovels slung across the dark pelts on their backs. Wooden handles. Flat bone blades with sharpened edges for digging.

The leader stopped suddenly and made a kind of waving motion as he arched several of his fingers. Then he blew through a horn that blasted out and throbbed over the plains.

More people appeared from the grasses all around them. Dirt-stained faces. Fur clothing. Spears and bows.

The leader turned to Calec, strands of gray flowing in his dark hair like rivers. "Now it comes time to see if you are worthy to walk the far country."

Calec swallowed, imagining being pitted against their

strongest warrior with only his bare hands or a spear, *not* his weapon of choice. Or pitted against some phantom in an unholy duel.

"I am Gomdon, leader of the clan of the Whispering Horses."

"I am Calec of the Woods."

"Well, then, Wolf Tongue." Gomdon motioned, and a hulking man approached from behind him, as well as a thin man—the one Gomdon indicated. "You will face Runik in a battle of wits. He is the best hunter and horse thief in all the clans. If you succeed, you may speak to me as an equal."

"I will not outhunt your best hunter," Calec said. "Nor out steal him."

Gomdon laughed, a deep and hearty rumble. "No, you will not. But because you ride one of the Whispering Horses and claim to not have stolen it, you have received a bit of mercy. It will not be a hunt or horse raid. Nor a duel to the death. You will only need to outdrink and outwit Runik."

Out drink?

Gomdon motioned, and several women stepped forward carrying ceramic jugs as tall as their torsos.

"Now, dismount. Only if you lose to Runik will you have to leave these plains forever and face the penalty of immediate death if you are ever spotted here again. Mitag will make sure of that." Gomdon pointed to the hulking monster of a man who glowered, and his knuckles blanched on the handle of his spear.

Calec's heart rattled against his ribs as he slowly dismounted. He was not a big drinker. Not compared to many, most men even, and several women. But if he lost this battle of wits, he would never be able to search the plains for the emerald city. He could never hope to outrun native nomads who hid in the grasses.

How do I outwit and *outdrink this nomad? And if I'm drunk, I won't be able to defend myself from any of these people, especially from some monster of a man with a spear. If it comes to that.*

Nomad women beat down and flattened an area in the grass with long poles, and others brought in torches and stood them on stakes in a circle around the perimeter. Then Runik stepped onto this arena, took a jug, and sat cross-legged.

Calec was ushered forward into the area of flattened grass, and a jug was forced into his hands.

"Now drink until I give the command to start the battle of wits," Gomdon said. "Your language, Wolf Tongue, is the same as ours even if you do not speak it quite properly and wield a terrible accent when you do. No allowances will be made for missed *gramdels*. Drink!"

Runik raised his jug to his lips and tilted it back. The bulge in the middle of his throat climbed up and down as he swallowed several times.

"Drink, I say!" Gomdon motioned to Calec. "Or you've already lost, and Mitag will drive you from our lands. Or if you resist, he'll fashion your hide into someone's tunic."

The nomad warrior stepped closer and snarled.

Calec lifted the jug. Acrid liquid poured past his lips and burned his tongue and throat, a smoky draught with a hint of fruit. Calec swallowed a gulp. Then another and another.

"Halt!" Gomdon said.

People around them muttered.

"Now," Gomdon said. "As the trespasser, Wolf Tongue will speak first."

Calec grimaced as he swallowed the pooling liquid around his tongue and wiped at his mouth. "And what do I say?"

"You insult the man before you. As best you can. To entertain us. To beat him down. To raise yourself above him in song."

Calec's gaze jerked over to the nomad leader. "Insult him?"

Gomdon nodded. "You know what that is? Just speak, like you did to the wind if you must, but do not bore all those watching."

Calec studied his opponent sitting on the grass before him: slight of build, deep-set and cunning eyes, short hair. Runik pushed a wolf pelt off his shoulders, and it slid onto the grass, exposing his bare chest and back to the bitter wind and late winter night.

What can I use to insult this man?

"One of the other two rules you must understand and cannot break," Gomdon said, "is that if you are pondering what to say, for that entire time you must be drinking and swallowing." His voice rose louder as he loomed over Calec. "*Now*, drink or speak!"

Calec placed the jug to his lips and swallowed one gulp. Then he lowered it. "If you steal horses, you are nothing more than a thief."

A silence passed over the plains as all eyes settled on Calec, all breaths held.

Gomdon burst out with laughter, nearly doubling over. "That is it? Your insult to an honored thief of the Whispering Horses?" He laughed again. "You are as dense as the ground beneath the grass."

An explosion of laughter erupted all around.

Runik's expression exuded bewilderment before he raised the jug to his lips and took only a small sip. Then he lowered his drink.

"If that is all you can find to insult, then you've the mind of a fool, not a chief," Runik said, "and when I kill you, your woman and children will feel no grief."

A low murmur of approval ran through the masses who stood like ghostly figures in the moonlight around them.

Anger rose inside Calec as he imagined Serileen and his unborn child. "We keep family and others out of this."

Calec moved to stand, but Mitag and Gomdon glared at him. Mitag lowered the steel tip of his spear and pointed it at Calec, appearing too eager to skewer him.

"That is not a suitable answer to his insult," Gomdon said. "Now, start drinking or answer appropriately."

Calec brought the jug to his lips.

"You lead this first bout, and so Runik's last retort was an escalating insult. Your opponent's last word must be a *gramdel*, a … it must sound like the insulter's last word," Gomdon said. "Like in song, our *gramdels*. You are creating lyrics to a song that will be sung only once. Only for those present on this night." He rubbed at his chin.

"Like a *rhyme*?" Calec stopped drinking to ask.

"I believe that is what outsiders call a *gramdel*. Runik must *rhyme* with you."

Calec raised the jug again and let the drink flow down his throat; he attempted to slow its passage by taking smaller sips. Too much time spent thinking and drinking and he'd fall over before he could even come up with a retort.

So strange are the ways of outsiders. But are they any more so than between the people of the city and those of the woods?

Calec hesitantly took another swallow, and another, his mind reeling with possibilities. He lowered the jug. Could he insult his opponent's family? Those he didn't even know? It seemed this man would use that approach, but Calec would refrain for now.

I need words that are difficult to rhyme with …

"Runik is as dull-witted and ugly as that which he carries on his back, a bone shovel."

A quick silence was followed by a murmur of disapproval that ran through the crowd as Runik drank. And Runik continued to drink and drink, his throat working as if climbing up and sliding down a ladder.

Calec suppressed a smirk. The nomad should have a hard time rhyming anything with shovel.

"They did not like that one much," Gomdon said. "You have used it, but your ranking as the initiator of this song has diminished. It is not wise to insult everyone and their ways. Nor is the format of your lyric well received. It did not rhyme with your first lyric, and it was not used in good presentation or in good order for a single line of song."

"They judge us?" Calec eyed those standing around like statues outside the ring of torches.

"They approve of good lyrics and detest poor ones. Like any song. You cannot sing a terrible song in these battles of the mind."

Calec's stomach tightened, and the alcohol sloshed about in a nauseating wave.

Runik lowered his jug and belched profusely as his head

bobbed a bit. "The people of the woods bugger woman and man and animal and tree, thus they love all."

A murmur of mild approval ran through the standing spectators.

Calec scoffed at the poor lyrics. "For one who so often insults mating, you'd think his own—"

"This first bout goes to Runik for matching that lyric of terrible taste that did not *gramdel* with our trespasser's own opening lyric, which he chose as 'thief,'" Gomdon said, silencing Calec.

Calec thought about protesting but decided it would likely get him nowhere.

"Drink or begin with your lyrics," Gomdon said to Runik.

Runik drank again, then he cast Calec a wicked smirk. "Then when those you love feel no grief, I'll force your woman to bed until she is sore, and only then will she feel much more."

A wash of anger seethed in Calec's blood.

"Now a new insult, Wolf Tongue, or drink more until your mind can conjure one up," Gomdon said. "And your reply must be only one line, and it must be related to Runik's last lyric. And the *gramdel* cannot be the same word unless it is of different meaning."

Calec drank. He started to swoon, and the land around him wobbled a bit. The drink was strong. Maybe a good thing as it was lowering his threshold and what he might say to another man. But if his mind slowed, the drunkenness would only progress faster and faster as he'd have to drink more and more while attempting to think.

"Runik took it far too easy on you with his first retort," Gomdon continued. "He is a kind opponent and has scored points with the watchers for it, also making his own future responses easier. Something you should have considered with the word 'shovel.'"

You didn't tell me all that to begin with, but no wonder ... using a difficult word to rhyme with would be too easy to use to win, and it would sound ridiculous in song. So, what good lyric and insult can I rhyme with 'more'?

Calec lowered his jug. "If only my woman wouldn't find you such a bore."

"She would still be fun to explore." Runik's retort was too quick, without even need of drink.

Calec drank. *He's practiced and has done this before—ah, 'before' rhymes, but no insult lies in that thought.*

"After a minute or less with you, she'd start to snore," Calec said.

"At least it is better than what she had before."

Calec gritted his teeth and drank again. His head swam. The many crescent and few small full moons seemed to tilt and wheel in the night sky overhead.

"She'd find less enjoyment with the men of the Whispering Horses than with a boar," Calec said and belched.

A muffled laugh arose from the onlookers. Gomdon's face remained stone. Mitag's snarl deepened.

Runik took a single drink. "Too bad there is another man other than Wolf Tongue with whom his mate is looking to score."

Images of Brenson immediately popped into Calec's mind and spiraled around. Damn it. He buried the thoughts and the distraction as he drank, and his stomach sloshed.

"If only Runik didn't ponder other men's women because he is generally ignored, and instead he focused on his duty of war," Calec said.

"And after I'm done with yours, for me, drink she will gladly pour."

The onlookers applauded that one.

Calec drank again before saying, "If only your skill with women could match my roar."

Was that an insult? Or just defense?

A few grunts sounded.

"After she's done with me on the floor," Runik said, "she'll ask me for it again times four."

"'He's easy to ignore, I never felt anything at all while lying with that man,' she swore." Calec's anger subsided a bit. This seemed like only jests between drunken men now, like in his days of knighthood. Maybe the danger wasn't as real as he first believed.

Some of the people outside the ring applauded by slapping at one forearm.

But something flashed in Runik's eyes. Anger? Frustration? Maybe he believed he'd have won by now, or maybe he really was self-conscious in that regard.

"Your woman hunts for what you cannot give her while you're away from her door, and right now she takes a man from every and any shore," Runik said.

Mitag bellowed with laughter and applauded louder than the others had before.

Calec drank a few gulps, and the torches spun around him. The faces of Gomdon and Runik and Mitag blurred and appeared to detach from their bodies.

Calec lowered his jug and placed a hand on the ground to steady himself. "My people's lore is that the men of the plains, namely Mitag, use Runik as their whore."

A gasp carried around the group, as well as several laughs. Gomdon grinned, but Mitag's snarl deepened. Runik's eyes narrowed, and a vein throbbed at his temple.

Runik sucked in a breath and lunged to his feet before jumping on Calec and knocking him over. They sprawled across the flattened grass. Runik gripped Calec's arm and tried to bend it backward at the wrist and elbow, attempting to snap his joints.

Runik was torn away by several of the onlookers and dragged back to the far side of the circle and then out of it, where he disappeared into the darkness.

Gomdon shook his head and said to Calec, "And, of course, if one loses his temper with their opponent and resorts to violence when the game is still of wits, he forfeits. Grappling or spear fighting have to be announced."

Gomdon turned and marched away.

"Bring our trespasser to the village." Gomdon's voice carried.

Mitag's snarl and the glare of pure hate in his eyes amplified as he lowered his spear and used it to prod Calec and drive him after Gomdon.

Calec stumbled in the direction Mitag ushered him, moving away from the gleaming spear tip as the ground swayed beneath him. And the grasses waved.

14

DESI STORMED AROUND THE SMALL LIVING CHAMBER OF HER house, her fists clenched as her shoes pounded against the black rock floor.

"You cannot go looking for reasons for the curse." Jaremonde sat on a chair at the table, tugging at his mustache between bouts of chewing on a few chunks of meat still stuck to a cut bone nearly the size of his leg. "I forbid it."

"Oh, so I can ride out to the pass in the west and try to abduct a witch hunter, but I cannot search my own city for reasons as to why these deaths are occurring again after all these years?"

"It is not a young woman's place to be involved with dead bodies and curses and danger. When you ventured to the pass, Lanigrad and Climson and Aonor and others accompanied you."

"And so it is my place to coerce men into helping Valtera? I can summon pity or love or lust in them? Thanks, Father. I hoped to be more in your eyes. And Aonor is a creep. He's old and wishes to wed me, the sooner the better in his mind."

Jaremonde shook his bald head. "You are much more in my eyes. That is why I do not want to put you in any danger. I do this for your safety, and one day you will understand. And Aonor would be a good husband. He could give you a good life.

He is master of collections in Valtera. Does that not mean anything to you?"

Desi folded her arms over her chest. "No. Aonor means nothing to me. Nor does his sickeningly sweet attention. Why not just set me up with Rimmell?"

"Rimmell could go either of two ways. He could become a good constable if he starts to use his head and fills out some. Or he could remain a blundering idiot. I wouldn't pressure you to consider such a potential lout. Aonor is a much more powerful man."

"Well, thanks for that, Father. But Rimmell is the only one of those men you hope for me to consider who is my age, and he is handsome, although I still do not wish to have him think of me that way. He does seem a bit thick."

"Then you will never be happy if no one is good enough for you."

Desi's anger flared in her cheeks. "And what if I just leave the house now? You cannot stop me."

"I will be *very* disappointed in you."

Desi paced around, her fingernails digging into her palms, her breath coming in quick huffs. "And so you are resigned that no one will be able to stop the curse."

Jaremonde sucked on a fragment of bone and used it to pick his teeth. "Of course no man or woman can stop the curse of the city, but we *will* stop the deaths. Rimmell and I are working tirelessly in that effort, whether I tell you much about my work or not. And Lanigrad is coming over again tonight. He *is* the most renowned scholar in Valtera. If there's something in our history that can help us, he'll know it. He could also be a potential suitor for you."

Desi shook her head. "I have no interest in him, and he none in me. He is kind and bright, but he is much older than me, and he knows it. Not as old as Aonor, but old enough. I respect him, but do not see him as a future husband."

"Your options are running thin."

"Why is my life about finding a suitor, Father? I could be of assistance to you. Like Rimmell."

Jaremonde scoffed. "You are much smarter than Rimmell. And I just wish to see you happy. Your mother doesn't seem to care much anymore since she's fallen ill, always very early to bed, late in rising. And you're always acting so hurt or angry. I have to be both parents now."

"Then let me go out with you tomorrow."

"No. You can go to the river with your friends for water, and to the market, but you are forbidden to go elsewhere until these deaths stop."

"Well, if you're waiting for the witch hunter to stop the deaths, I think we can keep on waiting. We never even got to show him the city. He'll never be able to find us. If he even cares and doesn't despise us. I'll be old before I can go about in my own city again."

"Then you'll be old."

Desi growled, flung the front door open, and stepped outside before slamming it shut behind her.

Jaremonde's shouts of protest were muffled, as well as his pursuing footfalls. Desi ran down the street.

A man was approaching steadily, a cloak about his shoulders. He stopped when he spotted Desi. It was Lanigrad, the middle-aged scholar, who was tall and fit, unlike so many of his profession. He carried a stack of books in his arms.

"Desi," Lanigrad said. "I was just coming to meet with your father. Do you wish to join us? There is much history involved with this curse, and not all the books pertaining to the event have been lost. Your help at Jaylen's Pass makes me believe you'd be a good asset in this work."

Desi stopped. She did want to know more about the curse and these deaths, but the last place she wanted to be right now was with her father. And he probably would not allow her to join them or converse with them anyway. He'd expect her to serve pastries and wine and be standoffish.

Desi nodded politely. "I wish to be part of it all, but I think Jaremonde has other plans for me."

"Ah, then I understand you and your father. But if you

decide to return, I will ask you to join all of us and partake in the discussions."

"*All* of you?"

"Aonor almost demanded that he be allowed to attend."

Desi's stomach turned squeamish. *Of course he did if he thought I'd be there.*

"And Rimmell," Lanigrad said. "As well as others."

Desi's heart sank. Not so much at the thought of seeing Rimmell, but this would be the most important meeting about the curse that she might ever be able to listen in on. She could probably put up with Aonor for the opportunity.

"Very well," she said. "I was thinking about returning anyway, before my father starts tearing apart the city looking for me."

Lanigrad motioned for Desi to take some of the books he carried, and he smiled mischievously at her. "Then lead the way."

15

GOMDON KNELT IN THE MOON-SILVERED GRASSES THAT SWAYED TO the rhythm of the wolf wind.

Calec waited for the man to rise, but this leader of nomads from the far country never stood. He simply vanished.

I must be beyond intoxicated.

Mitag prodded Calec with the sharpened tip of his spear, urging Calec to step forward. Calec did so and then was forced to kneel in the grass. At the base of the tussock before him, a hole had been dug into the earth, one large enough for a man to slip into. And earthen stairs led downward.

Calec wobbled as he stepped into the opening.

This is how these ghostly nomads arise from the grasses. Hence the shovels on their backs. Their most prized possessions must be buried beneath the plains.

Was that also how the people who'd abducted him disappeared? But with their *horses*?

Calec attempted to steady himself as best he could before he reached the bottom of the stairs. Mitag stomped down behind him. Gomdon's shadow disappeared around a bend in a passageway ahead—a tunnel outlined by firelight.

This tunnel was tall enough that Calec's head only brushed the ceiling as he stood. Mitag grunted, demanding he move faster. Calec followed after Gomdon, using a hand against the wall to steady the shifting floor around him. If only he'd sober up quickly.

They wound through a maze of branching tunnels where ensconced torches burned like those inside Duminborne castle. An entire network of caverns. A home. A civilization.

After Calec became lost beyond reckoning, he entered a chamber that spanned nearly the length of King Trithemore's audience hall. Stone pillars supported the ceiling in two rows along the length of it. A central fire burned, and a small hole above it allowed a plank of moonlight to lean in. The smoke mingled with the moonlight before rolling outward and escaping.

"Sit." Gomdon waited on a bench and motioned for Calec to have a seat opposite him at the fire.

Calec did as he was instructed, and Mitag sat immediately to Calec's right.

"Why now do you walk our lands?" Gomdon asked from across the fire, the flames and wavering heat and smoke veiling his features and distorting them.

"To find an emerald city," Calec said.

"Then you are another treasure hunter. Or a seeker of myths."

"I seek to help those who sought me first. A young woman stricken with fear."

Gomdon laughed. "Ah, for the young woman. I saw her as well. Beautiful. But her city is black now, not emerald. As black as shadow. Only our elders speak of an emerald city that used to live on the plains. If and when it is found depends on the ghosts who live there. We have no ... knowledge of how to locate it or where it will be."

"Then you've never seen this city? Nor been to its previous location before it burned?"

Mitag huffed a few times, as if attempting to contain an amused remark or to stifle laughter.

"Oh, we've been to its original location many times," Gomdon said.

"Then please tell me where that is," Calec said.

"Such knowledge will not aid you."

"Why not? I seek the city."

"But the city is not there."

"Of course it isn't, but its former people may be. Unless you know where they are."

"No one knows that either."

Calec sighed. "Your endless riddles are not helping me understand anything about this emerald city. I wish to find and aid its people. Can you assist me or not?"

Gomdon leaned forward, his eyes burning with the reflected flames. "No man can tell you where the city now lies or where it will lie. I cannot tell you where it is even though several of the clan members of the Whispering Horses have visited the place over the past decades. Others from the lesser clans have visited the emerald city as well. To trade. To barter for mysterious goods."

"Then you do know where it is," Calec said. "Or at least where they rebuilt it. Why will you not just tell me?"

Gomdon shook his head. "If you do not understand of what I speak, you do not understand the emerald city. The tales claim that the city can now only be found in the plains at night, but it never lies in the same spot twice. These tales tell of a glimmering emerald city whose people burned a witch alive, and the city burned with her. Most believe the city was cast into ruin and lost. But those who have stumbled upon it speak of ghosts and phantom buildings appearing under the moons somewhere out in the thousands of leagues of our plains."

Calec's forehead furrowed as disjointed thoughts wove circles in his mind. "What are you trying to tell me with all this strange talk?"

"That the city appears on the plains every night and vanishes again at the break of the next day. Only then to reappear in a different location the following night."

16

"THOSE WHO SEEK THE EMERALD CITY DIE TRYING OR TURN TO madness." Gomdon patted Calec on the shoulder as they exited the underground village of tunnels and stepped into morning sunlight. "Legends say the emerald city can roam hundreds of leagues in a single night. It has been seen at the mountains' edge, along the great river, the spotted lakes, and many other locations across the grassy plains. Its inhabitants are all ghosts. At least that is what those who have seen it claim. How else could people move with a traveling city?"

Calec rubbed the remnants of the lump on the back of his head. "They seemed real to me. As solid and human as anyone I know. The only oddity was that they appeared to be trapped in a past age. By the make and style of their clothing."

"The emerald city is now as black as night. The witch they killed cursed its foundations and its inhabitants and forced them to roam the plains for eternity. It is said that no man or woman from within the city or outside its walls can break the curse, and for at least a century this has held true. Those lucky enough to happen upon the city at night are well received as visitors to trade with, as the people of the ghost city rarely see outsiders. But none who have sought it have found it. The curse brings the city to only those who do not yearn for it."

"Then I am already lost," Calec said. "And where does the city go during the day?"

Gomdon shrugged.

Ghost waited nearby, his reins held by a nomad woman. Calec approached his steed.

"But, yes," Gomdon said. "You are lost. The chance that any man will stumble upon the emerald city with all the leagues of plains out here would be akin to finding one specific blade of grass in all the lands of the clan of the Whispering Horses."

A shadow heavy with doubt hung in Calec's mind.

"But I cannot give up so soon." Calec mounted Ghost and turned to the mountains. It seemed as good a direction as any.

"Then good luck on your journey, Wolf Tongue," Gomdon said. "And I advise you *not* to look for the city. If you know what I mean."

"Thank you for your ... hospitality." Calec nodded and rode off. It seemed like a fool's journey, but images of Desi's fiery and icy eyes haunted him still.

Several hours slowly passed, and Calec found nothing other than grasses and distant mountains and birds circling the skies. The wolf wind howled and skirled its cold breath across the lands. Snowflakes drifted from a gray sky and began to accumulate in the grass.

Winter was not over yet.

Calec tightened his cloak and rode on while the white powder frosted Ghost's mane. Calec looked skyward. One area in the distance seemed to shimmer through the white. The enlarging sky sea, according to all the tales, an eighth sea that would soon encompass all the sky. It would summon the Horseman—a claimer of murdered souls. A tormentor of victims. Some being from a darker age who wielded the arcane.

A falcon soared past Calec's head.

"What news of the emerald city?" Calec asked.

"Those who seek it will not find it," the bird seemed to say in Calec's pessimistic voice. "And you ride at the wrong time. It can only be found at night."

Calec and Ghost wandered the plains for hours and then

began to sleep during the day, continuing on their course for several nights, Calec slumped in the saddle, a dusting of snow still swirling in the air. Thoughts of Serileen and their future child whirled in Calec's mind for most of his waking hours and for many of those he spent sleeping. These thoughts were only occasionally interrupted by memories of Shep and Wyndstrom or of Serileen's mother's murder. Eventually, Calec realized he should return to the woods, but whenever he thought this, Desi's imploring eyes returned to his mind as if they were scorched into his soul. Those people traveled far for aid out of sheer desperation. And they failed in their abduction.

Some soft spot in Calec's heart grew tender and bruised. Those who had long suffered broke something within him like nothing else.

Darkness descended across the plains as if a sheet were laid out from east to west, a sheet splashed with blurred moons and moonlight. Calec packed up and threw dirt over his fire. He broke his fast on dried venison as he saddled Ghost. Then he spotted the glowing eyes of an owl in the brush.

"Do you burrow in the plains as well, my friend?" Calec asked.

"We all burrow out here." The owl's enormous eyes blinked. "What is it you seek?"

"That which cannot be found."

"And there is no one who knows of such magic?"

A strip of venison fell from Calec's mouth.

No. Not her. She wouldn't know this, would she? But she helped us before when Hillsvale's secrets proved too much.

The owl flapped and flew away on silent wings.

Calec glanced to the west. Did he have time to return to Westingsheer for a visit? It might be quicker than lingering and wandering across these plains for weeks or months without success.

17

CALEC PACED AFTER A SOLDIER IN THE LOWEST DUNGEONS OF Westingsheer castle. Dank and dark. A smell of mold and rotten straw. Torches barely fluttered with weak flames, and their remaining oils crackled as if on their last fumes. Moisture dripped from the walls and ceiling in slow runnels that plopped and splattered onto the floor or into Calec's hair.

Ahead, the tunnel flooded with darkness.

"The cell's at the end there." The guard pointed and handed Calec a torch. "We're ordered to stay back when she gets a visitor. Not that there's been many for this one."

Calec recalled Serileen leaving Hillsvale so she could speak with the person who now called herself the Enchantress or Noregana. Serileen had done so in hopes of aiding that village and its people. And it had been Serileen's suggestion to keep this Enchantress alive. If the Enchantress could aid Calec now, he would again be thankful for that decision.

Calec attempted to stride boldly into the darkness as he brushed his hair back from his face and ran a hand over his short beard, but some atavistic fear of the unknown, of the occult or the supernatural, thrummed in his veins.

A reflection of flames bounced off the steel bars near the top of a door ahead. Another opening and set of bars lay near the bottom of the wooden planks in this door. One opening to speak through. The other to pass food and waste buckets.

She is kept here in solitary. Permanently in the dark.

"It is not so dark here." As she spoke, her voice crackled and slipped between the lower bars of the door like a snake slithering from its den. "The torch at the end of the hall provides more light than I need."

Calec froze a good five paces from the door and cleared his throat. "I am Calec of the Woods, your visitor."

She laughed. "I know who you are. I will never forget. All the fire. The death. I think about you often."

An icy chill scampered up Calec's spine. "I've come as you've assisted us in the past. And you helped many children by doing so. You could still make amends for anything you've done and with whatever god you believe in if you help me again now."

A cackling laugh erupted. "Do not try to convince me of such foolish nonsense. The Horseman is the only god of the darkness. The only god of the sky sea. And he watches from his watery abode. His throne in the heavens. He sees all. I do not defy him. I only understand his ways. His teachings were brought to me."

Maybe he shouldn't tell her too much. If she still worshipped the Horseman, she might be opposed to assisting Calec.

Calec said, "There is a city in the plains of the far country that—"

"The emerald city. It resides in those plains. Its arcane spark is now the strongest in the land. The Horseman feels it like a bonfire. It's what he feeds on."

"Yes. And I seek this city. Something is occurring there that its inhabitants do not understand."

"Men may find it only at night. But who can understand such a city when its position and location is controlled by the Horseman's will? None can understand him."

"All I need to know is how I can find this city. How can a mortal know where it will be located on any given night?"

Silence exuded from beyond the door, as did the darkness inside the cell.

"Your offer of salvation for my soul is weak." A darting eye appeared between the upper bars. Along with strands of greasy hair. Most were blond, but one black lock lay over a scalp thickened by fire scars. "What else can you offer me?"

"I cannot grant you your freedom. That is beyond any means ... with your past."

"Then you'd better think hard, knight of the woods."

"I can offer you wine and fresh fruit. Vegetables. Meats. Pastries. Cakes. Whatever foods you desire."

"Your witch offered me the same. I did not care for it. So I took her hair instead." Pale and bone-thin fingers dragged over the black hair on her scalp. "To cover my scars. It was she who kept me alive. To experience this vile life."

"I am sorry for any suffering you must endure. But she did it to spare you."

"To spare a life such as mine is not mercy. It is punishment."

Calec's mind wheeled with other possible bribes. He could not offer her the book she'd found. Not the book of the Horseman. Even if there were another copy that hadn't burned in the fire. She was too dangerous already.

"I can offer you as much of my hair as you'd like." Calec pulled his knife from its sheath and raised it to his locks.

"I want more than just your hair." Two pale eyes peered out at him now, and a sickly hand gripped at the bars as if to assist the person inside with standing on her tiptoes. "I want your touch."

Calec's guts writhed like worms. "I must humbly pass, my lady."

"Do not try to endear me to you by referring to me as a lady. Not ever."

Calec nodded.

"And why not a touch?" the Enchantress asked, although Calec could still not see her mouth or lips moving. "I've never felt a man's touch before. I long for the sensation."

"I have a mate. One I am committed to."

"Don't use that excuse with me. Men will take other women

when they have the chance. Your witch often visits the necromancer. And she keeps these visitations secret. At least from *you*."

A feeling of missing a step when descending a staircase landed hard in Calec's gut. *How could this young woman know such things?* "You are also too young for me." *And far too repulsive inside and out.*

"Do not lie to me either, or our conversation will be over at once and you'll never find your emerald city."

"I do not lie, my ... Noregana."

"Oh, but you do. Is not the woman you pine over in the emerald city almost as young as I? You see her in your mind. She haunts you. And yet you are conflicted. Conflicted over your mate and your longing for another."

"I do not pine over the young woman for love. I wish to help her and her people. They came to me out of desperation."

"Say what you will, but I do not believe it. You may succumb to her if she attempts to seduce you."

"She must also be a few years older than you."

"If you wish to find your city, then you must make me a promise, knight of the woods."

Calec's heart trembled as if teetering on the brink of some cliff it had no choice but to jump off of.

"Do not be so dramatic," Noregana said. "I do not ask for a touch in the way you are thinking. All I ask is for you to touch my hand, and that you must promise to visit me each season of every year. You will be my most frequent companion. My man of sorts."

Calec's swallow sounded like a drowning man's gasp for air while still underwater.

"Swear it on your honor, if you have any left," the Enchantress said. "Or be gone and take all your offers of wine and fruit with you."

"I ... I will visit you." Calec's eyes quickly lidded with regret as he attempted to steady himself.

The eyes peering through the bars disappeared. Then a pale

appendage like a snake crept through the lower bars. A hand and arm as slender as bones. As gray as a winter sky. Its fingers unfurled as if part of some dead flower.

"Touch my hand, and I will tell you all you need to know," she said.

Calec hesitated. This might be a trick. But could she truly command magic with only a touch? No. She'd only been able to manipulate the details of memories. A touch should be safe.

He reached out.

"With your skin," she said. "No gloves."

Calec peeled off his glove, stepped forward, and again reached out. He hesitated as his hand hovered over hers, which seemed to sheet off an icy cold.

Was he going too far? Or was this gesture merely what it seemed and then he'd be able to help those people?

He closed his eyes again as he brushed his fingertips across her palm.

Her hand trembled, and she groaned.

Calec's stomach turned with revulsion.

"Now, was that so difficult?" she asked. "I only wished to feel it. Your skin on mine."

Calec snatched his hand back and wiped it across his leather leggings. His fingers felt cold, and his hand shook like an autumn leaf in the wolf wind.

"Where is the city?" he asked.

"The path to the emerald city is marked by one of the Horseman's moons. The one called Demon's Coin. But the moon is devious. Allow its hand to guide you."

"How can such a thing be possible? Does this hand move?"

"You will have to find out. But its secret is to not believe what should now be obvious unless you witness its true form. Your mortal eyes will deceive you before you find the truth."

"Your words are laced with deception as well. If I cannot understand their meaning, or if you are lying to me—"

"What? Then you'll return and punish me?"

"I will not return or visit you ever again."

"Then test my claim."

Calec wheeled around and marched away as fast as he could.

"And I will see you again in the spring, my knight of the woods."

18

Calec rode Ghost across the plains of the far country, his yellow ribbon woven around his fingers. The sun melted into the western horizon and a gray sheet of clouds there. The wolf wind howled out of the north and flung snowflakes about in spiraling clouds.

The Demon's Coin moon was veiled.

Curse the Enchantress and her treachery. Noregana. What was the meaning of the new name? And who took on a new name so long after birth?

Calec turned his face from the wind as he and Ghost plodded through the snow-speckled grasses. This snow had developed a hardened upper crust and crunched like dried bones when Ghost's hooves punched through it.

"Are you fulfilling your need for travel now?" Ghost seemed to ask Calec. "Or does this make you want to return to the woods, rider of the sword?"

"Do not call me that. That's how Wyndstrom refers to me. And no, this isn't what something inside me was longing for."

Hours wore away and faded under the plunging night. The wolf wind pushed clouds across the sky, and rents appeared in their gray cover. A moon emerged. The original moon of the lands, floating in its full state like a snowball suspended in the heavens.

As the night wore on, other pockets of sky opened. Stars sparkled against the darkness. And so did other more distant moons. Then the Demon's Coin moon revealed itself, along with its surface markings that could be construed as a monster's face above three scratch marks.

Allow its hand to guide you.

There did not appear to be a hand marking, but the three lines on the moon converged near the bottom of its lighted face, forming an arrow of sorts.

Scratches could be made by a hand.

But if that was the obvious answer and not a step beyond the obvious, then his eyes would supposedly deceive him when viewing the moon if it was not in its true form.

Calec studied its lighted surface for several minutes as he pondered any idea that would come to him.

Maybe the hand was at the top of the scratches, above where they converged. That way, this arrow of sorts would point him in the opposite direction of what the markings seemed to indicate. Not south but north, and pointing at the sky instead of the ground below.

Or maybe he was overthinking it, and Noregana only wanted to deceive him.

There was only one way to find out. He turned Ghost to his right and headed in the direction the arrow indicated. South.

They rode on as the snow swirled and the wind gusted. Atop each rolling hill, Calec had to shift the direction in which they traveled, either a little more to the east or west as they continued south and farther away from Jaylen's Pass and the woods.

Dark hours dragged along before dawn rose like an unwanted light.

"Damn the coming day," Calec said. "How will we ever catch the city if it moves again before tonight?"

"I pray for rest," Ghost seemed to say. "We should sleep during the day and only travel at night. Like before."

Calec grunted as he dismounted and made camp and a fire. Ghost grazed as Calec heated oats in water. When the oats were ready, he and Ghost consumed them, Ghost heartily, Calec distractedly and more out of habit. They were warm but lacked flavor.

After the sun rose in the east, they slept as best they could until nightfall. Then, when darkness settled over the plains again, Calec broke his fast and rode Ghost after the Demon's Coin.

19

Jaremonde forced the door to the old manor open. Its hinges squealed like one of Valtera's pigs did when being chased out of someone's house. Only darkness awaited him, the windows having been boarded shut.

The old manor of Valtera's witch.

No one had lived here since. Not in over a century.

But some presence still thrived within. He could feel it in the air, the walls.

Jaremonde marched inside, attempting to mask his fear with feigned boldness as he motioned for Rimmell to follow him. Jaremonde carried an old pike of the lord's guard in one hand, and it made him feel more akin to the ancient soldiers of Valtera rather than to a constable who was no longer needed in this moving city. No longer needed until recently, that was.

"What do you expect to find in this old place?" Rimmell held a lantern of his own, an old short sword now sheathed at his waist.

"Answers to all your foolish questions." Jaremonde inched along, casting light onto the walls inside the antechamber. It was all as black as the rest of the city. Although not as shimmery, as if a century of dust coated every surface. "But Lanigrad said it was already well searched. Several times. I just want to have another look around, given the change in the curse."

Rimmell wandered off in the opposite direction as Jaremonde, his light fading into the darkness.

"Don't go far," Jaremonde called as a deeper chill settled in the air of the manor. "We still don't know how this curse strikes."

"There's nothing here." Rimmell's voice sounded hollow and distorted as it echoed down a long hallway. "It looks like this place was cleaned out."

Jaremonde moved to follow Rimmell, hoping not to get separated.

It was true. No furniture or candles or lamps remained in the antechamber. A hearth against the far wall was still coated in soot. A grate sat inside.

"I was afraid of that," Jaremonde said. "There probably aren't any answers here, but I hoped it might be worth the visit. Some of the documents Lanigrad uncovered spoke of people raiding the witch's manor the day she was staked out to burn. Supposedly they weren't scared enough of her before they knew she could make an entire city vanish and reappear somewhere else. However, in the following decades, the people searched the place several times."

Rimmell continued down the hall while poking his head into doorways. Most chambers still had heavy wooden doors hanging on their hinges, but none of the doors were shut.

"And you thought the curse might be broken here?" Rimmell asked.

Jaremonde sighed to display irritation instead of dread, and his sigh was more than loud enough for Rimmell to hear. "I don't think the curse can be broken by anyone inside or outside of the city. But I'm hoping to find answers as to why the deaths have started up again."

"And you believe you can prevent people from dying? As if they're not linked to the curse?"

Jaremonde groaned. "What else, in all your wisdom, would you have me do? Just allow some ancient spell to continue to plague our people? To let worms breed and give birth inside people's skin and then burrow out once they've matured?"

Rimmell remained silent for a while as they continued

through the halls in the east wing. Jaremonde attempted to remember exactly where they'd gone so they wouldn't get lost.

"That was my idea," Rimmell said.

"What idea?"

"The worms burrowing out of the victims. I mean, that was my idea for all the holes."

Jaremonde shook his head. How had Rimmell ended up with him? The more they worked together now because they had a real issue, the more dim-witted Rimmell seemed. Rimmell was chosen for the position by the people, back when there were no mysterious deaths in the city. When the people probably didn't want him helping them with their duties. Valtera functioned quite well with its citizens sticking to their trades. The people had to work quickly and very hard to harvest enough food and goods at each daily stop on their city's eternal journey. That kept almost all of the more serious lawlessness down. And if something did occur, then the people banded together against the criminal. Punishment was swift and without debate. In Valtera, people rarely stepped out of line. Not much beyond petty theft. The same as it'd been for the century after the witch was burned, although there'd been a lord and an entire regiment of guards for the tens of thousands in Valtera before that time. Such things had no longer been needed.

The soldiers and guards of Valtera drifted to other trades or became food and goods gatherers as their enemies all but disappeared. The savage nomads who had at times raided their city now feared Valtera's people, believing they were ghosts. The nomads would only trade from a distance now, their terror wafting from them. And no longer could anyone plan a siege or attack on Valtera. Not with its curse.

"I don't think it's worms anymore," Rimmell said as they continued along the manor, everything still hauntingly empty. "There are no worm tracks crawling through the blood, and no worm bodies or moths or anything left behind. I'd think one would have died with a victim by now or have been discovered under their skin. Or they'd leave a trail."

Jaremonde shook his head. "I never thought it was worms. I was merely humoring you."

"Oh. Well, I have another idea."

"And what is that?"

"Spikes."

"What?"

"Like metal stakes. Some monster covered with spikes hugs each victim. That way it could still happen quick and not cause more than a scream."

"So burrowing worms or a spiked monster that can hug people from the front, sides, and behind, where all their punctures are? Keep the ideas coming. I think they're helping."

"Well, maybe it wraps around them, then. Like a constricting snake covered in spikes."

Jaremonde ignored him and continued his search.

They finished their brief inspection of the manor, then departed. Jaremonde closed the front door behind him and relocked a bolt on the outside.

Jaremonde led Rimmell back to their quarter as the sun hovered low in the west.

"That took longer than I thought it would," Jaremonde said. "That's all the investigating for today. We'll meet with the others again and see if they've discovered anything on their end."

They passed the saddle maker, Olinia, who glared at Jaremonde. He waved and planted a fake smile on his lips. She used a hammer and punch to work details into a cut of leather.

"That woman has always hated me," Jaremonde said.

"She treats everyone that way." Rimmell's slapping footsteps followed behind.

They turned down another street.

As Jaremonde passed a doorway, it creaked open, and a hand reached out.

A middle-aged woman stepped outside, smoothing her graying brunette hair under her coif. "Constable Jaremonde. How are things?" She glanced hesitantly at Rimmell. "I've just cooked a wonderful dinner."

Jaremonde glanced at Rimmell as well, then he cleared his

throat. "Well, Aprena, it seems the constable's duties have become much more than a trifle in terms of importance. We still hunt the cause for the change in the curse, but I've some hunches and we're getting somewhere."

"Oh, thank you, constable, for your persistence." The woman stepped out and took his hands in hers. "Would you like to come inside for a quick bite before returning to your work?"

Jaremonde faced Rimmell. "You go get some supper. Meet me at my house in an hour."

Rimmell glanced between the two and nodded as he swallowed.

Jaremonde watched Rimmell as he turned and walked dejectedly down the street.

"Oh, Aprena. It's good to see you." Jaremonde stepped inside and shut the door.

20

GHOST CRESTED A SMALL HILL IN THE EARLY HOURS BEFORE sunrise. The wolf wind smacked Calec across the cheeks with an icy gust. But this time Calec did not turn away from it.

Nothing but a pond and more empty plains lay beyond the hillside.

Calec had ridden after the Demon Coin's markings for two more nights and then in the opposite direction for another three. All without success. And now dawn was less than an hour away. Either the city was too far across the plains to reach in a single night, or he was still being deceived.

Anger clawed its way out of his heart and swam around in his blood.

Noregana.

She'd lied to him, or she deceived him still. But how could he ever take revenge on her? Only by not visiting her as he'd promised. Mayhap she realized this and was back in her cell laughing at his attempts. There were no real consequences for her.

Calec's anger flared as he urged Ghost down the gentle incline.

"Damn that woman."

"It seems hope is lost," Ghost said. "Do we turn around and

make for the woods? Before we become so lost we cannot hope to find our way, or at least your way, home?"

As they walked, Calec's anger fizzled out, and hope left him. He would continue trying a few more nights, but it seemed he would eventually have to give up. They only carried so many food stores.

The pond passed on Calec's left, and as he veered Ghost toward it for a drink, a flash of light caught his eye. He glanced down. The pond was frozen over in a sheet of ice.

He swung his leg over the saddle and dismounted to break up the ice for Ghost, but as he stuck his heel out and was about to stomp, something about the ice made him pause. The hairs on the back of his neck prickled like spines.

The moons overhead were reflected in that smooth sheet, and each seemed to float in its own sky. To slap him in the face with their vivid beauty. The first moon. Many smaller ones. The Demon's Coin. And the supposed scratch marks on that one's surface appeared different from what he'd been looking at this night.

Calec glanced to the sky and then to the pond again to confirm it as his skin tingled with realization.

It was true. The scratch marks in the sky that pointed south, or possibly north if he were following the opposite direction, pointed northeast in the moon's reflection in the ice. Or less likely southwest.

It should be impossible for a reflection not to point in the same direction as the actual object. But here it was.

Calec studied the reflection and moon for several minutes, taking note of the surrounding plains and distant mountains.

The moon is devious. Allow its hand to guide you. But its secret is to not believe what should now be obvious unless you witness its true form. Your mortal eyes will deceive you before you find the truth.

"Damn that woman," Calec said. "But she may have spoken the truth after all."

"So, do we head northeast?" Ghost asked.

"That depends on where the moon's markings are pointing

this coming night. The sun is about to rise. We will take our rest and try anew after nightfall."

As Calec made camp, he caught himself staring off toward the distant but looming mountains, hope returning and rising along with an inkling of fear and apprehension.

21

CALEC PULLED GHOST TO A HARD STOP AMIDST THE MOONLIT grasses of the plains.

There, in the distance of the valley, something glistened like light on water. But the reflective surfaces were black, and they could not be made out.

Whatever it was, it was not emerald. And Gomdon had said the city was now black.

Calec shivered, more from suspense than from the cold.

If that is the city, it is very difficult to make out even at night. Probably even if it is right in front of you. If you didn't know what to look for.

Ghost seemed to see it as well, or he sensed some disturbance. He shuddered beneath Calec and the saddle.

"Ride, Ghost. The true face of the Demon's Coin has led us to the vanished city."

Calec bounced his heels against Ghost's flanks, and they raced down the hill toward the reflected moonlight.

As the area drew near, the shimmering surfaces of outer walls and towers and houses and buildings came into view. Turrets. Black flags snapping in the wind. All painted with silver moonlight. Glistening like polished glass.

And the gates to the city stood open.

Calec's heart thudded inside his chest. What kind of power

could make an entire city vanish and reappear amidst all these plains? Power far greater than anything Calec had previously considered even in his wildest imaginings.

This city was supposed to be myth. But if this were true, what other magic might lurk out in the world? Such magic might only grow stronger and more potent as the sky sea spread and enveloped the heavens.

Calec shoved his fearful wonder aside and slowed Ghost to a walk, Ghost's footsteps quiet within the grasses outside the city's walls.

Only one guard sat beside the gates, and she appeared to be asleep. A robust middle-aged woman with short hair and a cap.

"I wouldn't have guessed that any inhabitant of a city only visible at night would sleep during that time," Calec whispered to Ghost.

"Maybe they are not human," Ghost seemed to say. "They may all be spirits."

"They sure did a number on my head if they were only spirits." Calec's lump was nearly gone now. "And why would ghosts abduct people?"

"Don't ghosts despise the living?"

The woman snored, a quick burst that cut off abruptly.

"Well, it seems there is a person here who sleeps at night. Like the kind we know." Calec patted Ghost's neck. "Probably not a spirit."

After a few minutes of waiting, and when the guard still hadn't roused, Calec used the flat of his sword to tap against the outer gate several times.

"And why in all the witch's hells are you knocking at ..." The woman's words trailed off as her bleary eyes widened, and she studied Calec. "Who are you? You're definitely not from Valtera. Nor a typical nomad."

She reached for something beside her, a long pike, although its craftsmanship appeared ancient. She gripped the weapon and raised it before her, along with a horn she brought toward her lips. But she paused.

"You're the first outsider who's ever approached the gates on my watch," she said. "Ever. Who are you and why have you come to Valtera?"

Calec attempted to show a friendly smile. "I am Calec of the Woods. Some men and a young woman from this city attempted to bring me here perhaps half a fortnight ago. A woman named Desi."

"Ah. This all makes sense, then, and there's no need for me to grow overly hopeful or optimistic." The shocked expression was washed from the woman's face, and hints of exhaustion overpowered anything else. "Name's Olinia. Leatherworker. And I heard about all that nonsense. Thought it a wasted effort. Seemed like it was, too, as it took you long enough to show up."

Now she appeared even less like a spirit left unto this world.

Calec smiled again and gathered himself up. "Pardon my intrusion at the hour, Lady Olinia. I was hoping to find your lord or king or his knights—"

"I'm not a lady, and we don't have a king or lord. Haven't for decades. And no knights. All we have is a constable and some of his men. And lots of workers. And a witch's curse."

Calec nodded. "My apologies. Where could I find this constable? You see, I was—"

"Don't go on and on at this hour. I'm no longer in awe of you. I'm tired, and this is the time for rest. The one who watches the gate at night is *never* bothered. And I've got a long day tomorrow. A lot of saddle repairs to make."

Calec suppressed his surprise, having rarely seen anyone, much less a woman, be so blunt with a visitor.

"Anyway," Olinia said, "the constable lives in one of the nearby quarters. You should talk to him first. He heads up dealing with the aftermath of the witch of Valtera. His father before him and so on. His house is not far." She continued with directions about streets and turns. "Now, if you can break our curse, I'll grovel at your feet and let the awe of your presence flow. But our curse cannot be undone. Such a feat has been attempted *many* times. In every imaginable scenario by many people. No man or woman inside or even outside Valtera can do it. That includes you. So until the curse is lifted, I must remain at my post this night and also take what rest I can find."

She stepped aside and allowed Calec to pass before she sat down, and her head fell back against the gate.

Ghost's hooves clopped on stone as they entered the vanished city. Black streets ran into the distance, choked with houses and loaded carts. No people. A few chickens clucked in the darkness, followed by the grunting of pigs somewhere down a street. A horse nickered.

But the city carried a clean scent, unlike any city Calec had lived in or visited. Unlike Westingsheer and Landing where the people's waste piled up. This was fresh mountain air, although bitterly cold.

Calec took in the city, surveying the streets as he and Ghost moved along. A few torches burned here and there against walls. Veiled lights also shone from inside some of the houses, most of which were single-story structures packed together.

Mayhap these people feared venturing out at night. But there was only one sleeping guard at their gates. If they were afraid, whatever they were afraid of was likely already within Valtera.

Calec steered his steed down a few streets and made what he thought were the appropriate turns before arriving at the house he suspected was the constable's, although all the houses appeared similar.

"Do I knock?" Calec asked.

"You may want to, after all the trouble we had finding this city," Ghost replied. "Even if the gate guard was less than cordial with our arrival."

Calec's blood spiked with apprehension. What would they expect of him if these people had already tried so much? He dreaded the hope and optimism they would likely associate with him.

Calec dismounted, took a deep breath, and knocked on the door—solid wood surrounded by black stone, like all the others.

He waited a few minutes before knocking again. No answer.

He stepped away and knocked at the adjacent house that definitely had a light burning inside.

Footsteps pounded around within this house before the door opened. Light spewed out. Several torches burned inside and outlined a man with a potbelly and mustache, both of which extended beyond his silhouette.

"Who? What are—"

Someone inside released a gasp. "It's him! The witch hunter of Duminborne."

About a half dozen people were gathered inside this house, all dressed as if they'd emerged from some drawing in an ancient book. Strange tunics, trousers, and caps. Most crowded over a table, but one of them stood off to the side. The young woman with the pleading eyes of sky-sea blue.

Some tender spot in Calec's heart throbbed with pain. "I am not a witch hunter. I am Calec of the Woods, former knight of King Trithemore Simblade."

Calec quickly explained about witches and the people of the woods and how he was one of them, but no one seemed to be listening. They all gawked at him.

"And how did you arrive here?" the man who answered the door asked.

Calec briefly summarized in a few short minutes how he'd found the city as well as his trials.

The bald man with the mustache shook his head and waved him over to the table where the others were all gathered. "Welcome, Sir Calec. I am Jaremonde, the constable of Valtera, the emerald city. We've gathered a few people together here and are working hard to try to stop the deaths of our people. Lanigrad, our most learned scholar"—he pointed to a tall and svelte man in middle age—"believes the answers may lie in Valtera's history."

Calec stepped forward, and the half-dozen men around him nodded to him.

"Join us in our discussion of what plagues Valtera and what we seek," Lanigrad said as he motioned for Calec to sit. "We are overjoyed that you've found us. That you persevered through all the trials you claim to have faced. None before you have done so. And I would be lying if I admitted to merely being surprised that you now stand before us."

Calec slowly took a seat as his eyes wandered about the group and settled on the young woman who stood beyond them. She stared back at him.

22

CALEC GLANCED OVER THE BOOKS BEFORE HIM, HIS EYES RUNNING over images and stylized words. Drawings of a jade city so pristine it glimmered under the sun. So majestic it couldn't have been real, unless in Heaven.

The men of Valtera were gathered around Calec at the table, gnawing tough meat and drinking. Discussions and disagreements about the meaning of words or stories rose like storms and then faded into silence.

"Just try to keep it down," Constable Jaremonde said. "My wife is sick and needs her sleep. She's just in the other room."

The constable's hand clamped down on Calec's shoulder.

"Again, we're still mighty impressed not only that you found Valtera," the constable said, "but that you came at all. Even if you cannot help us, I'll still call you friend till the end of my days. And I am truly sorry for how we went about it. We heard about a man referred to as the witch hunter who lived near Westingsheer. And the woods you reside in were not far from where our city was located on that fateful day when the others found you. I ordered them to return with you as quickly as possible, as we need assistance with our curse. And we needed someone to lure you to the emerald city"—he glanced over at Desi, who watched from the edge of the room—"to get you to visit and then hopefully make you never want to leave."

Calec smiled and sipped on a sweet mead that filled his tankard. "I will try to aid all of you." He avoided looking directly at Desi.

"Perhaps if you marry Desi, you will wish to never leave," Jaremonde said with a straight face.

Thick tension descended around them in an instant, but its weight and solidity were quickly shattered when Desi said in a clear and distinct tone, "I will not be forced into marrying any man."

The tension and awkward silence returned, and it lingered for a minute.

"I apologize again about your head," a narrowed-shouldered man with an overhanging stomach said and cleared his throat to dispel the silence. Climson, their blacksmith. Perhaps more muscle for this small group of investigators, although it appeared it might have been a while since his muscle was needed. "Wasn't sure how else to get you back to Valtera."

"Unfortunately, we ran out of time," Lanigrad, the scholar, said as he leafed through pages with a gentle touch. His jaws worked on some strip of salted meat. "This curse takes the inhabitants of Valtera along for its ride whether we try to flee it or not. We don't have to be inside its walls. Many have tried to escape it. None have succeeded."

"Let me understand a few things," Calec said. They'd already been over Valtera's curse and how it began with the burning of a witch. "What was this witch actually accused of?"

"Witchcraft," Lanigrad said. "There are reports of her strange doings inside her manor. People saw her up on her roof at night seeming to speak with something. Some false god. We now believe she was communing with the ancient Horseman of the sky sea."

"Bah," Climson said. "There's no such thing as a sea in the sky. And no Horseman. Worms eat us as soon as we go to ground, and then they shit us out. What worse afterlife is there than to become nothing but worm shit?"

"Then what do you think that watery thing growing in the

sky is?" Lanigrad asked. "The oldest texts often mention an eighth sea."

Climson shrugged. "It's only a sunspot. A trick of the eye."

"Then why is it enlarging every season with the coming of many new moons?" Lanigrad asked.

"Well, water can't just sit up there. It'd fall." Climson shook his head. "You'd think a scholar would use common sense sometimes."

"Moons have a pull of their own." Lanigrad swallowed his meat but didn't look up from skimming a tome. "And clouds must be composed of water, or hold water, or why would rain ever fall from them?"

Climson grumbled something and sliced off a hunk of dark meat from a platter.

"But that was all?" Desi stepped forward and hovered just behind Rimmell and Lanigrad as if she could no longer contain herself. "They burned a woman alive because they thought she was up to mischief and was seen on her own roof? That's absurd. They must have had some solid reasoning."

"The books mention some occurrences, but it seems their writers did not wish to record those in detail," Lanigrad said. "As if they were afraid of what they might evoke with such records."

"No wonder she cursed us." Desi's eyes burned with something other than entreaty now. Calec tried not to stare. "If it were a man, the people or lord would have held a trial at least. With a single woman, all it probably took was one man's word against hers."

"Desi! This isn't the time for your arguments about women's fairness," Jaremonde said in a scolding tone. "You may remain in the room *only* if you do not interrupt us."

A scowl deepened in Desi's features, but she took a step back from the table.

"I wish to express my agreement with young Desi," Aonor, the master of collections, said. Then he fell into a fit of soft coughing. "But I will also note that the curse is killing women as well. The witch's anger cannot only be directed at the men who accused her."

"Maybe the curse cannot be directed at any one person when an entire city is made to appear at a different location each night." Desi folded her arms with disgust but would not look directly at Aonor.

"That's enough, Desi." Jaremonde waved her away, but she only stepped back a couple paces and stood near the wall.

"I've heard tales of her eating children," a young man named Rimmell said to Calec, speaking for the first time since Calec was introduced to him. "That story and others like it are still passed around when you grow up in Valtera. The rest of you may be too old to remember, but I am not."

"Children's horror stories." Jaremonde shook his head. "To give 'em a good scare and make them behave is all."

"She ate their brains as soup," Climson said. "A delicacy for witches."

A hand settled on Calec's arm. The master of collections leaned over and pushed back a feathered cap on his head as if to whisper in Calec's ear. Aonor's breath was as sweet as lavender, a scent like roses perfuming the air around him. So sweet it made Calec think the man must wish to cover a smell as pungent as rotting flesh.

"Oh, please help us so I don't have to spend another night with these men," Aonor said only to Calec. "Desi is so distraught by it all."

Aonor sat back upright and brushed something from his white sleeve laced with gold. Then he coughed into a kerchief.

"Well, we've established that we don't really know much about what this witch did to deserve to be burned," Calec said, and all eyes turned to him. "And the people who have recently died from these punctures, what do we know about them? Does it happen when the city vanishes? Has anyone seen anything? Are the victims related, and if so, how? What do their friends and family have to say about it all?"

Rimmell cleared his throat. "It has been my duty to question everyone around the scenes as well as the victims' friends and families. Under Jaremonde's guidance, of course." He tapped his knuckles on the table as if waiting, but Jaremonde didn't interrupt or add anything. "Screams have been heard, but there have been no sightings of magic or worms emerging from bodies, or spiked monsters running away. It is as if they've just been chosen and struck dead and found later. Many women. Some men. No children. No connection other than these people all live in Valtera. The deaths seem to happen at night, but more specific timing is hard to pin down as many of them have just been found in the morning. However, these deaths don't seem to occur immediately after the post-twilight vanishing."

Calec brooded on that for a moment. "And where does Valtera go during the day? If no one can see it in daylight?"

"We can see it just fine in daylight," Jaremonde said. "Our scenery doesn't change until after twilight. We feel nothing. We just look out from the walls and see something different from the hour before, or we wake to a new sight."

"I guess we would not be the ones to describe why Valtera cannot be seen in the sunlight, if that is truly the case," Lanigrad said.

Calec nodded. "Agreed. I heard it from the nomads. If the city could be seen in daylight, they'd have likely seen it at some point. Far easier to find a black city under sunlight than moonlight."

Lanigrad nodded his agreement.

"How do you find enough food for everyone in an entire city?" Calec asked. "When your location is constantly moving?"

"It is not easy," Climson said. "That is why we work so well together and partly why we need so little from a constable. We're always busy with each new area outside our city. We've a river that still always runs through the center of Valtera, but otherwise there are many whose trade is to go out and harvest whatever foods grow in the area. They also hunt. They plant and seed the plains in hopes of the emerald city returning to a location nearby around the time of harvest season. That seldom happens, but we've gotten lucky and have gathered large food stores when the timing is right. *If we arrive before the crops have gone bad or before they are eaten by birds and bugs.*"

"Where does your river flow to?" Calec asked. The idea of a running river in this city did not mesh in his head.

"Only the witch and her eaten children know that." Climson laughed. "Seems to end just beyond the city walls."

"It was once the river that roared down out of the mountains," Lanigrad said. "The Rogue River. A small portion of it travels with us."

"And has anyone been back to the original site of Valtera?" Calec asked.

"We don't have a lot of time for distant traveling, sir knight," Lanigrad said. "You witnessed firsthand what happened when we tried to find you in one day and night's time. Some have seen the site when it's been close, but there's been no detailed surveying of the area since these deaths have occurred. Any intentional sightings of the area are born more out of longing for what once was. And all the records I found on the matter mention that the site is empty except for a stake that still rises from the area where Stake Square once resided. Patches of snow and ice are also mentioned, but those are not unusual for the location. And all who made note of the stake claimed there was nothing more than ice in the area surrounding it."

"Then what is your plan thus far to understand this new part of the curse?" Calec asked.

"We've been taking evidence from all the bodies." Jaremonde sat up straight and pulled at his mustache as if he were under scrutiny. "Questioning people. Visiting the witch's old manor. Holding these meetings each night where Lanigrad fills us in on history and we all share what we've learned."

"And piecing together these legends and children's horror stories with history hasn't revealed anything?" Calec sipped at his mead.

The others all eyed each other, but no one said anything.

"I'd like to see any more bodies that are found," Calec said. "As well as visit the original site of your emerald city, the witch's manor, and the abandoned site where she was burned. I'd also like to help Lanigrad comb through historical tomes, if you are all willing."

Lanigrad gave Calec a nod. "I applaud your reasoning and need for thoroughness. Does a knight enjoy reading? There are shelves and shelves of books in the old citadel."

"My father was the king's sage. I've spent my fair share of time reading and assisting in finding works of the pen."

Lanigrad smiled. "Then there is something I will show you before we continue digging deeper into old tomes."

23

LATE THE NEXT MORNING, AFTER THE CONSTABLE AND THE MEN assisting him took a brief rest and insisted Calec do the same, Calec followed Lanigrad and the others as they rode through the city. Aonor was absent, claiming he had records to make and other scribe or collections work to do, and Desi had been ordered to stay behind at Jaremonde's house.

"One of the sites you wished to see." Lanigrad pointed across a short but wide bridge. "Just across the Rogue River. The waters run deep and narrow through the canal here, but on the other side is where the witch was burned. Stake Square."

Calec urged Ghost to cross the bridge, and his hoofbeats sounded hollow as they passed over the river.

"No one comes here still?" Calec asked once they'd reached the square—actually a circular area nestled between the backsides of buildings. It appeared more desolate than the plains at night. Except for a stake standing in the middle.

Lanigrad shook his head and dismounted, his long legs making the movement easy for him. So fit for a scholar. "Not often since the burning. At least that's what all the books say. And the people claim it's bad luck to walk this square."

Calec studied the blackened stones in the vicinity. Nothing stood out as noticeably different from the rest of the city.

"Valtera has more than bad luck already haunting it." Calec

approached the stake, a pole that stood straight out of the stones and rose twice the height of a man. "Have any of you ever been here before?"

Jaremonde, Climson, and Rimmell remained on their horses at the edge of the square, their expressions at least seeming to appear patient as they waited.

"Once in the past month or so," Jaremonde said as he tugged at his mustache.

"I have not been here recently," Lanigrad said as he followed Calec. "But I've visited several times. Wouldn't be a very good historian of the city if I hadn't seen its sites."

Calec held his breath as he ran a hand over the stake. Its surface was rough against his glove, and it seemed to grab at the leather. But no sparks or flame leapt out of it to light him on fire as perhaps his subconscious feared.

He knelt at the base of the stake. There were areas along the corners where something—probably rope—had rubbed the wood smooth. All the faces of the stake were weather worn and cracked. Pale gray. Only the base was still blackened.

He whispered so quietly he almost couldn't hear his own voice, "What did they do to you? To cause you to curse the city in such a manner? And to cause all this death so long ago and again now?" He exhaled as he pondered it. "I vow to find out what happened, and I will attempt to right whatever wrongs were done in your name. *Or* I will find your source of power, and if it is evil, I will break it."

The wind died for a few heartbeats but then returned in a raging blast.

"I recently learned of an innkeeper's tale about the witch's burning," Climson said to the others beside him, although he spoke loud enough that Calec could hear him over the wind. "Back when Valtera had innkeepers. Anyway, this innkeeper had supposedly been drinking a heady brew of hops and honey."

"You remember any tale with drink in it." Jaremonde raised a waterskin with steam pluming from its opening, and he took a swig.

The blacksmith grinned at the constable. "Sure enough. And so now I understand my true calling in these matters."

Climson waited for the constable to pass the waterskin over, and then he drank as well.

"The witch burned right outside this innkeeper's tavern here on Stake Square," Climson said and nodded to Calec. "The tale this innkeeper supposedly spun after the fact claimed that he had more patrons that night than on any other night of his life. At least until it got dark. They had trouble lighting the fire to burn the witch. So the watchers all came inside to get warm and fill their bellies with liquor. The wolf wind howled like the dead that night, but colder. Snow flew in flurries. Ice fell from the sky too. Valtera saw several feet of drifts overnight. It's said that these patrons could hear the witch's skin crackling like logs as she burned. It also said that if you're brave enough to venture here at night, you can still hear the crackling of her flesh on the wind."

"I heard another—" Rimmell began, but Calec cut him off.

"Who told you this tale?" Calec asked Climson as he studied the backs of the surrounding buildings. "Pardon my intrusion, if you will, Sir Rimmell."

Rimmell nodded and smiled politely.

"I heard it from the oldest mason in Valtera," Climson said. "He thought the story was close to how his father used to tell it. I questioned him a bit about his father and if his father was a witness to the event. The old mason eventually and abashedly admitted to actually hearing the tale from an old woman. The oldest person in the city."

Calec examined the markings of an ancient fire around the base of the stake. "And who is this woman?"

Climson shrugged. He looked to the others, but no one answered.

"The story I heard was that the witch went up like kindling," Rimmell said. "That the people doused her in as much oil as Valtera's torches could burn in a month. Her blaze warmed the entire city all through the night."

"But none of Valtera's dead bodies have ever been found here?" Calec asked.

"I don't know every detail of the deaths from long ago," Jaremonde said over the wind, "but of the more recent victims, there haven't been any at Stake Square. However, one body was found under the bridge we just crossed over. Rimmell and I found it. It was a young woman."

"Who was she?" Calec asked.

"No one who stood out in Valtera," Jaremonde said. "Recently married. No children. Her husband was out harvesting roots when she was found. They lived in a house a few streets away from here."

"No witnesses?"

"Only claims that a scream was heard echoing as if someone was trapped in a tunnel. That's why they sent for me."

Calec rose and paced around the square for a few minutes.

"And what structures surround us now?" Calec motioned to the walls of the nearby buildings.

Lanigrad glanced about and then pointed at the walls in turn as he spoke, as if reading off a list. "The backside of an old church. Houses. Abandoned shops on Walderdorf Street."

"No tavern? Like in the innkeeper's tale?" Calec asked.

Lanigrad shook his head. "Not currently."

"And have there been any problems with any of these buildings?"

"Not in terms of anything linked to the occult," Lanigrad said. "None of the houses are currently occupied, and no deaths have been found there. None at the church either, as far as I know."

"But any windows that may have once overlooked the square are now bricked over."

Calec faced one of two areas of the square where there was no surrounding wall. North. The other was a smaller opening to the east where he could see the bridge they'd crossed over. The wolf wind howled down from the mountains through the northern gap. It swirled about the square, tugging at and throwing Calec's cloak about.

"Do Valtera's cardinal directions ever change?" Calec asked.

"Does that gap always face north? Or does the city ... rotate on its axis with the vanishings?"

Lanigrad didn't ponder the question long. "The city moves about the plains, but the north wall of Valtera always faces north. Same with the other walls."

Interesting.

It might be of no consequence but was still a strange detail that could have gone either way.

"There isn't much to see here." Lanigrad mounted his gray mare.

"I wouldn't say that." Calec finished his rounds of the area. "There isn't much here now, but for me to paint a picture of what might have happened, it helps to have an image of the original scene in my head. Now, unless the city's present location is close to the original site where Valtera was founded, may we visit the old manor of this supposed witch?"

Lanigrad turned his mount around and followed the others as they headed back over the bridge under the gusting of the wolf wind.

24

CALEC RODE BESIDE LANIGRAD, THEIR HORSES' HOOVES CLOPPING on Valtera's stones as they ascended a hill. Light dwindled in the west. The sun slid toward the horizon, throwing long shadows across the streets and around the houses and buildings.

Enormous estates and manors sprawled across the margins of the hillside, overlooking the city. A few of these manors had towers and turrets, as if these nobles wished to pretend they lived as royalty in their castles. But all were as black as shadow and as shimmery as glass.

Jaremonde grunted as he stopped before one boarded-up manor and heaved himself out of his saddle. He fumbled with a ring of keys that rattled, and he searched for a specific one while approaching the door.

"Rimmell and I were here very recently," the constable said. "I didn't perform a thorough search of every room of this place, but there didn't seem to be anything left inside. It was cleaned out long ago. So, I do not believe there's anything here that will help you, witch hunter."

Calec dismounted. "I'd just like to look around."

The constable unlocked the door and eased it open, the hinges creaking so shrilly it seemed they hadn't been parted in decades.

Jaremonde lit a torch as Calec stepped inside.

Inside, it felt as if some ancient presence slumbered in its dark lair. The eerie quiet summoned a feeling that if Calec spoke too loudly or his footsteps echoed, some beast would awaken and come slithering or crawling out of a shadowed corner.

Thin blades of sunlight swung through gaps in the boarded windows and painted stripes across the floor.

Jaremonde entered behind Calec, but he stumbled over a lip in the doorway. The constable cursed as he dropped his torch. It thudded against stone and sent a hollow echo reverberating around the antechamber.

Calec held his breath as he glanced about. The torch rolled in a tightening circle, its flames wavering but always reaching straight upward as it moved.

Then it happened.

The walls began to shake, to grow ethereal. Like mist only blacker.

Calec stepped back toward the doorway, his hand reaching for his sword.

"What magic is this?" he asked.

But no one replied.

The walls melted away. Night seemed to surround him, although he could make out a plank of red sunlight on the distant horizon. But that light faded quickly, leaving only moon-light and several moons hanging overhead.

Calec's heart raced as he leapt back for what should have been the doorway to the manor.

Then he understood.

Valtera had vanished and left him behind. Even after finding the emerald city and spending time within its walls, he would not travel with it.

The city disappeared so soon ... How am I to ever help these people if I must locate their city every night?

Plains and grasses surrounded him, the blades rolling in waves under the wolf wind.

25

GHOST STOOD NOT TWENTY PACES AWAY FROM CALEC, HIS EYES closed as if he were resting while Calec took his tour of the witch's manor. Nothing of the city remained.

Calec ambled over to his steed and patted his neck. "I was hoping once we were inside the city, we'd just go along for the ride with the locals. I don't understand the ways of magic."

"Those who came to abduct you vanished, but I didn't," Ghost seemed to say. "Just because you leave the city or ride into it doesn't mean the curse applies any differently to you."

"Then, for as long as it takes, we will have to chase the vanishing city and its curse."

Calec heaved and pulled himself up into the saddle before turning Ghost toward the Demon's Coin moon and the direction marked by its three scratches. South tonight. Then he paused. Amidst all the distraction of the past day, he'd forgotten.

That was not the true direction.

He glanced around for water, but there were no ponds or sheets of ice around the area.

How would he find the true face of the Demon's Coin? If he dumped his waterskin out into his hand, his water stores would probably be gone long before he found the city. His hand squeezed his sword's intricate hilt in frustration.

"Is your blade not polished to a mirror-like sheen?" Ghost seemed to ask.

Calec held his breath as he drew his sword. He laid it across the flat of his other palm.

Moonlight danced along the length of the blade.

Calec tilted it and angled it until the face of the Demon's Coin moon came into view near the hilt. The moon's scratch marks pointed northeast.

He veered Ghost in that direction, and they rode off into the night.

But every time he looked upon his blade, the moon's markings seemed to have altered a bit, almost as if the moon were changing position to indicate Valtera's location in relation to wherever he was. Hopefully that was it, anyway.

He guided Ghost on a slightly different course.

A disappearing city that changes location each night.

As Calec rode on, memories of people who'd disappeared from his life haunted him: his mother, his father, Frallec, Eristin, the unborn child from Serileen's earlier pregnancy.

He imagined words spilling from the mouth of the necromancer, Brenson. The necromancer's words like poison as he spoke to Serileen, declaring that any child by Calec would be too weak to survive in this world.

Calec's heart twisted about itself.

"What if the man's claims or prophecies are true?" he asked Ghost. "What if there is some potent defect in my blood? Mayhap it *was* my fault the first child did not survive. And not only because I was not there with Serileen when she was attacked."

Guilt writhed inside his chest and dropped one side of the twin scales he imagined there.

"If the second child does not make it, you could always decide for yourself," Ghost replied.

Calec furrowed his chin as he slowly shook off the notion of his guilt. "The death of the first child could have been all the necromancer's doing. Some evil curse to sway Serileen and advance the workings of the Horseman's dark magic."

"Could have been."

Calec's blood seethed with anger.

He tied his yellow ribbon about his wrist and hoped with all his soul for two things. One, that nothing would interfere with Serileen's pregnancy. And two, that this and any future child by him and Serileen would not be too weak to survive in this world.

26

FIRELIGHT GLOWED IN THE DISTANCE OF THE PLAINS, ARISING FROM just to the right of where Calec was headed to find the city.

He veered Ghost off in that direction as the wolf wind tormented their eyes and hair. The looming mountains in the north had grown closer.

Calec glanced at the reflection of the Demon's Coin moon in his sword's blade and then back to the firelight.

"It's the nomads," Calec said. "This time we'll be the ones who choose to visit them. I'll just ask if they have seen the city or know how far off it still is."

Ghost only grunted in reply this time.

As they approached, the firelight grew brighter, a raging blaze with a spit over its center.

The smell of freshly cooked meat wafted in the wolf wind and made Calec's stomach grumble.

But something was different. These men and woman did not appear similar to the other nomads. These were all dressed in white furs.

Calec pulled Ghost to a halt.

One of the men stood and turned the carcass roasting over the fire. The meat that wafted those scents came from a *human* body. It was a man's carcass spitted over the fire, his arms and legs pinioned. Muscle and skin searing.

Cold fingers seemed to grip Calec by the throat and clamp it shut so he had to struggle to breathe. He studied the people around the fire much closer: probably two score, large and slouching, with spears.

He would not stand a chance against their numbers.

"Easy, Ghost." Calec's voice came out as a strained whisper. "These are not the nomads we've encountered before."

He steered Ghost away and waited for the gusting of the wolf wind to hide the sound of faster and louder hoofbeats.

Every few strides, Calec glanced back at the firelight. None of the people seemed to have noticed him, but he did not stop watching his back for a few hours.

The night grew old and faded to the dark hours of morning before Calec found the vanished city glistening under moonlight. He rode past another sleeping guard and through the gates. Down the blackened streets to the constable's house.

After he hitched Ghost outside, he knocked on the door. A minute later, Desi opened it.

"You've returned already," she said, the light in her sky-sea blue eyes brightening.

Calec nodded as he explained the reflection of the moon in his sword.

She smiled. "Then you can always find us ... unless the city travels so far in a single night it'd be impossible to reach before we vanish again." Her smile faded. "And that does happen. The jumps we take about the plains seem to be completely random. Some vanishings must move us a hundred leagues or more from our previous location."

Calec waited.

"Oh, I'm sorry," Desi said. "Come in. Take a short rest. We do not have another bed, but Jaremonde will rise soon. Perhaps I could get you some blankets and you could sleep on the floor here?"

"Thank you. That would be sterling."

After Desi prepared a bed for Calec, and Calec made sure he was not watching her while she went about it, she disappeared into her own chamber and shut the door.

Calec sprawled across the blankets and soon shut his eyes. But images of burning human bodies assaulted his thoughts, both over spits and at the witch's stake. He tossed about.

A pounding knock sounded at the front door, and Calec's eyes popped open. He'd fallen asleep, but only for what'd felt like an hour or so.

"Jaremonde!" someone shouted.

Desi hurried out of her chamber in a slip and rushed for the door.

Calec's gut tightened and cramped. *A body was found.*

Jaremonde entered the main chamber, rubbing at bleary eyes as Desi opened their front door.

"Constable." A man stood outside, his voice wavering with anxiety or impatience. "The herd has been spotted not far from here."

Jaremonde's hands fell to his sides, his voice thick with sleep as he spoke. "About time. And we've still got the morning hours and a full day to catch one."

Jaremonde gathered up a pack and a few things. Desi furtively did likewise, and Jaremonde didn't seem to notice her.

"You've already spoken to the other hunters?" Jaremonde asked.

"I've sent others for them," the man said.

Jaremonde faced Calec. "You coming, Sir Calec? Hunting?"

Calec glanced around. "I wished to see the witch's manor. We've a curse and a vanishing city. Is hunting so important now?"

"As I've said before." Jaremonde ran his fingers over his mustache. "I've recently visited the witch's manor, and there is not much to be found there. We can visit it at any time. If *you* lived in a city that appeared and disappeared around the plains with no stable farmlands, you'd understand. If we do not hunt or gather food when we can, many more than one will die. That is partly why we've fallen from a city of tens of thousands to only a thousand or so people over the past century. That and the fact that babies have become scarce in Valtera."

"What prey animals could supply so much food for an entire

city?" Calec asked as Jaremonde picked up his supplies and headed for the door.

Desi stood still, holding her own pack behind her, as if waiting for her father to leave.

Jaremonde snatched a pike from beside the door and hefted it. "Big ones."

———————

27

CALEC RODE GHOST AT A STEADY TROT, REINS IN ONE HAND, A torch in the other. He trailed behind a score and a half of people from Valtera as the last hours of darkness waned.

"What do we hunt?" Calec asked the two who rode in front of him, Rimmell and the only woman in the group.

The woman was thick of arm and girth, the one who'd slept beside the gates when Calec first arrived. She appeared disinterested in conversation, but she turned and her face flickered with shadows, making her eye sockets look like a skull under her torchlight. "The mammoth."

Mammoth? Calec's mind wandered over images from his childhood: great beasts as tall as buildings, huge tusks, thick woolly fur.

"The herd is ahead," the man who'd come to Jaremonde's house said from the front. "But the nearest canyon is half a league to the east."

"And how did the people of a city that moves about the plains learn to hunt mammoths?" Calec nudged Ghost into a canter until he rode alongside Olinia and Rimmell, then he slowed to a trot.

"We use the ways of the nomads," Olinia said. "Our ancestors learned a thing or two from them, before we became their ghosts of the plains. Now they only trade with us outside our walls. But at one time, our ancestors were friends with many of the clans. The people of Valtera learned how to breed horses for speed and endurance from them as well."

"Not to mention the *gramdel*." Rimmell flashed a smile. "Not that a knight has probably heard of it, but it is our most common tavern game. I think it came from the nomads. Or at least someone told me that once."

Highlights from that fateful game against Runik replayed in Calec's mind. "I know of it."

They rode on in silence as the wolf wind keened off the mountains and blasted their cloaks and any exposed skin.

"So, do we run these mammoths into a covered pit filled with spears?" Calec asked.

Olinia laughed. "You haven't been paying attention. Valtera moves, remember? We don't have time to spot the herd, then dig pits for them, and then set up a hunt. We have to improvise. Not all the teachings of the nomads fit with our current situation."

Calec raised an eyebrow as he pondered how else they could hunt beasts as massive as mammoths.

"You should've seen the last female we brought in," Rimmell said.

"We took in two mammoths on one of the hunts I've been on." Olinia stiffened, and her tone grew hard. "And we claimed the largest mammoth in recorded history on the hunt I rode with before that."

They continued riding for another hour, and Ghost drifted behind again. Calec would conserve his mount's energy for the actual hunt. Calec's mind wandered over all the described events of the burned witch as well as the recent deaths he'd heard about. But he had a hard time focusing on all he'd learned now that they were about to hunt mammoths. In the dark.

Something rustled through the grasses to Calec's right, and a wave formed and rolled beneath the blades before carrying over the hill away from the hunters.

What creature would move in such a manner? Through the grasses like a worm mining through soil?

Calec turned Ghost for a moment and followed after the

rustling, but he kept the hunters in view so he could easily catch them again if and when he needed to. He gripped his torch tighter as he ascended a small rise, and memories of the last fire he witnessed out in the plains struck him.

"'Tis a long winter, this one." The voice came from the night.

Calec's rein hand found his sword as he turned.

Gomdon sat bareback on a horse before a troop of clansmen under moonlight. Runik, who appeared to not have suffered at the hands of his people for losing the drinking game, and Mitag flanked their leader. Another nomad emerged from the grasses before Calec where the wave ended.

Of course it was a nomad. A trick to lure me away. Calec expelled a breath of relief and nodded in their direction.

"So you've somehow managed to find the ghosts of the emerald city," Gomdon said as he rode nearer. "And you've joined them, or you are now a ghost yourself."

Calec shrugged.

"But you've had no luck with their current hunt?" Gomdon asked.

Calec shook his head. "I do not even know if we travel in circles. How is it that I've mostly ridden toward the mountains to find the city and yet you have caught up with me? You must be far from home."

"We hunt, and we have many villages in these plains. We are nomads. We travel between all of our homes." Gomdon gave him a look as if Calec were as dense as a rock.

Calec suppressed a wry grin.

"He could *not* have found the emerald city so soon," Mitag said in a guttural voice.

"Ah, but he already rides as one of the ghosts themselves." Gomdon eyed Calec curiously. "Either he is no longer of this world, or he has discovered some secret of the ghost city." Then he indicated Ghost, the horse. "And you still ride *Nomisent*, Wolf Tongue. He is older now, and he became infertile before we gelded him. But in his day, *Nomisent* was the swiftest of our herd. He still has some spark left when it is needed. We do not trade only rounceys when the ghosts of the emerald city ask us for aid."

Calec studied Ghost: long and shaggy now with his bay winter coat that hid much of his build.

"We will let the ghost people hunt tonight," Gomdon said. "It is not long that they will be in this land. We shall hunt the following day, or we will give the mammoths a rest and try the following week."

"Do you think you will aid them?" Runik asked Calec. "Or do you only hope to wander as a lost soul amidst the grasses until winter's hand eventually pulls you into a cold grave?"

Calec motioned to his bow strapped to Ghost's saddle. "I often hunt in the woods and am a fine shot."

Mitag bellowed with laughter. "Mammoths are far from harts and squirrels of the woods."

"You are falling behind now, Wolf Tongue." Gomdon raised a hand in farewell. "Help these ghosts find peace."

The nomads turned and disappeared into the night.

28

"THE GREAT HERD." THE LEAD HUNTER CREPT THROUGH THE GRASS and pointed with a javelin as the sun's morning glow splashed the horizon. Stars and the many moons began to fade.

Ahead, on a vast swath of plains, beasts the size of houses roamed, tearing at tufts of grass, scratching, chewing. They were coated in piles of long hair. Massive males roamed around the margins of the herd while smaller females with young scoured the grasses and a wetland inside their perimeter.

Jaremonde rose from the grass with Climson, Olinia, and Lanigrad. The renowned scholar even wished to hunt ... Somehow that seemed odd to Calec. Rimmell trailed behind them.

"On my command," Jaremonde said, his chest swollen with pride. "If we take a mammoth, our food stores will be stocked beyond the need of Valtera's people for another season." Jaremonde patted Calec's arm. "Ride when I say, and try to keep up. Your steed is a little long in the tooth. Of nomad breeding, but still a dud. Those people of the plains pulled a fast trade on you, thinking an outsider would never know the difference."

Calec glanced down at Ghost. He was no Wyndstrom, but Ghost could actually go farther and faster than Wyndstrom could. Ghost probably wouldn't have ever been able to carry him in full plate armor, but that was no issue now.

Calec only nodded. *Wasn't it your friends who acquired Ghost from the nomads?*

One man stood off to the side, drawing Calec's attention. The man's hood covered his face, and he kept to himself.

"There!" The lead hunter waved. "A large male has broken from the herd."

A single mammoth was grazing at the rear of the herd, facing away from the others.

"Ride!" The lead hunter jumped onto his mount and kicked it into a full gallop as he brandished his torch.

The others mounted and stampeded after him. Calec followed at the rear. They made straight for the gap between the male and the rest of the herd, the muted thunder of their horses' hooves pounding like drums on the plains. When their horses raced into the gap, the people of Valtera all began waving their torches and shouting.

The lone male spun about and bellowed through a long trunk. Others in the herd answered, but Valtera's lead hunter hurled a javelin at the beast and galloped straight toward it as if neither he nor his steed could comprehend fear. He waved his burning torch, and its flames roared as they whipped in the wind.

The mammoth bellowed again before turning east to flee.

The other hunters whooped and stampeded after it. The mammoth called out a third time and tried to veer left or right, to circle around its pursuers and return to the herd, but the men on horseback fanned out and cut off its line of retreat.

The beast continued its lumbering run. This carried on for less than a quarter of an hour before massive cliffs rose from the plains at the base of the mountains. The mammoth headed straight into a wide crevice cutting into the cliffsides.

Jaremonde shouted in glee. "We've got the big bastard now."

The mammoth trumpeted again as it barreled into the gap. The riders pursued it.

"Now comes the most dangerous part," Olinia said to Calec. "Be ready if it turns around before the crevice becomes too narrow."

They pursued the beast into the canyon. Other shouts and yelling sounded from above.

"No! Too soon!" Olinia said.

Javelins rained down into the trench from the clifftops as many men waiting up there leaned over and threw. Other waiting men swung pikes down into the canyon and contacted the top of the mammoth's back or head. The beast reared and trumpeted as it shuffled about, trying to shift its massive bulk and turn around as it finally realized it was trapped. The sides of the canyon pressed in against the mammoth, but it contorted and twisted its head, its enormous tusks gashing into the hillside and causing dirt to cascade around it.

More javelins flew through the air.

Then the beast seemed to fold inward, and soon it was facing Calec and the others, a look of madness swirling in its small dark eyes. Its breath plumed from its mouth and trunk, and it bellowed. The walls of the canyon quaked. Its feet pounded the earth and seemed to shake everything around Calec as it charged them.

The lead hunter flung another javelin and readied his pike to swing. Most of the other thirty men Calec didn't know remained beside their leader, also hurling weapons.

Calec charged forward, ripping his sword from its sheath. Something deep stirred within Ghost, and he and Calec tore past the hunters like the swiftest of all horses as javelins sailed from the hunters' hands and flew into the beast's face and toward its eyes. Most of the hunters' javelins were exhausted when Calec drew near to the beast.

The mammoth's legs were the size of two massive tree trunks in one, and they pounded the earth like boulders plummeting from mountains.

Calec veered Ghost off to the side as the beast stampeded past; then he wheeled Ghost in a tight turn and veered back. As the mammoth's hind legs lumbered past, Calec swung for the tendons at the back of the leg, just above its hock.

His blade slipped through mats of hair and cut into flesh.

The beast bellowed.

Something flashed like fire in the sunlight at the edge of Calec's peripheral vision.

He spun about.

A javelin tore through the air, flying straight for his chest.

Calec raised his sword and turned, attempting to knock it aside, but he'd seen it too late and it was flying too fast.

Metal pinged as the javelin struck his blade. The attempt deflected the javelin only a little, and its tip plunged into Calec's upper arm. Blinding pain lanced up into his chest, and Calec toppled from Ghost.

The mammoth tumbled as well, crashing into the earth and sliding to a halt over a few horse lengths.

Calec flexed the fingers of his left hand as he released his sword from his right. The javelin was buried into the flesh on the inner aspect of his arm, and blood spewed around it.

Where the major vessels to my arm run.

Calec's hand settled around the shaft of the javelin, and he tore it out with a ripping sound. A shout of pain escaped his lips, and he mashed his cloak against the wound to stem the blood loss.

He attempted to steady his breathing, but the world started to spin. He glanced at the others, who were riding toward him, all without javelins. One other he recognized now, but he hadn't known she was here. Desi's eyes of ice and fire shone beneath the hood of the hidden hunter.

Calec's head flopped back onto the grass, and the early light of dawn faded.

———

29

ULMA HOBBLED ALONG A NARROW STREET, HER FOOTSTEPS STILL not ringing true on the stones beneath her. Still off-kilter. Her walks were prolonged now with her bad ankle, and twilight was already settling in around the emerald city. Tomorrow, Valtera would have a new setting.

Today, she had trouble remembering what the scenery looked like the day before, as well as the angle of the wind. She also couldn't recall any details of her most recent walks or what time she'd actually gone or returned, but she vividly remembered those children and what they had done to her.

She passed the saddle maker's shop and house. Olinia, the stout middle-aged woman with short hair, worked outside. She used some kind of press or punch on a strip of leather and squeezed with both hands. Whatever muscle she carried in those thick arms lay hidden under layers of softer flesh.

Ulma raised a knotted old hand in an attempt to wave, but Olinia only watched her as she passed. This time Ulma didn't stop. She kept on marching right up Branber's Hill.

More than a week had passed since her initial injury after one of those children pushed her, but at her age, injuries seemed to linger and rarely ever healed completely. However, Ulma would not use a cane, no, not her. Other old women used canes. She was a walker, a brisk walker, and she'd rather die than have that taken away from her too. She'd already lost any and every audience for her stories. The day she could no longer go out for walks morning and evening was the day she'd lie down in bed and just die.

The sun slipped below the black stone towers to the west. It would be completely dark soon. Maybe she'd at least have to compromise with her walks, either start earlier or make them shorter. But no cane. She'd be remembered in Valtera as the woman who walked more leagues of its streets than any ancient patrolling soldier. The people would remember her pacing by their homes morning and night without the aid of a cane. A tough old woman. That's what they'd say in years to come if anyone ever spoke of her. A tough old woman with a soft spot for children ... at least for most of her days.

Her ankle started to throb as she moved. Those children had betrayed her. Turned on her as she neared a century of age. Those children she spoiled with sweeties at her own cost. They soured now and wanted—no, demanded—more from an old woman. The newest generation might bring down the mighty heritage of Valtera. After all these decades of living and some-times even thriving with the curse, someday soon, the streets of Valtera might only be roamed by the posterity of its city-living farm animals: chickens, pigs, goats, horses. Those animals that lived inside the walls and moved with the city. Soon there might be no people left. At the height of Valtera's reign, just before the burning of the witch, tens of thousands of inhabitants lived in the emerald city. Now there were probably fewer than a thousand people living here, although the city still had as many buildings and houses and towers as it did in the time of the witch. Nothing seemed to crumble or rust. But so many of those structures remained empty. Soon Valtera would become nothing more than a ghostly city of forgotten animals.

Ulma neared the last stretch of her walk, the part she dreaded now. Down the far side of Branber's Hill. She felt in her pouch. Plum full of sweeties.

She breathed a sigh of relief. Her other hand squeezed something else tighter, her knitting. An unfinished scarf and her two needles. She couldn't remember why she decided to bring these with her on her walks lately, but they made her feel more in control. Like the streets were still as comfortable as knitting inside her manor.

Children ran about, shrieking as they chased after one another through the streets.

"Hey, it's the old lady." Kirya, the girl with the twin braids, pointed.

"Sweeties!" several children yelled as the group turned like a flock of sparrows wheeling in the wind. They rushed straight at her.

The old warm sensation that children brought, the fuzzy memories buried inside Ulma, had turned stale. Even a bit cold. Her knees trembled as they ran at her, and she clutched her hands to her ears.

"What's wrong with you?" Kirya pushed past two boys to stand at the front of the group. "You're not going to die, are you? Not out here in the street, I hope."

Ulma heaved and expelled a few prolonged breaths as all the children stared. Some of them started to whisper.

"She's going to die!" Kirya said.

Other children yelled and backed away.

Ulma shook her head. "No. No. I'm quite all right."

She forced a smile as she reached for her pouch full of sweeties. The children clambered closer.

As she unfolded her wrinkled hand, the children lunged forward and snatched the sweeties out of her palm. She pulled more out of her pouch as those children who served themselves first unwrapped theirs and popped them into their mouths, their sucking sounds ringing out like some broken song with moist lyrics.

A smile crept back onto Ulma's lips, one she hadn't felt in the last week or so, as all the little faces around her turned distant. Glassy eyes. Contentment. Red stains at the corners of their lips.

"Hey, she's got a lot more today." Kirya pointed at Ulma's still bulging pouch. "Can we each get one more?"

Ulma hesitated. "I, uh, need to save some until tomorrow. There's only so much to go around."

"She's lying," a little boy said. "She's got all the sweeties in Valtera. No matter where we move to, she must always get all the syrup and honey."

Kirya stepped closer. "How come you always get all the sweeties? There's never any left when my mother goes to market. She says you must buy them all up and hoard them in your manor."

"Well, that's not true." Ulma's tone turned, like the limping beat of her footsteps. "I only buy enough for you children. I enjoy seeing you happy and giving them to you on my walk each evening."

"I'd be *really* happy if I could get another. Just one more. Only *this* time." Kirya stepped closer, and those around her followed.

"If I give you more today, you won't get any tomorrow." Ulma grabbed and sealed her pouch with her fist.

"She's stashing them." Kirya reached for the pouch.

Other children joined her, and it seemed like a hundred small hands were grabbing at Ulma. Ulma stumbled back, but still they pressed closer.

Ulma shrieked and struck out at them with her other hand. Once. Twice. Maybe more.

A girl screamed. So did other children, and they all backed away as one.

Kirya held her arm with one hand as if she were hurt, her face ghastly pale, tears welling in her eyes as she wailed. Blood drained between her fingers. A boy also held one hand in his other palm and clutched the presumably wounded one close to him as he shrieked.

"She stabbed me!" Kirya moved her hand and looked at her upper arm as she sobbed. Three holes were punched through her tunic. She lifted the tunic up, revealing circular puncture wounds in her skin, each draining rivulets of blood.

Ulma's stomach turned, and she gasped.

"She stabbed me!" Kirya wailed again, tears streaming down

her cheeks. She pushed the others back. "The old lady stabbed me!"

"She stabbed my hand, too," the boy said between shrieks of pain.

All the children screamed and turned and fled as if the witch of Valtera were chasing them.

Ulma glanced down. She gripped her knitting needle as if it were a dagger, its tip enameled with blood.

And a ruby of liquid slowly gathered in size along the shaft of the needle before it formed a droplet and plummeted onto the black stones.

30

CALEC DREAMT. A DOZEN WOMEN CRAWLED ON THEIR HANDS AND knees about the plains, tearing through the grasses, hunting for something. The black silhouette of a man in a mask with horns of writhing flame stood atop a hill nearby, his arms folded across his chest. His shadow horse with the red eyes pawed at the grass and chomped on some twisted bit, globs of blood-tinged saliva stringing from its lips.

Moonlight, light from the Demon's Coin—Calec didn't know how he knew this, but he did—reflected off a ring on the masked man's hand. Its insignia glowed with intricate detail. The golden skull and ribcage of a man with a black heart trapped inside its ribs.

One of the women yelled something unintelligible. The other women crawled over to the one who'd spoken, and they uncovered a mound of freshly turned soil that'd been piled up. The grave they'd been searching for.

One woman scooped up the dirt and lifted it to her face. She sniffed at it and then bit into the dirt and chewed as if it were bread. Dark spots stained her lips and filled the gaps between her teeth. Rivulets of soil then sifted past her teeth and drained from her mouth.

The other women joined her, and the man in the mask laughed, a low and echoing rumble that shook Calec's head.

Calec gasped. His eyes fluttered; his head felt light. Everything swooned and swayed. Daylight streamed in through some window overhead.

Memories of his recurring dream faded quickly, but others returned: a charging mammoth, riding Ghost, a thrown javelin. The ride back to Valtera had been a blur of fading light and darkness while being dragged on a makeshift sledge. The blinding pain of a burn to cauterize a wound had been thrown in there somewhere as well.

Calec rolled over so he could assess the pit of his left arm. A mass of bandages lay in a heap beside him. The wound in his flesh was stitched closed with gut. Red burn marks encircled the area.

"Be still," a voice said. A young woman—Desi—wrung out a cloth in a basin, the water dripping from the rag dark red. "I'm sorry to have woken you, but I had to clean your injury. You lost a lot of blood. Some are surprised you're even alive."

Calec's head flopped back down, and his chest heaved as if the simple movement caused him to run out of air.

"What happened to the mammoth?" Calec asked.

Desi returned with the rag and wiped at some of the blood stains around his wound. Pain lanced up Calec's arm.

"We got it." She forced a smile. "There are a hundred people out there now cutting and carving it all up. They should be able to haul it all back before twilight."

"And how far off is twilight?"

Desi wouldn't look him in the eye as she bandaged up his arm. "Not long."

Her hands were tender, and a tingle, possibly of excitement, thrummed along Calec's skin.

No. It is nothing.

She was beautiful but probably a decade and a half younger than he. Too young. Even if such differences rarely stopped other men, Calec would have none of it. And if his body did not follow all of his wishes, at least he would not allow any emotion to be revealed. Most importantly, Serileen was his mate, and she now carried his child. He had to focus on that. He looked away.

"Is anyone else hurt?" Calec asked.

Desi shook her head. "Nothing serious. Scrapes and bruises. Some cuts. You are the only one unfortunate enough to be bedridden."

"And you are a healer?"

Desi chuckled. "I'm whatever my father needs me to be in any pressing situation, and I'm what he doesn't want me to be the rest of the time."

Calec tried to ponder that, but his head spun.

"It was a javelin," Calec said. "Not a mammoth tusk."

Desi nodded. "I saw it after you fell."

"Who threw it?"

Desi shrugged. "No one claimed to have done it."

Disbelief circled in Calec's mind. "If they had claimed the throw and admitted error, I may be less suspicious. Even in the midst of terror, each person probably saw where their javelin struck."

Desi remained silent as she tied off the bandage.

"It came from the group of riders," Calec said.

"As long as it doesn't take on an infection, you should live. And we already cauterized it. Climson did, with hot iron. An infection should be staved off."

She doesn't want to talk about who threw it. "And most of the hunters I didn't know had already run out of javelins."

Desi swallowed, and her face drained of color. "Like I said, no one claimed to have thrown it. It may have been an accident. Only nerves while being charged at by a great beast."

Calec's eyes closed. "I will need more than one person around me at all times here if I'm to trust anyone. Someone didn't take well to my coming."

Desi didn't answer.

"And when I looked up after being struck, the first thing I saw was you, hiding from your father in a cloak." *Or at least I hope you were hiding from your father and not hiding because you wished to impale me without anyone noticing you.*

Calec waited a moment longer, and then he opened his eyes and raised his head.

He lay in the plains atop a bed of grass now, and no one was around.

The last rays of twilight were gobbled up by the horizon, and night fell across the far country. Moonlight shone from several of the larger moons. And the wolf wind howled in his ears.

Calec's heart sank.

His head fell back onto the grass.

31

THE GRASSES OF THE PLAINS GLOWED WITH MOONLIGHT, appearing similar to a night at sea. Calec struggled to find his feet, and his chest heaved for air.

I must be very low on blood.

He took a large drink from his waterskin and glanced around. Ghost stood not a hundred paces away, sleeping as if he'd been tethered to something and didn't realize he was no longer tied. Nothing else of the city remained.

Calec staggered over to his steed and patted his neck. "This madness will surely kill me, but you seem to be doing well with it."

"I sleep when I grow tired of the world," Ghost seemed to say.

"Well, I must ask you to kindly carry me to the city, or I may not survive for long."

Calec paused for a moment. Did he even wish to return to the emerald city again? He sought it out to help its people, but he was attacked and almost killed for doing so. His thin blood spiked with anger.

Maybe he should return to the woods instead. To safety. Not risk his life if at least one of the people of Valtera wanted to see him dead.

He brooded on this as the wolf wind set the grasses dancing around him.

But he didn't know for certain the javelin throw struck him on purpose. Someone might have not wanted to admit to almost killing him on accident. And if the throw was purposeful, Valtera's people might be in more danger than he initially suspected. That would mean someone didn't want him there, and that possibility made him want to return more than ever. *Someone* might be behind or linked to the curse.

Calec heaved and pulled himself up into the saddle, then checked his sword's reflection. He turned Ghost in the true direction the Demon's Coin moon and its three scratches indicated. East.

He angled Ghost in that direction, and they rode off into the night, Calec too dazed to press Ghost into a trot or gallop, Ghost happy to take it slow. Hours passed as Calec drank as much fluid as he could.

He needed to look into exactly how and why this curse came about. There had to be some reason. Like in Landing. The book of the Horseman. Something like that. But at each location he traveled to, something much different reared its ugly head. This would likely not be easy.

"Just steer clear of any cooking fires in the plains," Calec said to Ghost. "And move as silently as you can under the moons."

32

SOMETHING TRUMPETED IN THE DISTANCE, AND CALEC AWOKE from a daze, still wobbling in Ghost's saddle as his steed bore him along. Ghost's movements were sharp and tense beneath him, and Ghost's ears flicked about. His nostrils flared as if seeking a faint scent masked by the direction of the wind.

Ahead, upon a field of moon-frosted light, silhouettes of a mammoth herd crowded together. The largest of them faced outward from their circle and raised their trunks and tusks.

Calec gripped the reins tighter.

"Do not fear the mammoth, Ghost," he said. "We do not hunt them, and they are the kind of beasts that would not harm or chase us unless ..." He stopped cold.

But they're acting as if something is *still hunting them. And they must've traveled far from where we hunted them, unless this is another herd.*

"But there is something else out there," Ghost seemed to say. "Something that does not smell of herd animals. Something that hunts."

Calec drew his sword and checked the moon's reflection again. Still headed in the correct direction.

"It may only be the nomads." Calec glanced around as something seemed to breathe on the back of his neck with the gusting of the wolf wind. "Or those more savage peoples we ran into the other night. Every day we linger here, we move deeper into the wild of the far country and farther from the woods, my friend."

A rush of cold ran along Calec's arms as other silhouettes appeared in the distance, stalking through the grasses toward the herd. Hunched four-legged beasts with powerful front quarters and smaller hind ends. Calec could not tell what color they were or if they were dog or cat-like, only that they prowled about in the likeness of predators.

Calec angled Ghost far to the south.

"We will circle around this region," Calec said.

Ghost's eyes rolled wildly, and he blew a plume of cold breath through his nostrils. His feet lifted higher in the grass as they moved more quickly.

One of the predators darted at the mammoth herd, and the herd bellowed and packed more tightly together.

Then a dozen more of the stalking beasts emerged from the grasses on the far side of the herd, charging the mammoths at the rear of their circle.

More bellowing erupted from the mammoths as they spun about and broke their formation. They barreled away.

The pack or pride of hunting beasts gathered into a knot and chased the herd. And, as if in a final sacrifice for the group or one last act of desperation, the slowest but largest of all the mammoths wheeled around. Great tusks flashed in the moonlight like blades as it reared on its hind limbs and released one last cry.

The predators surrounded the lone mammoth and bit and clawed, soon climbing over it and appearing more akin to a nest of ants than animals, a swarm. They felled the beast and writhed atop its body.

Calec kicked at Ghost's flanks.

"Ride, Ghost. The lands grow wilder yet."

But Ghost needed no more urging.

They galloped away over the plains as Calec hunched over Ghost's neck and his saddle, clinging to his steed's rocking form, afraid that in his wounded state he might fall and be left behind.

33

CALEC TROTTED GHOST INTO THE GLEAMING BLACKNESS OF Valtera not long after midnight, Ghost lacquered in sweat and foam.

No guard sat on duty this night, and that sent a prickle of worry coursing through Calec, stirring him further from the light plane of sleep or heavy state of rest he'd found over the previous several hours.

"Your return is swift." A man stepped from behind the gates, fully awake as if awaiting him. Lanigrad. "For someone who almost died and was left out on the plains. Some may be surprised you decided to return at all."

Something inside Calec shouted a warning. Someone in the group of hunters had tried to kill him. He didn't want to be taken by surprise when alone with only one of them, but he also wanted them to believe he wasn't too concerned about the threat or didn't suspect it.

I will not turn my back to any one of them.

"My steed can race like the wolf wind, when it is needed," Calec said.

Lanigrad approached, reaching out to clasp his forearm. "We honor your actions during the hunt. You helped bring the beast down. And I speak for all of us when I say I am *very* sorry a stray javelin struck you. We are also very grateful for your return."

Calec accepted the man's grip, but his other hand found the hilt of his knife under his cloak. He forced a smile. "I am sorry as well. But I am glad to be back."

"I'm to take you to Aonor's manor." Lanigrad eyed Ghost. "For you and your horse to rest and recover. The others are still helping many of Valtera carve and prepare and smoke the mammoth's meat so it will last. They labor and celebrate. Over our victorious hunt. And you will receive an ample share of the spoils."

Ghost's misty breath billowed into the night, and Calec forced himself to let go of his knife.

"But do not despair," Lanigrad continued. "The festivities primarily consist of only drinking and music, and your injuries and recent travel surely require that you rest the remainder of the night, if not well into the morning. Once you feel better, I will take you up on your previous wishes and show you the empty witch's manor. That place is not going anywhere."

Calec nodded his assent. "I do not have enough vigor for merrymaking at the moment."

Lanigrad mounted a horse and led Calec through sections of city that seemed to span across the entire plains. Pigs snuffled as they rose and hurried away. Chickens clucked in the darkness. Ghost steamed and cooled off from his hard ride across the plains.

Soon, they rode up a familiar hill. Near the top, huge manors crowded around the hillside in the moonlight, overlooking the city.

Lanigrad stopped outside one turreted manor Calec did not take note of on their last visit and dismounted.

"The house of the master of collections and our master scribe, Aonor," Lanigrad said. "A fine estate."

He led Calec through double doors and down a hallway to an antechamber lit by many candles and a massive chandelier that dangled overhead. Somewhere, a bell rang. Two men with pikes at their sides arose from sitting and waited like statues near the entrance of the antechamber, their attention focused straight ahead. The walls inside this manor were painted emerald, and the contrast of color—or at least the lack of darkness—seemed to smack Calec across the face. But the walls did not shimmer or appear as true stone. They were merely covered in thick coats of paint.

Busts of marble or jade lined either side of the chamber, and paintings framed in gold-stained wood hung from every available space, as if Valtera had too many paintings to be displayed and not enough walls.

A long table waited at the far end, where empty plates and tankards sat.

Hallways ran off to either side of this chamber as well as straight ahead.

"Ah, our witch hunter has returned." Aonor shuffled out of some hall, coughing as he doffed his feathered cap. He clapped, and four servants appeared. A smell of roses suffused the air around him. "Get our guest a platter of meat and mead."

The servants departed.

"No celebrating yet," Lanigrad said. "He must rest first."

Calec smiled. "I appreciate all your concern, but I do not mean to impose."

"No, the scholar is right, of course." Aonor dusted off a white sleeve trimmed in gold. "You must rest. Then eat heartily. You have earned it, and you cannot help us with the curse if you are exhausted or dead. And *we* still have a lot of work to do in recording and dividing up the spoils of the mammoth."

Inside the warm building, weariness settled over Calec like a heavy blanket.

"You are exhausted." Aonor clapped again and motioned to a servant. "Find the witch hunter a suitable bed. He must recover so he can assist us again. And the sooner the better."

Calec followed the servant down the west wing of the manor, and he was shown to a room: small but also painted emerald inside, a feathered mattress, candles burning on a table. Paintings in gilded frames littered the walls of this room as well. And there was a theme to the art; the paintings appeared to be related to a certain time period in history. Either blurred or distinct images attempted to capture the scene of some lord standing on the balcony of a shining emerald manor. The man watched over a meeting between the nomads and the people of Valtera. All the paintings in this room seemed similar, but all were different. Different angles, perspectives, or the people in them varied both in number and appearance.

The servant departed, and Calec latched his door. He undressed and lay on the bed, his thoughts becoming tangled inside a turbulent swarm in his head.

He fell into a deep sleep, and the nightmare of the women eating grave soil returned to haunt him. But this time, the women were pursued by a pack of shadowy beasts roving the plains. And the masked man with flaming horns watched it all.

34

DESI HURRIED DOWN THE STREET, OFTEN GLANCING BACK OVER HER shoulder. Flutes played in the distance, and people danced under torchlight. Hopefully her father wouldn't realize she'd left the area as he was celebrating with at least a hundred other people over the spoils of the mammoth. Jaremonde was overly drunk, and some woman kept trying to talk to him. Desi's mother was still sick in bed, had barely gotten up in the last month. But even before that, she hadn't appeared too interested in Jaremonde. Not for years.

"Where you going?" a voice called after her.

A sinking sensation pulled at Desi's insides as she slowly turned around.

Rimmell stood there, swaying just a tad. "You're leaving already?"

Rimmell had been watching her during the celebration, so it wasn't too surprising he noticed that she'd departed. He seemed to notice a lot more than her father let on, probably wasn't as dense as Jaremonde believed.

Desi walked back a few paces. "I'm going. You can come with me, or you can let me be. But I can't just sit around and drink and celebrate a turn of luck when someone's bound to become the next curse victim at any moment. I'm going to look into something."

Rimmell slowly nodded. "And what do you want to investigate? Where the latest body was found? We've already been over it. You want to discuss possibilities? I throw out a lot of ideas, but Jaremonde just dismisses them and never offers others."

"I'm going to find a little girl. Rumors have surfaced that some old witch stabbed her a few times, but this girl escaped. Over on Branber's Hill."

Rimmell nodded. "We've heard of it as well, but Jaremonde thought it was just rumor. Told me to look into it myself as soon as he had no need of me in the coming days. So I wouldn't really be disobeying his orders by going with you now."

Desi hid a grin.

"I can't sleep anyway," Rimmell said. "Not with all the excitement of the hunt and celebration still coursing through my blood."

Rimmell appeared a touch intoxicated, but more handsome than usual in the torchlight. Much less dense. Desi would feel safer if he came along.

"What?" Rimmell asked. "I really am trying to help. I know Jaremonde won't be around forever."

Desi shook her head. "Let's just go."

They hurried away into the city as gales of laughter erupted from the celebration behind them. This laughter echoed and seemed to chase them through the streets, but the sounds died out as they neared Branber's Hill. The rest of Valtera's streets were empty. It had to be getting close to midnight.

"How do you hope to find this girl?" Rimmell asked. "I heard about Branber's Hill, but not much more. I wasn't sure where I'd start."

"A parent of another child came and told Father about it. I overheard it all while pretending to be cooking and cleaning up: in the neighborhood where the girl lives, some old woman used sweeties to tempt children, and this old woman also carried a stabbing weapon of some sort. We just have to find the exact house."

After almost half an hour passed, they arrived at the neighborhood in question.

Desi raised her hand to knock on the first door.

Rimmell grabbed her hand and asked, "What would you do if someone came knocking at nearly midnight?"

"I'd be scared." Desi's hand fell. "But if we don't find out what exactly is causing this deadly part of the curse and why it's happening, others are going to become victims, too. Others like the little girl who barely escaped."

Rimmell nodded, puffed up his chest, and knocked.

A rustle and clatter arose inside. Then footsteps.

A man threw the door open and glared at them. "What's all the racket for? Got seeds to sow early in the morning."

"I'm sorry, sir," Rimmell said. He almost glanced down and watched his feet, but he clenched his jaw and looked the man straight in the eye. "I work with Constable Jaremonde, and we've heard that a little girl in this neighborhood was stabbed in the past couple days."

The man yawned. "Heard something about that. Down the next street, take the first right. They are in one of the houses on that lane."

"Thank—"

The door banged shut.

Rimmell and Desi headed for the street. It ran off into the darkness, torches only mounted near every fifth house or so that squatted against one another.

"So many," Desi said.

"I'll go to the far end and work my way back." Rimmell started off. "You begin here and work down. Call out to me if you find her house."

He disappeared into a pocket of shadow before emerging into the torchlight down the way.

Desi turned and knocked on the closest door.

A slouching old man answered, and after Desi explained why she was there, he said, "Yes. Poor child. She lives in the house three down from here. They've been holing up in there for the past couple days."

Desi thanked the man and hurried to the house in question.

It stood in darkness, as the nearest torches were a couple houses away on either side.

"Rimmell," Desi quietly called down the street. "I found the house."

There was no answer from Rimmell, and she didn't want to yell and wake or scare everyone in the neighborhood. Desi stood tall and knocked. She waited for a few minutes and knocked again before a latch slid and *thunked* against wood and stone. The door slid inward no more than a crack.

"Who's there?" a man's voice asked.

"I am Desi, and my father is Constable Jaremonde. I've come to speak to the girl who was attacked."

"She's sleeping."

Another muffled voice sounded behind the door.

"This is important," Desi said. "We need to find out what happened and why. To stop any more deaths."

"So my little Kirya can end up dead? I don't think so." The door slammed shut, and the sound of a bolt latching followed.

Desi knocked harder. "If we don't find out what happened, it might happen to another ... or to her again."

The latch slid back, and the door creaked open again. "Keep it down, or she'll hear you."

"Who?"

"The witch."

"Then let me speak to Kirya."

"Are you alone?"

Desi nodded, and a moment drew out and lingered as the hair on the back of her neck stood on end. "I have the constable's assistant just down the way though, and—"

A hand reached out and grabbed her wrist. Desi nearly shrieked as she attempted to fight it off, but the man yanked her inside and swung the door closed behind her. The air seemed thin in the darkness inside as Desi struggled for breath.

The man said something to someone else before looming in front of Desi. "Kirya stays inside, and so do you. No one can see us talking. If anyone comes by, you'll leave immediately afterward and I'll lock the door and not open it again."

Desi forced a nod as she attempted to steady herself.

"Ask Kirya what you need to and be off. The witch's curse still lingers in Valtera, and her curse has ears." The man's face was lit only on one side from a taper in his hand. "I'll be right here."

Desi nodded, and a little girl crept forward, her small face appearing under candlelight.

"Are you going to stop the witch?" Kirya asked.

"If the witch's curse is responsible for killing people, we surely will." Desi knelt before her.

Kirya started crying, her chin wrinkling up and rising against her lips.

"I don't want to die," Kirya wailed.

"I'm trying to make sure you don't," Desi said. "Can you confirm the rumors I've heard about you being attacked?"

Kirya shook her head and stared at the floor.

"If you will not tell me, I cannot protect you," Desi said.

"No one can protect anyone from a curse." Kirya sobbed.

"Unless we can break—"

"The curse can't be broken." Kirya covered her face and trembled. "Not by anyone inside or outside the city. Even I know that. I'm as good as dead already."

Desi took Kirya by the wrists and eased her hands away from her face. "But deaths from the curse are not new. They have only returned, and they were stopped, or they halted on their own before. They can be stopped again. If you help me."

The father grabbed Desi's shoulder and said, "Let her be. I think it's time for you to go now."

Desi ignored him, but Kirya remained silent.

The father tugged on Desi's tunic to get her to stand.

"She attacked me!" Kirya stepped toward Desi, but her father's large hand held her back.

"Stay away from her," the father said.

"She should see it," Kirya begged.

The father sighed, and after a moment, he rolled Kirya's sleeve up to her shoulder. Three circular wounds were scabbed over and rimmed in dark bruises.

Desi gasped but covered her mouth. It sure appeared how her father described many of the dead to the others who came to their house for those nightly meetings.

"Tell me all about it," Desi said.

Kirya sniffed a few times. "An old lady hurries down our street in the evenings just before the vanishing. Every night. Or she used to. She walks with a limp and brings treats with her and hands them out. Except this time ... she didn't have enough. I asked her if she had any more, asked politely, I did. So did some of the other children. That's when she got this mad look in her eye and started stabbing us."

"Do you know who she is?"

"She doesn't live around here, but she used to walk here every evening. She hasn't been back since her attack. Real old, but she walks fast. You can hear her coming from a long way off."

"And which way is she coming from and where's she going?"

"From the city and then away down Branber's Hill."

"What did she stab you with?"

"Some kind of spike. It looked like a knitting needle, but it was as sharp as a knife. It's all a trick. She tries to lure children in with sweeties and then she stabs them. She got one other boy on the hand, but we ran away before she killed us all."

Desi nodded, picturing some feeble old woman with knitting needles, incredulous as to how such a woman could kill so many. "And this old woman moves fast? Not just in her walking, but fast enough to stab you before you saw it coming?"

"She caught me while distracting me with sweeties."

"And you said you've seen her many times."

Kirya nodded.

"She never did anything before?" Desi asked. "Never attacked you?"

Kirya shook her head. "Only brought us sweeties to lure us in and trick us. To make us trust her. Been doing it as long as I remember."

"I think you should leave now," the father said, and this time he yanked Desi to her feet.

Desi nodded and thanked the girl and her father before slipping outside. The door closed and latched behind her. She headed down the street, keeping an eye out for Rimmell.

She walked for less than a minute before she stopped. Some sound carried over her breathing and her own footsteps. It paused.

Then it came again. A stilted clatter of someone pacing up the street.

Desi's throat felt as if someone were attempting to strangle her.

A dark form emerged from the shadows and appeared in a sphere of torchlight. This person paced along in Desi's direction. A hunched figure in a dress. She clutched something at her side. A pouch and something else, long and pointed.

Desi's heart thumped in her chest as she stepped backward, but the woman was advancing rapidly. Maybe it was only because it was dark and Desi was alone, but her mind conjured up images of her body lying dead on the black rock street, stab wounds riddling her skin.

"Rimmell!" Desi shouted.

No answer. And the woman didn't even pause. She just kept coming with the irregular beat of her footsteps.

Desi might be able to outrun this woman, but if she carried some curse, how might that work? Could she still kill Desi without having to actually stab her?

As the woman drew within one house length, she raised her hand holding the needle—long and sleek. Black or shadowed.

"Be off!" this person said in an old woman's crackling voice. "You're not supposed to be out here at night."

Desi turned and fled, and she raced down the hill. But the footsteps kept coming after her, following her as she turned onto the next street.

"Rimmell!" she shouted back.

Desi ran, and as she approached the Narrows Bridge, she glanced back. The woman paced down the hill behind her.

Maybe her father was right—she shouldn't have gone out on

her own, especially at night. This woman might follow her home, or anywhere.

The old woman kept coming, faster and faster it seemed.

Desi glanced around.

In a desperate attempt, Desi sucked in a breath and dived from the street into the river. She splashed into icy cold water that felt like a smack to the face and caused a clamping sensation around her groin and armpits.

The current grabbed her and took her, and she swam along with it down through the canal.

35

CALEC AWOKE TO A POUNDING ON HIS DOOR.

He sat up and blinked, his armpit feeling swollen but less painful. A gritty feeling rubbed at his eyes. He must not have been asleep for more than a couple hours.

"Sir Calec." A man's voice carried an anxious edge.

"I am awake," Calec answered.

"I was sent to bring you into the city. Something has happened."

Calec dressed, strapped on his blades, and unlatched the door. The servant who'd shown him to his room waited outside. Calec followed the man down long corridors and out of the manor to a stable in the back, where Ghost was brushed, saddled, and eating.

"What has happened?" Calec asked.

The servant climbed onto a gray palfrey. "I do not know any details. Only that I was asked to bring you."

Ghost's ears flicked back in irritation when Calec approached, and the horse reluctantly took the bit before they rode off through the city.

A wash of light arose in the distance. Not far. And it was too much light for anything Calec had seen here before. They rode in that direction. Down narrow streets. All but the pigs and chickens and an occasional stalled horse were quiet, as if the people of Valtera sensed some impending danger.

Ghost veered around a corner into an open square. A massive hide hung from stakes before a fire, rising like a hairy giant. The mammoth's hide, drying. Bones were heaped in a pile beside it, and the curving tusks were leaned together and rose like an archway before the fire.

But there were no cheers and no music and no dancing. No one was sleeping or passed out either.

The people in the square all stood in silence, staring bleary-eyed at a smaller group huddled around something on the ground.

Some warning banged at a door in the back of Calec's mind. He dismounted and slowly approached, his balance still off, his head feeling light and swimmy. His armpit released a dull throbbing pain.

Jaremonde stood in the center of group.

"Where's Rimmell?" Jaremonde shouted.

"He seems to have wandered away," Aonor said from within the inner group.

"Looks like this one was stabbed a hundred times by an icepick." Climson eyed whatever lay on the ground and drank from a tankard, foam frothing around his lips. "Or a hundred snakes slithered out of his bones and skin."

"Bloody curse." Olinia paced around the circle of people. "Not as many holes as the last one I saw. Must've been a thousand in that one. Why haven't the good constable and his people not stopped the workings of one dead witch?"

"We're trying!" Jaremonde snapped. "I don't see you helping at all. Working leather day and night. That's all you do."

"You've never invited me into your gatherings," Olinia replied. "I might be of more aid than yourself."

"No place for a woman." Jaremonde's cheeks flushed with anger. "You're lucky you're allowed to hunt with us at all. Only because you're bigger and tougher than many of the men. And I don't see you stopping any curse here either."

Calec eased through the crowd, and people around him muttered.

"The witch hunter survived," one man whispered behind Calec, his voice full of awe.

"Not only that," another replied, "he even returned to Valtera after what happened."

"Praise the old gods," the first man said.

A subtle warmth flowed through Calec as he approached the center of the group and attempted to focus in spite of his light-headedness.

The people there hovered over a body. The victim lay on their stomach, their arms and legs partially folded. Blood pooled beneath them.

Calec knelt beside the body. It was the lead rider and javelin thrower from the mammoth hunt. His tunic sleeves and trousers looked as if a leather punch had taken on a life of its own and ran rampant over them. Blood ran out of each puncture. Many smaller holes were present near the extremities of his arms and legs. Larger holes on the upper arms and legs. An image of a javelin piercing the man's skin popped into Calec's mind, but he dismissed it. Even smaller punctures with bloodstains riddled the man's hands and feet. Jagged marks like scratches dotted the man's neck.

Calec glanced around: no drag marks through the blood, no bruising on the victim's exposed skin, no weapon lying near him.

"Did anyone see anything?" Calec stood. His head swooned, and he was forced to steady himself against Lanigrad, who clutched his arm.

Lanigrad shook his head. "Jaremonde's already been questioning us for the past hour or so. I came over to relieve myself. That's when I saw the body just lying here." His voice lowered to a whisper. "And Rimmell and Desi are gone. Jaremonde might be blind to Desi's behavior, but we are not all so easily fooled. I know she rode with us on the hunt. And she was here at the celebration earlier."

Calec knelt again, pulled his knife, and cut open the victim's tunic. He peeled the cloth back and undressed him.

"What are you doing?" Aonor said and fell into a fit of coughing. "Let the dead be, sir knight."

"I'm looking for anything." Calec searched the man's back. No holes there, only more jagged marks like scratches. His front bore similar marks, and his abdomen was distended as if full of fluid. Mead or something else—like more blood? He cut off the man's sleeves.

There was something on the man's wrist.

"What is that?" Calec asked.

A black swath of skin, like a rash, ran in a circle around the body's left wrist and lower forearm.

"That is the burn mark of the witch," Jaremonde said. "We've seen it on all the victims. Along with the holes in their skin."

"A burn mark?" Calec pondered that.

That hadn't been mentioned in their meeting in the constable's house. Did everyone else already know? And why would burning create holes in flesh in some areas but not in others?

"Was he carrying a torch?" Calec pointed to a burned-out torch lying on the ground nearby. There was also a bucket filled with a small amount of frozen water an arm's length away.

Jaremonde shrugged. "He could have taken a torch away from the fire to see better over here."

Drunken men seldom carry a torch to go relieve themselves in the dark. Unless he'd meant to do something else. Either way, that torch shouldn't be able to create a circular burn mark around his wrist. It'd create a burned patch of skin.

"And what is this water bucket for?" Calec tapped it with his foot.

"Father!" Tromping feet rang out in the square. Desi hurried over, her hair and dress dripping. Her lips were blue, and her jaw chattered.

"What in all of the emerald city's holds?" Jaremonde stood and spread his arms as Desi rushed closer and collapsed against him. "What happened?"

"There was an old woman," Desi said. "She chased me into the river."

"Where was this?" Jaremonde asked.

Desi trembled. "I went out. To see if I could look into the rumor of the little girl who was stabbed."

Jaremonde pulled away from her. "You did what?"

"I aided her." Rimmell paced into the square. "It was her idea, but I didn't stop her. I assisted her."

Jaremonde's piercing glare could have killed a man then. "You," he said to Rimmell. "I will speak with you later. What did you both do?"

"Where did you go?" Desi turned and asked Rimmell. She still trembled.

Calec removed his cloak, his wounded armpit burning and aching as he wrapped it around Desi. "Stand near the fire. It is still winter in these lands."

Calec ushered Desi over beside the blaze, and the people followed.

"One of the house's doors I knocked on had a middle-aged woman inside," Rimmell said to Desi. "Her name is Belith, and she invited me in, claiming she'd seen the entire thing. The stabbing of the children. It took a while. We had tea, but the more she talked, it just seemed she wanted someone to talk to, not that she'd actually seen the attack. She did mention another boy who got stabbed in the hand though. When I came out, I called for you, but you didn't answer. So I went up and down the street. I couldn't find you. That's when I heard the splash in the river."

36

CALEC KNEADED HIS BLEARY EYES AND THEN RUBBED HIS ARMS TO warm himself as he sat and rested on a street in an area the locals referred to as Branber's Hill. He also waited in hopes of spotting the girl who was stabbed or perhaps the old woman who'd done the stabbing. This now seemed more important than returning to have a look through the ancient witch's manor. And much more important than resting another day.

Dawn shone in purples and oranges against a matting of clouds in the east, and Calec tried to ignore the ache in his armpit between bouts of dozing off. He drank waterskins of fluids and rested as he waited, and he felt less lightheaded than the day before, although not normal.

A book lay open in his lap, and he thumbed through the pages, attempting to discern which legends about this witch were true and which were myth. His right hand was ungloved to help turn the pages, but the cold tormented his fingers. Pictures of the city as emerald and gleaming filled the pages, along with dates in chronological order. Important happenings of each month or season were listed.

Seasons.

Calec's blood became turbulent in the canals of his veins as the word struck him. Each season he would have to visit the Enchantress, Noregana. To share a bit of time, maybe a few words. He'd sworn to it. But more importantly than breaking some honor he'd tarnished long ago as a knight, he might need that evil woman's help again in the future. He'd have to comply.

He shook off the memories and tried to focus on the book before him. But other thoughts wandered in. The city vanishing with every nightfall would cause him to lose precious time, time he couldn't use for sleeping or investigating. He'd have to ride Ghost around the far country and find Valtera after every sunset.

Calec glanced down the street. Ghost was eating hay at a cross street out of the way.

Never leave Ghost far behind.

If Calec could become a citizen, then would he vanish with the city like all the others? But how could he accomplish that? Maybe someone had to be born in Valtera. And even if he could, he wasn't sure he'd really want it. If the curse could never be broken, would he ever be able to renege on this citizenship and leave the city? The woods were his home, even if he felt the need to travel and see the world at times. Serileen lived in the woods as well. Along with his unborn child.

He released a long breath. The wasted time spent on locating Valtera each night would likely lead to more people dying before anything could be stopped, if stopping that aspect of the curse was even possible.

Children emerged one by one from houses in the neighborhood and slowly went over to greet one another, a quiet and timid display that quickly turned into laughing. As they grew louder, more and more children joined them. Within an hour, a group of children, probably all between three and six years old, ran about the streets chasing each other. The older children probably had chores.

But there was no little girl with twin braids.

Calec chewed on roasted meat that smelled of smoke and char. Mammoth. As tough and gamey as anything he'd ever tasted. He flipped through pages and skimmed their contents. His eyes settled on a spot where several pages had been torn from the book. He ran his finger along the jagged edges close to the base and wondered what information they'd held.

Then he read on but found nothing mentioning a witch's burning. Either records of that event were removed with the missing pages, or the event had occurred in a different year.

Footsteps sounded to Calec's left.

Desi approached with Rimmell, both holding clay mugs.

"Here, try this." Desi handed Calec a mug. She wore knitted gloves. "It's nettlebrook tea. It'll keep you awake and alert. But be careful. It's hot."

Calec attempted to chew faster and swallow, but the chunk in his mouth was still too big. So he talked around it. "Thank you."

He took the mug with both hands. It was so hot it nearly burned his skin, and he winced as he set it down.

"I told you," Desi said. "Rimmell boiled them a bit too long, but all the people of Valtera love their tea scorching."

"Ah, it'll keep winter's lingering chill away." Calec watched the steam billow off it and create a haze in the bitterly cold air.

After blowing on the contents of his mug, Rimmell took a sip. Desi took a drink from hers.

"Have you found anything?" Desi pointed to the book on Calec's lap, now closed, its back cover facing up.

Calec shook his head.

Both Rimmell and Desi sat down and placed their mugs on the street to cool.

"The children who have seen the old woman say she always comes from that way." Desi pointed down the street. "But no one knows where she lives."

Calec studied the children at the far end of the street before asking, "And where is Jaremonde?"

"With his team of investigators," Rimmell said. "Still questioning all those present at the celebration last night. There were at least a hundred people there."

Calec held his hands over his mug, and the liquid's warmth crawled across his skin.

A song rose from the children in the street. They held hands and ran around in a circle. A burned-out torch lay on the street in the center of their ring.

. . .

The witch is dead, the witch is dead
    Couldn't get a fire bu-urning
    Too cold to burn, too cold to burn
    At least she'll be gone by morning

The stake holds her, the stake holds her
    The wolf wind's breath is roaring
    Snow falls down, snow falls down
    The cold season's in forewarning

Calec's ears itched, and something turned over in his mind. "What is that? That song?"

"It's nothing," Desi said. "Something all the children of Valtera sing whenever a torch goes out. Usually because its oil wasn't refilled soon enough. Some old superstition. I used to sing it when I was a little girl."

Rimmell stared at Calec. "Does it mean something to you?"

"Sometimes there are darker truths or a dark history in the origin of children's songs." Steam from the mug gathered into droplets on Calec's hands as he remembered something about a plague and how children learned to carry flowers to drown out the smell while they sang about it. "I don't know what it all means in relation to the burned witch, but hopefully we will soon."

37

Hours wore away as Calec waited on the street, skimming through another book he'd loaded onto Ghost and brought with him.

His nerves tingled. This was taking too long, waiting for what he came to find in this neighborhood.

"Well, I hope you find what you're looking for in those books as well as here." Rimmell motioned around them before he stood and brushed off his trousers. "But I can almost hear Jaremonde cursing my name and asking everyone where I am and what could I possibly be doing out here for so long. Saying that there is *real* work to do."

Desi smiled.

"I meant no offense to your father, please, Desi." Rimmell bowed.

Desi shook her head. "None taken. I understand your worries completely."

Rimmell nodded to Calec, glanced back at Desi, where his eyes lingered for a moment, and then he departed.

"How long do we wait for her?" Desi asked. "This limping old woman with the sweeties?"

"Hopefully she'll arrive before twilight, considering me and this city that leaves on trips without me."

Desi laughed and leaned over toward him, her shoulder

brushing his. "I never thought it would be so hard *not* belonging to Valtera and its curse."

Calec's wounded armpit throbbed harder, but he grinned and sipped his tea. Floral and honey flavors clung to his palate. He ignored any other thoughts trying to slip into his mind.

"What is it like to live in the same place all the time?" Desi asked. "To wake up and see the same trees and hills or mountains around you?"

Calec sighed. "It is ... beautiful. But also, with it comes a need to wander. To travel. To see what other canvases the world has to show you."

Two horses clopped up the street carrying Aonor and Lanigrad.

"You two whiling the day away with reading?" Lanigrad asked as he dismounted and removed a satchel of books and an armload of scrolls from the saddlebags of his horse. "You should both become scholars."

Desi grinned, and she took on a distant expression as if considering it.

"Not Desi." Aonor coughed softly. "She is far too beautiful to waste her talents on books. She could become the light of any manor in Valtera."

Desi's expression dropped.

"We come bearing drink." Aonor lifted a waterskin and poured its contents into a mug. "Care for tea?"

Desi shook her head and motioned to the three clay mugs already on the street. "That's kind of you, but we already have tea."

Aonor poured for Lanigrad, and both men sat with them.

"Here are a few more books I found in the citadel." Lanigrad handed two other tomes to Calec and one to Desi. He passed another to Aonor and opened one for himself. The scrolls he piled up beside him. "Ones I thought might be of interest and keep you occupied during your watch. They are not the standard references or accepted historical texts used by most."

"The texts I've seen have had pages removed," Calec said.

"And the missing pages are those that would have information pertaining to events around the time of the witch's burning."

Lanigrad gave him a bemused look but furrowed his chin and nodded.

An hour passed as the group skimmed works, and children ran about the street or in and out of houses. Calec flipped through pages of his second book, which appeared to be staggered entries, as if the writer used the book to take notes. This writer appeared to pose questions to witnesses and then record their testimony in relation to specific strange or questionable events. Many of these pertained to the time of Valtera's witch and attempted to establish her whereabouts on certain days. None so far mentioned any crimes she'd committed, nor anything suspicious.

Lanigrad marked something in a book with a stylus and then shuffled through his scrolls, the papers rustling against his callused fingers as he unrolled several of them.

"This is interesting," the scholar said and cleared his throat. "The books you're all looking at now are accounts taken by scribes and collectors in the year prior to the witch's burning." He looked at Aonor. "Not that scribes' accounts are not accurate. But they have a certain ... procedure to follow."

Aonor's thin lips turned down at the corners. "It is the duty of the scribes and collectors to note what we are told as well as take detailed records. We cannot discern the truth in matters we did not witness firsthand. There must be trials and judgments and votes by the master scribe and the council to determine what are actual truths and what should be entered into the texts."

Lanigrad nodded. "And have any of you come across anything about the Dusking Festival?"

Dusking Festival. Calec recalled that term amidst so many others inside the book he was currently evaluating.

Calec flipped back several pages and skimmed the entries. "I saw a page referencing the festival. Just didn't note anything of interest."

"Well." Lanigrad held up his book. "This says the festival

that year had some incidences. Many became sick, and a few died. One of the attendees even swore to the old gods that they found dead chickens and pigs in the streets on their walk home. The animals appeared sacrificed, their blood dribbled across the emerald stones and smeared into strange markings or ancient words. Many more animals were missing." Lanigrad held up a scroll. "This same witness eventually admitted, although it seems from the scribe's notes that the witness was obviously fearful, that they'd seen the witch lurking about the festival. They saw her by the soup cauldron and believed she dropped something in it before leaving in a hurry."

A tingle of apprehension ran across Calec's skin, and he suppressed a shudder. His roaming finger paused on a line of passage when he found what he was looking for. He read aloud, "'I tried to keep watch on her during the Dusking Festival. Because many were concerned she would use her dark magic when all of Valtera was gathered together. She never left her manor during the festival. I never once even saw her look out a window to try to catch a glimpse of the festivities.'"

"So the witch poisoned people *and* never left her manor?" Desi asked. "Or the person watching her was not very astute."

Lanigrad shook his head. "These are the kinds of debates I worried we may run into with such works. Where truths were not judged by the council. I was hoping we'd find something lost in the texts, as the council was probably not always correct in their decisions."

"So there is no way to be sure about any of this," Desi said. "We hunt for answers but will not be able to find supporting evidence."

"We are merely seeking information that could be helpful in understanding our curse and, more importantly, the return of the deaths linked to the curse," Lanigrad replied.

A few minutes of contemplation and reading followed.

"There's an entry here that is very interesting." Aonor jabbed a finger against a page. "The witness goes into detail. It says, 'The guard was too afraid to speak to you scribes or to anyone about it. And now the guard is gone. But the guard told me this: "I saw her leave through the front door, latch it, and glance about nervously. She was alone. I still had the lord's key. I waited until she passed over the hill, and then I snuck inside. After hours of searching, I found it. The attic. The walls were bathed in the blood of chickens and pigs. Carcasses hung from the rafters, and there were strange markings depicting some unholy god of the ancient sky sea. Then I heard them. I ... I can't go on.'" The scribe then made a note about a lot of weeping from the witness who'd spoken to some guard that went missing. The witness eventually continued: 'There were women up there. Chained to the walls. Skeletal starving women. The ones who we thought were taken by the clans.'"

Lanigrad inhaled swiftly.

Women were abducted? But that is not part of the recent events.

Aonor dragged his finger along the page. "The people gathered outside the manor, demanding their women be released. They waited with stakes and fire."

"But there are claims to similar types of events here," Desi said as she rifled through a few pages. "This entry says many women of Valtera were taken in those days, but the abductions were attributed to clan raids, not the witch."

"Well, either someone has a very vivid imagination, or they were hallucinating with fear ... or lying," Lanigrad said as he pored over a few other scrolls. "Many historical texts accept that there were raids in those days before the curse. Some of the clans were vicious. They took women as spoils."

"Then we know nothing more for certain." Desi sipped her tea, and they all returned to their work. "May I see your book, Lanigrad?"

He shrugged and handed it over, and Desi gave him the tome she'd been sifting through.

Hours wore away before Aonor and Lanigrad conversed quietly and closed their books. They both stood.

"We have to be off now," Aonor said. "There are more pressing matters with these deaths than waiting for someone who may not show. More books at the citadel to look into. More witnesses from the celebration whose testimony must be recorded."

Calec and Desi bid them good luck.

Desi sighed, and some tension fled her as she returned to reading and watching her surroundings.

A few minutes passed before Desi stiffened and sat straight.

"There she is." Desi pointed to a little girl with twin braids who was coming toward them, the little girl looking as if she'd been waiting for a while. "The girl who was attacked. Kirya."

Calec glanced over.

"I'm surprised to see you out here," Desi said when Kirya neared.

"I don't want to be." Kirya scowled and stuck out her lower lip. Then she held out her hand. A folded parchment was tucked between her fingers. "Father made me. So I wouldn't be killed."

Be killed? "By whom?"

Kirya held the parchment out for Calec. "Take it!"

Calec reached for it but then pulled away, making Kirya lean over and extend her arms even farther. The sleeves of her winter tunic slid up her wrists to her forearms.

No punctures dotted either of her hands or arms, the skin there smooth and clean. Desi gave Calec a quick look of bemusement.

Then Calec took the parchment. "And what is this?"

Kirya stared at him. "There was another note that said I had to bring you this one. Or else."

She turned and fled back down the street. Calec watched her go before unfolding the parchment.

Witch Hunter,

I brought you into our world so I could remove you from it forever. Your name and your fame have grown. The Horseman despises it. You were brought to Valtera for one purpose. To die. To rid the world of your arrogance and false beliefs. Now you are the hunted.

Recall the javelin?

Emotions spun around inside Calec as he attempted to remain and appear calm, his fingers growing slick on the parchment. Anger and even fear stirred his blood with their wicked hands. Pain lanced through his wounded armpit, and his lightheadedness returned for a moment.

"What does it say?" Desi leaned over against Calec to read the letter as he tried to fold it back up.

She turned and studied him. "But how? The message is for you? From some witch?"

"You know as much as I do." Calec shrugged. He glanced around the street and hunted for watching eyes.

Desi leaned back, her face pale as she picked up a mug. "Ouch!"

The mug tumbled from her hands, and the fired clay shattered when it hit stone. But there was no liquid inside. A round block of ice rolled across the blackened street.

Desi's lower lip trembled as she peeled off her gloves and turned her hands over. "It was *so* cold."

Her fingers were white.

Calec grabbed her icy hands and rubbed them between his. He'd seen frostbite before, in the highlands, at least the beginnings of it. If blood wasn't returned soon, her fingers would turn black. But he shouldn't warm them too quickly either, or it'd cause excruciating pain as well as damage to the tissues.

Do not warm them with fire.

Calec cupped her hands in his and raised them to his mouth. He blew gently on her fingers to warm them.

The small round of ice ran out of momentum and toppled onto its side on the street, resting there beside the burned-out torch the children had been circling.

38

Ulma stood before her window, staring out at the emerald city now blackened. If she were to go on her evening walk, she should have left an hour ago. It might be too late now.

But she couldn't force herself to open the door. Instead, her hands worked her knitting, her needles bobbing and weaving like a pair of dancers. Stitch. Throw. Stitch.

Some dark anxiety crept up her throat every time she considered leaving her manor. She glanced to the still bulging pouch of sweeties near her door. Those children. Not to mention what she'd done to them.

Images of blood gathering and then dripping off her needle played in her mind as if it were all some demon's cruel weapon intending to break her down. She also could not forget the sweet sensation of revenge that'd flowed inside her after she'd punished one of those greedy children. Those memories hadn't left her alone for more than the span of a restless night's sleep. However, she found herself less and less able to recall most of her days.

Her hands stopped working, and her needles clacked against each other as her fingers trembled. She scratched at a red rash that had risen on her wrist. It itched all the time now. Probably because of all this new anxiety.

She believed she'd missed her evening walks for two of the

past three days already, but she was no longer sure. And walking made her who she was. The old woman who walked briskly without a cane. No longer a spinner of old legends. She shouldn't remain trapped in her manor and miss another evening strolling the city. Those children shouldn't be able to take her walking from her.

Anger mingled with the anxiety in her chest and turned acidic like chronic heartburn.

The sun set over the plains beyond the walls of Valtera, and Ulma forced a deep breath. She didn't have many years or even months left. And if she let those children take the one thing she still lived for, then she wouldn't have many days left.

Her hands trembled, and her knitting and needles fell to the floor with a clatter.

Maybe she should only continue with her walks at dawn. There were very few to no children running about at that time. Hardly any people about, actually. But if she was forced to change her ways after all these years ... well, then, she was already dead.

Ulma turned and hunted out her longest and strongest knitting needle, grabbed the pouch of sweeties, and flung her front door open. Twilight hit her eyes like sharpened sticks, causing her to squint as she slipped outside and closed the door behind her.

She pocketed her needle and sweeties and limped off, her footsteps still off-kilter. The rash on her wrist itched like drawers full of hay, and she scratched it vigorously.

The old boarded-up manor on the hilltop immediately adjacent to hers passed by on her right. She would not turn into the old woman who'd holed up in her manor and started talking to the sky, would she?

39

CALEC WAITED THE DAY AWAY, RECOVERING AND SKIMMING through several more books. Desi remained at his side assisting with other old tomes filled with entries. The color had returned to her hands slowly over an hour or so, and now her hands appeared normal.

Evening fell across the city, and Calec's anxiety started to work at his stomach. He might have wasted an entire day waiting for this possible witch woman to show, and she might never again come to this area.

His mind wheeled with other questions. About the parchment and message Kirya had handed him. Was there really someone who had lured him to Valtera? To kill him? The stitched wound in his armpit ached with the thought and with any movement. If so, it might mean Desi or at least one of those men who abducted him had an ulterior motive.

As time wore on, his eyelids drooped. Other than when he'd passed out for many hours after his injury, he hadn't slept much. He drank more of his tea, although he checked it first with a fingertip before grabbing the mug. It was cold now, but no colder than the winter air and wind howling through Valtera.

In the book he currently skimmed, he found a few references to a witch burning about a century ago, but the entries were short and only mentioned fire as judgment. The entries claimed she'd used witchcraft, but none documented exactly what her witchcraft was. For all Calec could tell, she might have been accused by some who were upset with her. She could have been staked and burned based on accusation alone.

"What is the yellow ribbon for?" Desi asked. "The one you wear about your wrist?"

Calec's attention settled onto the ribbon, an item from a missing girl whom he'd returned to Hillsvale. It had already come to mean much more to him now. His child.

"A token from a previous—"

A clatter arose from down the street. Sunlight dipped below the houses to the west, and shadows stole out of the corners and splayed across the neighborhood.

The children fell silent. Then they huddled together and whispered before glancing around. As one, they all turned and fled, running for their houses and disappearing inside like cockroaches when a torch is lit at night.

Desi gripped Calec's shoulder, her fingertips digging into his leathers.

Calec stood, and his hand traveled to the hilt of his sword.

The staggered beat of someone walking with wooden shoes on stone echoed around them. This sound rolled off the faces of the surrounding houses and sped along, as if portentous of the arrival of some great beast.

"She comes," Desi whispered. "The witch."

Calec pulled his sword a handsbreadth from its sheath with his unwounded arm.

A woman in a black dress and hat came clomping up the hill, one hand on a pouch, the other gripping something tightly against her waist.

Calec's blood ran cold. Could the witch who was burned by this city still be alive?

The woman's clattering steps didn't pause or even slow as she came within a house's length.

"Please, lady." Calec held up a hand for her to halt. "I wish to speak with you."

But the woman didn't stop.

Desi's breathing grew fast and raspy. She backed away, and the sound of her footsteps came in quick claps as if she were turning to flee or already fleeing.

Calec drew his sword. "I asked you to stop!"

The woman came straight for him, almost collided with him, but she turned ethereal, intangible. As if made of nothing but light.

Calec braced and stiffened his arm, preparing to shove her back. But his hand passed through nothing but air as this specter of a woman floated along the length of his arm and vanished altogether.

Then there he was, standing again in the plains under the light of many moons. The grasses swayed and threw the moonlight back with their soft underbellies.

Demon's Coin crouched among a nest of clouds and seemed to leer down at him. Mocking him.

40

————————

CALEC HURRIED FOR GHOST AND CLAMBERED ONTO HIS STEED'S
back. He drew his sword and found the reflection of the
Demon's Coin and its markings in the blade.

Tonight, those markings were hiding in the clouds, but Calec
now knew the moon's surface well enough he could guess in
which general direction the scratches ran in regard to the still
visible demonic face.

After surmising to head northeasterly, he wheeled Ghost
about and dug his heels into the horse's flanks.

"Run, Ghost. Run like the wolf wind."

Ghost's ears flicked about; his eyes swiveled as if hunting
for whatever adversary hounded them. His nostrils flared,
and his massive breath expelled fog into the bitterly
cold air.

"But we'll avoid any fires *and* the mammoth herd," Ghost
seemed to say. "And in turn hopefully avoid the predators who
hunt those beasts."

Calec ignored the pain in his arm and some lightheadedness
and leaned forward in his stirrups as Ghost's hooves thundered
across grass and dirt. The wolf wind screamed in his ears and
dragged its icy fingers across his cheeks. Ghost tore through the
night.

They ran for almost half an hour as Ghost's breathing came

in heaving bursts, his legs a blur under the moonlight. But the vanished city never came into view.

Calec eased Ghost down into a steady trot.

Hours wore on until Ghost was forced to walk the plains.

"The city has leapt far this night," Ghost said between blowing out long exhalations.

"I fear that as well." Calec stroked Ghost's neck. "I pushed you too hard, thinking we might come upon the city soon. But it is as if the Horseman has concealed his moon and has also thrown the city fifty leagues or more across the plains. As if he finally understands our intentions and now hopes to defeat us."

"Either the Horseman or the witch who walked through you is onto you."

They continued at a steady walk for hours. Midnight turned to the wee hours. Ghost's pace dwindled.

Finally, something glinted under moonlight far away, an entire city glowing on the plains.

"Ghost." Calec pointed. "We've almost arrived."

"Thank the old gods and the Mother, as I could go no farther this night."

Then it happened.

A ray of orange light broke out on the eastern horizon.

Calec shivered.

"*No*. Ghost. Run. Run like the predators of the mammoths are on our heels."

Ghost dug in with his rear hooves and leapt forward, although not with the power he'd displayed before. And it was already too late.

More spears of sunlight broke from somewhere beneath the far horizon. The city turned ethereal. Like the old woman. It wavered and sparkled.

Then it was gone.

"No!"

Not thirty minutes later, Ghost cantered over the area where the city had been, but they did not collide with any walls or enter any gates. They zigzagged back and forth many times before Calec pulled Ghost to a halt.

The city was not only invisible during the day, it was not present, as if it traveled to some other realm.

Calec glanced about.

Empty plains stretched around him for as far as he could see. Grasses bent under the heaving breath of the wolf wind.

Calec couldn't tell if it was real or only in his imagination, but he thought he heard derisive laughter rippling under the keening wind.

41

JAREMONDE SIPPED MULLED WINE. HE SAT AT A TABLE INSIDE A tavern near to where the mammoth celebration had taken place. Fires burned hot in the hearths along each wall. They'd been working on questioning everyone all the past day. Then Jaremonde had tried to rest, but with all the thoughts and anxiety running rampant through his head, he barely slept. Now, day two of working through and recording any accounts of the people who had been at the mammoth celebration was dragging.

"You need to take a respite." A middle-aged woman with a protruding bosom approached and smiled. Aprena, the same woman who'd invited him in for supper the other day. "There's too much strain placed on you with all these deaths."

Jaremonde nodded and smiled. "You sure know how to take my mind off things. But people are looking to me now for answers, and I can't let them down."

She ran a hand along his back. "What about letting me down?"

"Aprena." Jaremonde glanced around to make sure Rimmell and the others hadn't seen her touch him. "Not so obvious. My wife is sick in bed. I can't be seen with another woman now. I'll look roguish. Like no one can trust me with what's going on."

Rimmell sat at a nearby table questioning a group of men

who were dirt-stained and carried hammers and chisels in their belts. Carpenters. Aonor sat alone and pushed beads across a counting machine—an abacus was what Jaremonde thought the master of collections called it. Olinia and Climson sat at a third table with more potential witnesses of the latest death, conversing as if they were all having a friendly meal, Climson's way of attempting to make any potential suspect feel at ease so that they would hopefully let something slip.

Questioning over a hundred people in detail and hunting for subtle clues of guilt or lies was exhausting. And it was taking too long.

But at least even Rimmell was trying now. He'd given up skulking around behind Jaremonde and was trying to take charge. However, it was yet to be determined if his actions and attempts would turn out helpful.

"I'm still here." Aprena set another cup before Jaremonde.

"I'm sorry." Jaremonde turned to her and gave her his undivided attention for a moment. "You are looking beautiful this midday."

Her cheeks reddened, and she whispered, "Now who's being too obvious? Maybe you can stop by tonight before heading home."

Jaremonde nodded and took a drink. He glanced around to make sure no one was watching as he set his tankard down and fondled her breast for an instant.

Aprena scowled at him, but the corner of her lips lifted. She turned and hurried away to another table. Jaremonde sighed and tugged at his mustache. Everything was so complicated now. Before, only Valtera itself was complicated. Now there were all these dead people. Not to mention his sick wife who never had the energy to even speak to him. Also Desi and her disobedience.

Jaremonde drank again, brooding over all of it and how he could possibly stop a curse that killed without warning.

"Hear, hear!" Climson took a swig and slammed his tankard down. The redness in his eyes suggested that more than morning tea or mulled wine filled his tankard; the blacksmith had either been celebrating their successful hunt for far too long or he was growing too careless with his charade of appearing like every witness's friend.

Rimmell and Olinia—neither of whom had redness in their eyes—also lifted their tankards and drank.

"And where is Desi?" Climson shouted over to Aonor.

"She is still sleeping at the constable's," Aonor said. "Exhausted, the poor thing."

"I think Aonor and the witch hunter *both* wish to be sleeping in Desi's bed," Climson said and bellowed with laughter.

Aonor's brow wrinkled.

Jaremonde shot Climson a dark look, and the blacksmith quieted and returned to speaking to several men at his table.

"One of those men knows the old witch who walks Branber's Hill," Rimmell said from an arm's length away, startling Jaremonde and causing him to bump his drink. Liquid sloshed over the side of his tankard.

Rimmell appeared out of breath as he almost ran into Jaremonde's table but instead leaned over and rested his elbows on it.

Jaremonde raised an eyebrow.

"He sees her walking past his house every morning and evening, wearing a black dress. And he mentioned her limp." Rimmell's eyes flared and vibrated with excitement. "She lives near the ancient witch's manor that we visited. We should go. Now."

Jaremonde waited a moment, just to show the lad who made the decisions. "Did he tell you which house she lives in? Or is he going to take us there?"

Rimmell's expression contorted into one of confusion, but only for a heartbeat. "He told me enough. I can find it. He said he doesn't like to go near the place."

Jaremonde glanced over at the men Rimmell had been speaking with. One large man watched them, but he raised his hand in an amicable acknowledgment. Jaremonde nodded in reply.

"Tell me where this house is," Jaremonde said.

Rimmell listed out directions and road names that would take them to a hilltop. Manor Hill.

"We will head to …" Then Jaremonde paused. "No. Go there as fast as your young legs can carry you, but wait for me outside her manor. If she's there, don't go in without me. If she tries to leave, don't attempt to stop her. Just follow her. From a safe distance. I'm going to tell the others where we're headed and try to get some of them to join us."

Rimmell nodded and rushed for the door.

Jaremonde downed his mulled wine. *A real living witch.*

After quickly telling the others about the old woman and Manor Hill, Jaremonde departed the tavern followed by Olinia, Aonor, and Climson, each carrying a pike. Aonor's awkwardly stiff posture made it appear as if he'd never held such a weapon before in his life.

Rain composed more of ice than water pelted the city as they marched through the streets, huddling under their caps.

"Wait," Olinia said, stopping them for a moment. "There's something I have to do first, and it's on the way. A bit of something at the shop that has to be finished before nightfall. Nothing much. It'll only take me a few minutes. I'll meet you all at the manor."

She departed swiftly, her pike rising and falling as she jogged off.

Climson laughed. "Probably about to piss her drawers over fear of this witch."

Aonor scoffed, and they all continued on their way. Across the Narrows Bridge. Up the hill. The ancient witch's boarded-up manor loomed ahead.

We were so close, but how could I have ever known a witch lived next door?

When Jaremonde arrived at the front door of the manor in question, the door was already ajar. And it was dark inside, the windows shuttered.

"Rimmell was supposed to wait outside," Jaremonde said. "Damn lad. He's trying *too* hard now. Not the sharpest tool I've worked with."

"Maybe the witch saw him outside and got him," Climson said. "Made worms crawl out of his eyeballs. Or wrapped him in a spiked blanket and sat on him so no one could hear his screams."

Aonor silenced the blacksmith with a glare.

"Hello!" Jaremonde shouted into the manor's open doorway. "We've come to speak with the owner of this residence. You may have seen a young man about."

There was no answer.

Jaremonde glanced back. Climson pulled himself up to an ensconced torch on the manor's outer wall, tore the torch down, and lit it. He passed this torch to Jaremonde and then grabbed others for himself and Aonor.

They all crept inside. A fire burned in a hearth at the back wall.

And a scream sounded from somewhere deep inside the manor.

42

THE BLACKENED CITY APPEARED AND SHONE LIKE CRYSTAL ROCK ON the plains ahead, moonlight silvering everything around it. It was a little before dawn the night following the one when Valtera had disappeared right in front of Calec and Ghost. And that failure made for a wasted day of being able to do nothing but rest on the plains.

By the time they entered Valtera's gates, Ghost was lacquered in sweat and foam.

Lanigrad waited just inside the gates, seated and thumbing through a tome. "And so you return again, my devoted friend. But a day has already been lost."

"We tried as best we could, but the city had traveled too far," Calec said.

Lanigrad shut his book with a thud. "The others are still questioning all the potential witnesses from the hunt celebration. The old woman you saw has long disappeared from the vicinity of Branber's Hill."

Calec's eyes closed in regret. But something inside him shouted a reminder of warning. Someone in the group of hunters had tried to kill him. They'd also left him a message through Kirya.

"We've placed a few people on watch on Branber's Hill since the night after your encounter, but the old woman has not returned." Lanigrad stood. "We'll catch this woman and see if she has anything to do with the curse, but first, I believe I still owe you a tour—the manor you never had the chance to see much of."

Lanigrad mounted a horse and led Calec through the city. Icy rain began to pelt the streets and rooftops around them, as well as their backs and heads.

After riding up the hill and approaching the ancient witch's manor, Lanigrad unlocked the door and handed Calec a torch. Calec waited to step inside after Lanigrad, so Calec wouldn't have to worry about getting stabbed in the back.

After the incident with the javelin, Calec wanted at least two of these people with him at all times, but he also didn't want to appear frightened of being alone with anyone in particular. So he didn't comment and merely kept his distance from Lanigrad. He also kept a hand close to his sword and would be ready if there was ever the need to throw javelins again.

The manor was eerily quiet and utterly dark. Only thin slats of sunlight filtered through the gaps between boards covering the windows. And the light made the dust motes hovering in the air sparkle. So stagnant. As if the place couldn't be touched by the people or city outside.

"I am just reminding you that Rimmell and Jaremonde were here recently." Lanigrad held his torch high as he marched around the periphery of the empty antechamber. "Not long before your brief first visit when the manor and city vanished on you. They didn't find anything. But I understand you like to see the sites yourself. However, it may take a while to examine this place thoroughly."

Calec didn't respond but kept his distance from the man and, in these close quarters, one hand now on his knife, ready to pull the blade in an instant.

"I'm not going to be so thorough as to get on my hands and knees and search about for any hidden crevices." Calec studied the walls looming around him. They were the same blackened volcanic glass as the rest of Valtera. "Not yet anyway. I just wanted to visit the place. Get a feel for it."

Lanigrad's footsteps echoed around the chamber and grew so loud in the quiet of the manor that the noise seemed it might wake the dead spirit of the witch.

"I'm going to head down the west wing," Calec said. "You may accompany me or stay here, but do not come upon me without warning. I will have my knife at the ready in this place, and any sudden surprise could be deadly."

"Thank you for the warning, sir knight." Lanigrad stooped over and studied the old hearth in the wall.

Calec headed down the west wing, the sound of his footsteps echoing off the ceiling as he went. Over the next hour he entered and exited many empty rooms. These chambers were in the same state as the rest of the manor: dust furred, lacking furniture, only slits of daylight creeping in through boarded windows. Eventually, he found a staircase leading to the upper story. He ascended the stairs and searched more empty rooms. At the end of the second story hall, he arrived at a ladder that climbed up to a latched door in the ceiling.

She used to walk on the roof and speak with the Horseman. And women may have been kept chained up in the attic.

Those were some of the old legends, although Calec was running out of ways to corroborate the stories. The history tomes' accounts, which supposedly had relied on some council, seemed to be expunged. It was as if the emerald city wished to forget what'd caused it to turn black.

As Calec climbed the ladder, splintered edges around cracks in the rungs pulled at his gloves. The ladder groaned and creaked as he ascended, and he tested each rung with partial weight before stepping up to the next.

When he neared the latched door at the top, he pulled his knife from its sheath and smashed a rusted lock with its handle. On the seventh blow, the lock snapped. It plunged into the darkness below and clanged against the floor. The echoes it released barreled down the hall, and the sound shook all the nerves inside Calec's bones. He held his breath and listened.

If Lanigrad was about, he'd probably soiled his trousers. Calec shoved the overhead door upward and climbed into an attic, his torchlight barely able to work its magic against the darkness lurking above.

He walked carefully along a wooden plank supporting the ceiling of the second story, heading in the direction of the outer walls. If there were chains still here, they'd have to be anchored to the beams or walls.

Calec's torchlight chewed at the darkness, but he couldn't see more than a few feet in any direction. He crept along, brandishing his torch often before he arrived at the outer wall. Slats of wood supported the outer roof, but there were no rusty chains or skeletons waiting. No arcane markings written in blood. No animal carcasses or obvious blood stains at all, although some areas of wood appeared to be dark and rotting.

A rattle and a bang carried from somewhere off in the darkness.

Calec whirled around and stood silently, listening, his hand on his sword's hilt.

"Hello?" he called out. "Is there anyone here?" He pulled his knife instead.

The outer walls creaked as the wind shoved against them, and the roaring of falling ice or rain drummed overhead. No other sounds.

Calec eased his way back toward the north wall.

When he arrived, he followed the tracks of beams along the periphery. Again, there were no chains, but within a few minutes he found something—another door. It was positioned in the outer wall and appeared latched on the inside.

He paused. It would lead outside, not into some dungeon. And if there was a way to the roof, it might be from out there.

Before trying the door, he turned back and searched along the last two walls. After finding nothing of interest, he returned.

Calec lifted the latch and slid it over, unbarring the door. The handle felt cold and dead in his hands as he tugged on it. The door slid inward, and sunlight burst in from outside, blinding him for a moment. But the light was a muted gray, and the patter of rain sounded beyond the doorway.

After his eyes adjusted to the light, he stepped out onto a

balcony where a short ladder led to the roof. He climbed and then hauled himself up onto the top of the manor. Here, it seemed he stood upon the summit of all of Valtera.

The wolf wind herded clouds across the sky in great flocks, muting and graying the sunlight. Snowflakes whirled in the wind, and icy rain pelted the slate of the roofing around him, making the footing slick and treacherous.

From this vantage point, the city sprawled outward for a league or more in every direction. Then the plains extended to the horizon everywhere beyond the city except northward, where the range of mountains stood watch over their valley.

If ancient royalty wished to gaze upon their city, this view would be fit for a king. But why was the witch's manor located here?

"I am on high, like upon the tower in Landing, Horseman," Calec muttered. "If you wish to speak to me, do so now. I detest you and your ways. How you claim the souls of the murdered. How those souls must have vengeance before they can find freedom."

Calec glanced straight upward as darkening clouds seemed to push against the sky and the area of the sky sea. The wind gusted and tore at his hood and cloak, flung his hair, and whistled in his ears. He lost his balance for a moment and slid onto a knee.

He clutched the edges of the slate tiles around him and took a few breaths before standing again.

If there is a Horseman, he has answered me. He watches Valtera now.

A scream pierced the wind, coming from the city below. Then another scream followed, as well as shouting. Calec hurried over as fast as he could to the far edge of the roof of the east wing while attempting not to slip and plummet to his death.

He knelt and peered over the edge.

Near the adjacent manor, a group of people huddled around someone.

He recognized all of them.

43

CALEC EXITED THE ANCIENT WITCH'S MANOR AND RUSHED TO A manor nearby.

The group of people surrounding someone lying on the street included Lanigrad, Aonor, Rimmell, Olinia, and Desi. Climson stood near the wall of the manor and kept watch on an old woman whose hat was being tormented and deformed by the wind.

As Calec approached, details of the person who lay on the ground became clearer—Jaremonde's protruding belly. His mustache. He was sprawled out. Still. Lifeless. A torch with a dying flame sputtered in the rain beside him.

Desi had a hand clamped over her mouth. Tears streamed down her cheeks, and she sobbed silently.

Calec slipped past the others as he scanned the area for anything of interest and knelt at Jaremonde's side. Small puncture wounds covered his hands, and his hands rested in pools of blood. A chill rose from his remains. It even seemed to form a barrier against the bitterly cold wind and rain.

"What happened?" Calec rolled up the victim's sleeves. A blackened circle of flesh surrounded the constable's left wrist and hand. Other punctures continued up his arm, growing larger but sparser.

How Jaremonde claimed every victim appeared.

All those who died of the curse were marked with a burn from the burned witch.

"I ... I sought out this manor after a carpenter at the tavern told me he knew where the old woman lived." Rimmell's face was pale and drawn as he motioned to the old woman who sat against the wall of the manor. "The one who walks Branber's Hill. The constable wanted me to go as quickly as I could. I waited here outside, but then I heard strange noises coming from around the back. So I went back there to have a look around and see what was causing all the ruckus. I couldn't find anyone or anything back there. And not long after that, there was another commotion coming from the front of the manor. Once I returned, the front door was open and the others were already inside."

"Sterling work in tracking the woman down, Sir Rimmell." Calec nodded to him.

Rimmell blushed furiously.

Aonor pursed his lips and tapped them with a finger before speaking his version. "Jaremonde went inside first. We all spread out to search for the old woman, but we made sure to keep at least one other's torchlight in view. Still, we weren't close enough together. All I heard was a scream."

Desi sniffed. "I just arrived. After the fact. I overheard that everyone was headed here, and I didn't want to miss the encounter with the old woman."

"Who told you about it?" Climson faced Desi as he asked her. "If you were at home and Rimmell went straight to the manor? It wasn't your father."

Desi glanced away. "My mother. She told me someone came by to let her know about Jaremonde and the impending danger. My mother made me promise not to go inside the manor before she'd tell me about it."

Her mother? Why would a bedridden woman be told the most recent information? And who would stop by to tell her? Calec stared at Olinia and waited for her answer.

"I arrived a bit later as well," the saddle maker said. "Had to make a quick stop along the way."

So either Rimmell or Olinia wanted Desi to know.

Unless perhaps Desi was spying on the group again, under a cloak somewhere at the tavern. But then why not admit the fact now? Her father would be the only one who'd be furious about such a thing.

Calec considered that any one of these people could have killed Jaremonde without the work of some age-old curse born through completely magical means. Even Lanigrad could have hurried over to this manor after Calec left him behind and climbed to the roof.

Only Jaremonde was cleared of guilt now. And one other would be very unlikely *if* this return of an ancient death curse needed a physical body to enable its magic.

Calec furtively studied each person there as he stood and pretended to survey the area. Then he strode over to Climson where the old woman huddled against her wall.

"Give her a blanket at least," Calec said. "It's freezing out here, and she's probably seen about a turn of a century."

"Witches don't get cold," Climson said. "We should burn her here, right outside her manor. That will keep her warm. And maybe it'll reverse the curse and change Valtera back into the emerald city again. At least it should stop the deaths."

"You cannot burn her without evidence of her guilt," Calec said.

"We should burn her." Aonor stepped closer, holding a pike in his hand similar to how someone might hold a big stick. "It is not for you to decide, witch hunter. Valtera has long relied on its people to enforce its laws and serve judgment and sentencing. Since the time the first witch was burned."

Calec faced Lanigrad. "Is that true, scholar? Was that the beginning of the end for Valtera's soldiers and for trials?"

Lanigrad nodded. "That's when the people took up the power and banded together, as they quickly found they no longer had any outside enemies. They also had to fight to survive in an everchanging environment. There were many thieves and scoundrels in those early years, but they were dealt with. Valtera has been this way ever since."

"And look what burning that first woman got you." Calec turned away and gave the old woman his cloak. "A vanishing city of blackened stone."

"You disgust me." The voice came from the woman, a raspy old tone. "The mighty people of Valtera have sunk low now. Children shove and accost old women in the streets. And the people want to burn an old woman for it. If this is what Valtera has become, I no longer wish to be part of it. Do what you will."

Aonor's anger raged in his heavy breathing; Climson's flared on his cheeks.

Calec raised a hand. "No one is being burned today." He knelt before the old woman. "Would you accompany me inside your manor, lady? I wish to learn what tales you know of Valtera. Surely there are few within these walls who have seen as many years as you."

The old woman peeked out at him from beneath her hat, her face as wrinkled as parchment that was soaked, crumpled, and then dried.

"There are none in the city as old as I," the woman said.

Calec reached out to help her up. "And what is your name, lady?"

"Ulma." She took his hand, and Calec assisted her in standing.

"She's a witch," Desi whispered. "Be careful. It is she who chased me into the river. And the one who almost ran into you that past twilight as you disappeared."

"I must not have seen him, as I certainly didn't run into anyone," Ulma said, eyeing Calec and squinting.

"She may have frightened you and the children." Calec took her arm and guided her into the manor. "Mayhap she even hurt some of them, but we'll get her story and her side of things. I am confident that she is *not* responsible for Valtera's deaths."

"How can you be so sure?" Aonor raised his pike as if he wished to decapitate the woman, but instead he followed them into the manor.

"Call for someone to take and prepare Jaremonde's body in whatever manner he and his daughter and wife prefer." Calec motioned for them all to follow him. "Then come inside. We will discuss it, and you will see. To me, the more pressing circumstances revolve around which tales from the time of the witch burning are true and which are myth. And this woman may better be able to tell us than anyone."

44

CALEC MOVED TWO CHAIRS INSIDE THE ANTECHAMBER CLOSER TO its hearth, and he helped ease Ulma onto one of them.

Olinia entered the manor last and slammed the door behind her to shut out the wolf wind, and most of the tapers on a chandelier snuffed out. She latched the door, and the wind that'd howled into the chamber and stirred the flames in the hearth became trapped. It died where it was, and the chamber turned quieter and still and dimmer. Only the crackle of the fire and the thrum of icy rain pelting the windows and roof surrounded them.

Calec took a seat beside Ulma before asking her, "Do you need anything, lady? Tea perhaps?"

Ulma shook her head. She removed her long-brimmed hat, and hair as silver as starlight spilled out in thin strands. "I don't eat or drink much these days."

The others dragged more chairs closer and sat, and most set their pikes on the floor.

"Is there anyone else inside this manor?" Calec asked Ulma. "We will check, but I am asking first."

She shook her head. "It's only been me for over thirty years now. And I didn't harm those children on purpose, if that's why you all came to burn me. They accosted me, tried to rip my sweeties away from me, and they shoved me."

She lifted a leg and slid up her dress. Her ankle had swelled over a wooden shoe, the area twice as thick as it should be. Her skin was discolored—deep purple. Twisting veins rippled along its surface.

"Been passing out sweeties to children for three decades," Ulma said. "Since I stopped being able to help much with sowing seeds. Since my husband passed. Since my stories died."

"Then what weapon did you carry that you could use to stab a little girl with?" Desi asked, her face still stained with tear tracks, but she was holding it together, at least for now.

Ulma lifted a hand. In it she held a long and pointed needle.

"For my knitting," she said. "It's about all I do these days besides walk and attempt to cook and clean for myself."

"And why were you carrying a knitting needle on one of your walks?" Rimmell asked politely.

"I needed some defense after those children made me twist my ankle and nearly took away the one thing that still brought me pleasure in this life. My walks."

No one spoke for a minute, and if not for the murmur of the rain, a silent awkwardness would have risen and lingered.

"I can't do this right now." Desi stood and hurried to the exit of the manor. "I have to tell Mother what's happened."

Calec watched the door close behind her.

"And why would you believe this woman's account of her interaction with the children over the little girl who was stabbed?" Aonor asked Calec.

"I do not believe Ulma is the reason for these curse-linked deaths primarily because that little girl, Kirya, had no burn mark or rash." Calec leaned back in his chair and let the warmth of the fire bathe him. "I looked for the marks specifically after tricking Kirya into revealing her arms. And if all the victims develop holes in their skin"—Calec glanced around in an attempt to assess everyone's emotional state—"then I figure Kirya, who was stabbed thrice, should have also had some marks prior to receiving her punctures. *If* Ulma could indeed curse her."

"You believe the punctures on Kirya were completely unrelated?" Climson asked. "Pure coincidence?"

Calec nodded.

Climson grumbled some indiscernible reply as he brushed his hair over his shoulder.

"A very convenient coincidence," Aonor said, his pike resting in a threatening pose across his lap. "What if the burn mark is placed after death?"

"In Jaremonde's instance, would someone have had time to place the mark after making all those punctures?" Calec asked. "Before the rest of you arrived? Or would you like to believe there is some additional part of the curse floating along in the wolf wind and marking victims at random?"

No one answered.

"Now, if everyone is at least partially satisfied for the moment," Calec said, "the most pressing matter I wish to discuss with Lady Ulma is in helping us corroborate the legends of the burned witch. It seems that most of the old books from the citadel here have been relieved of this portion of Valtera's history, and there are many conflicting accounts in other books. Also, many of the tales you all told at Aonor's manor seemed to have stemmed from the memory of Valtera's oldest resident."

Calec made a flourish to indicate Ulma.

Ulma pursed her thin lips. "My mother and father told me about the witch when I was young, only a few years after the matter. They were both present at the tavern outside Stake Square that night, when it was still a tavern. Before being converted into a church. They witnessed the entire affair. So what is it that you wish to know?"

"I have a few questions concerning the tales I've heard," Calec said. "Not to mention questions about children's songs and the sites I've visited. The story everyone accepts is that the witch was burned. But the children's song says it was too cold to burn. Also, there are only scorch marks around the *base* of the stake in Stake Square. And the woman was accused of witchcraft, but other than her supposedly walking on her roof and perhaps talking, there is no definitive indication of what she'd done. Only conflicting reports from witnesses of her possibly poisoning soup at a festival and stealing women."

Ulma tapped her lips. "These things go farther back than my life, but my memory of all I heard in those following years when it was all fresh are much different from the stories that are now told around supper tables. Only no one has cared to hear my tales for decades. I will have to bring together many old legends and memories to weave it all together ... Maybe I will take that tea first."

Calec stood and glanced about as if to find tea, but Ulma waved him away.

Over the course of what felt like an hour, Ulma rose from her chair. She shuffled about the manor, gathering ingredients and water and pouring it all into a pot over the fire.

Impatience ate at Calec as he attempted to assist her and smile, but she only waved him away and took far too long to retrieve anything. It was no wonder people no longer had the patience for this woman's ways.

Finally, Ulma handed out clay mugs to everyone. Her hands trembled, her knuckles and finger joints appearing like cancerous lumps. Then she sat down and sipped her tea.

"Every tale I've heard told about burning the witch," she said, "although they mentioned how cold it was that winter. I have no knowledge to contradict a burning. But I do know that this woman came from the nomad clans. The two peoples— those of Valtera and the nomads—were much closer back in those days. At least Valtera was closer with some of the clans. Those who traded with the emerald city at the base of the mountains. But of course, there were other more savage and warring clans that Valtera had to defend against. This particular tale is older than I. It has a different spin than most legends where war begins between two men and their kingdoms over the love of a woman.

"It is said that a wealthy nobleman of Valtera was tending his crops in his fields beyond the city's walls. You see, the people of

Valtera didn't use serfs like other kingdoms did. This man profited more than his workers, but he toiled alongside them.

"And one winter day, this man spotted a nomad woman hunting river otter or perhaps fishing along the shores of the Rogue River. She waded out onto a shelf of ice as if she didn't know better, as if she almost wished to die. As if she desired for the river to take her. The ice cracked, and she plummeted into the frigid waters. The nobleman came running and called all his workers to her aid, but they raced down to the ice shelf and were too late. The current was already stealing her away. But the nobleman didn't head for the shelf. He was already running in an attempt to head her off downstream, and he arrived at the bank before she passed him by. The man used his sowing tool to anchor himself to the bank. Then he waded into the river. The cold struck him like a jolt of lightning, as nothing burns like the icy winters in the northern plains. He grabbed the woman as the current carried her past, her skin already deathly cold, and both of them were almost taken. But the man's grip did not falter. He pulled them both to shore. The woman was barely alive, her face and lips as blue as mountain ice. In an attempt to revive her without other means available, he kissed her and blew the breath of life into her lungs.

"That was when some say the cold took her for good. Others preferred a second instance. But the man revived her nonetheless, calling his men to him. They built a fire, but the wolf wind struck the flames down. Thrice it died before one man was able to keep a flame going and nurture it. The workers warmed the nobleman and the clanswoman there that day, afraid to remove them from the warmth of the fire and bring them to Valtera. Some stories claim the woman's skin never regained its hue.

"That was when the clansmen arrived. The nobleman had already fallen in love and begged the chief of the clan for the woman's hand in marriage. But this woman was the chief's daughter, and so the chief gave the woman a choice: to leave her clan and live with the people of Valtera and this man, or to return home with them and forget this day forever. The woman chose to return to her people.

"But a hot spark flared inside the nobleman. He'd fallen as madly in love as any man ever had, but that love was linked more to an idea of himself and what he was around this clanswoman—a hero. And there was another woman of Valtera who had long vied for this slightly older and much wealthier nobleman's hand. At this time, and after several years of pursuit, she nearly had him. But now he shunned her. She grew bitter and resentful. We will call her the discarded woman.

"The nobleman made offers to the clan's chief for his daughter's hand, and his offers grew larger and larger until he promised the chief all of his farmlands. The chief finally accepted and ordered his daughter to leave her people and go live in Valtera as a city man's wife. Soon, she and the nobleman were married, and this is when the other storytellers—the ones I used to call old—would say she turned cold. On their wedding night. When the nobleman gave the clanswoman his seed. They say the cold seeped into her womb then, into her blood, her heart, her future children, and she became his frozen queen."

Calec glanced around. The breaths of the others didn't rise above a whisper. All eyes were locked on this old woman who spun her story with more skill than anyone he'd heard.

"Not a year later," Ulma continued, "the nobleman died, and his clanswoman wife was left with nothing but their manor. No farmlands to sow beyond the walls of Valtera. No clans people of her own. Others say there was a child, but she kept it hidden from everyone, locked away inside the manor. And so she began walking on the roof where she could see the plains all around her. It would be as close as she would ever come to returning to her people. That is when the discarded woman took her revenge, although most have since claimed the discarded woman only spoke the truth about this clanswoman. About the clanswoman's witchcraft and the wicked ways of her people that she could not let go. About unnatural ceremonies and deeds. About how this witch clanswoman caused the winter to linger on for months longer than any winter in history. Snows piled as high as men, and the people of Valtera starved.

"A hungry mob soon came and dragged the clanswoman to what is now known as Stake Square. My mother and father watched as the executioners started a fire many times, but the wolf wind repeatedly snuffed out its flames. People inside the tavern claimed the clanswoman called down her witchcraft to dispel the fires and invoke a winter that would not stop until she was dead.

"The discarded woman then arrived and faced the clanswoman, urging all those around them to disperse until they'd talked. What all they spoke of none now know. But some overheard the discarded woman claim that once the fire started, it would take nearly twenty to thirty minutes of being burned alive for the clanswoman to actually die. That was with a typical burning, but this burning would be prolonged given the cold and the lack of heat the fire would attain. Then the two women shared whispers of conversation. Some claimed the discarded woman was the true witch, that she delved too deeply into the occult at the citadel and found old tomes that taught her how to summon the Horseman of old. Others said the discarded woman simply mocked the clanswoman and the savage ways of her people. They said the discarded woman boasted about how this was the clanswoman's fate for stealing her nobleman away and taking the manor and farmlands that should have rightfully been hers. She spat in the clanswoman's face and said the clanswoman should have died that day in the river as she'd intended, whether it be to avoid some other fate or man she'd been promised to.

"My mother even claimed that before the discarded woman departed the square, any fires all but died before they raged. Only a few wisps of flames remained and chewed at the woman's feet as she screamed. Then a dark shadow of a man with flaming horns appeared behind the clanswoman in the swirling snow blasting down from the mountains. Those attempting to light the fires fled the square. And this figure whispered in the clanswoman's ear as she was tied to the stake and writhing in pain. This belief was shared by many in the tavern, although my father rejected the vision. Rumors then rose around the subject of the Horseman's propositions and the clanswoman's promise to him. The most accepted of these musings came from the discarded woman, who was the only one who could have overheard their deal making. And the discarded woman would not leave the square, even out of fear, as she enjoyed the scene of the clanswoman's long suffering, and she reveled in the clanswoman's pain and potential damning of her soul.

"This version of the dark transaction between the Horseman and clanswoman was that the Horseman offered the woman a gift. The Horseman proposed that if the people of Valtera were to burn the clanswoman alive, he would offer her a curse in return. And the clanswoman, amidst raging anger, pain, and desperation, accepted his offer, making a pact with evil. The city of Valtera would then be cursed to wander the plains for eternity, like a nomad clan. The curse would be fashioned so that no man or woman inside or beyond the city would be able to break its spell. Valtera would also become as black as the hearts of its people, the emerald they loved so much stained over. The city would become lost and would only be seen by the light of the moon. But that was not all the Horseman desired. If he was to offer this mighty gift, he must be able to expand upon it. If she indeed wished this fate upon the people of Valtera, he could make it so, but she would also have to accept a curse of her own. A curse of witchcraft. She would have to accept that the power of the fire burning her would remain harbored in her bloodline. Any future descendants of hers would feel this dark power when they came of age, *and* when they found the path of the Horseman, whatever that was supposed to be.

"The clanswoman then rescinded her desire for all of it. At least at first.

"But she was bold. She negotiated with the Horseman *himself*. As her feet burned, she made a counteroffer, asking that the curse should only affect the men of her bloodline so that no other woman would be wrongly accused and burned for witchcraft.

"And so the Horseman accepted, and the flames sprang to life."

Ulma folded her hands and stared straight into Calec's eyes, as if she could read his every thought.

Silence seemed to stalk out of the corners and darkness of the room and swim in the air about them, swelling into a presence all its own.

45

CALEC DEPARTED ULMA'S MANOR AFTER THANKING HER PROFUSELY for her story, but he stopped outside the door and turned back.

"And what was the discarded woman's name?" he asked.

Ulma thought for a minute. "Lady Norella."

Calec nodded his thanks as he gazed out over the city. Everything about Valtera seemed much more vivid now, more visceral. The sun sank in the west, and the wolf wind's song rose in volume, as if heralding the coming night.

"Where are you going, witch hunter?" Rimmell hurried to catch up to Calec. "Jaremonde's no longer ... I no longer have someone directing me ... and I feel a bit lost."

"Then perhaps it is time for you to take initiative," Calec said. "Maybe lead the others. They will be looking for someone to spearhead this entire affair."

Rimmell slowed his pace, but Calec continued on his way as he watched the young man.

Then Rimmell's posture straightened, and he seemed to grow a handsbreadth in height. "And what will you be doing?"

"First, I wish to visit Desi and her mother and pay my condolences." Calec paused. "Desi said she'd heard about this manor from her mother. Did you stop by to tell her mother on your way out here? Or to tell Desi?"

Rimmell shook his head.

"There is no harm if you admit to doing so," Calec said. "You couldn't have saved Jaremonde."

"I didn't tell her," Rimmell said. "I headed straight for the manor to keep an eye on things as Jaremonde ordered."

"And you, Olinia?" Calec faced the saddle maker. "You admitted to having to do something before arriving here."

Olinia couldn't hold Calec's gaze, and she seemed to find something fascinating on her boot. "Only some pressing customer issue. With one who wouldn't understand if his items took another day. I just needed to deliver the leather and thought it would be a good opportunity, as it was on the way here."

Calec studied her but nodded.

She's lying about something.

A slow, tingling feeling from the possibility that Jaremonde didn't have a sick wife floated its way through Calec's thoughts. He'd never seen her, only heard the claim. In these enigmatic affairs Calec found himself in, the most removed of those who were still in contact with the main players often seemed to harbor the largest secrets.

"And what about us, sir knight?" Lanigrad asked. He stood with Climson and Aonor. "Where do we all go from here? Our one lead for the witch and her persistent curse seems to have fizzled out."

"Follow Rimmell, for now." Calec mounted Ghost.

"First," Rimmell said and then thought for a moment, "we search this manor and rule out another person as Jaremonde's killer."

Calec departed by urging Ghost into a steady trot. He was fairly certain they would find no one else inside the manor.

After a long, brooding ride retracing steps and winding through several quarters and streets, Calec found himself standing before Jaremonde's door. He knocked.

The door opened a crack.

"Sir Calec." Desi opened the door fully, revealing her reddened eyes and tear-stained face. She wiped at her cheeks. "You may come in if you wish."

"Thank you, lady." Calec bowed his head and stepped inside. "I wished to stop by and tell you how sorry I am about your father."

Desi flung herself at Calec and wrapped her arms around his neck. She sobbed against his chest.

Some tingling sensation, some warm feeling of belonging and wanting to help and maybe even something else rose inside Calec. He smothered all the emotion in a manner similar to how he imagined the wolf wind smothered weak flames.

After a couple minutes, Desi pulled away and wiped at her eyes. "We were too late in coming for you. We all tried to stop the curse, but there's no hope in that. If my father was killed, and you're convinced it wasn't the old woman's doing, then this curse must strike those unfortunate enough to live in Valtera like invisible lightning. We are the cursed people."

"And why do you say this? Why do you claim if it isn't the old woman who carries and uses the curse, then it is lightning?"

"Because no one else in that group would have done it. Not to him."

"I was struck in the arm by a javelin within that same group. A javelin meant to impale my chest."

Desi studied him. "You still don't believe it was only a throw corrupted by terror when a hulking mammoth was charging straight at everyone?"

Calec paced around the room. "I wish to speak to your mother, if she will allow it. Is she well enough to talk?"

The color drained from Desi's face. "She's probably sleeping. There is nothing to be gained there."

"I will wait, if you will." Calec folded his arms over his chest as if he would stay all night, although that would be an impossibility.

Desi appeared ready to argue, but after a moment, she nodded and went to a far door. She opened it quietly and disappeared inside the room before closing the door behind her.

Calec paced about, wondering if Desi would make an excuse, wondering if there really was a woman back there or if she'd died long ago.

The chamber door opened again, and Desi peeked out. "You may come in, Sir Calec."

Calec's mouth felt as dry as dead grass when he approached the doorway, and he placed one hand on his knife beneath his cloak. Desi stepped back inside and opened the door farther.

"You'll have to excuse her," Desi said. "She hates people to see her like this. She was once so beautiful and took such great care of herself. She has ... just been sick for so long now."

Inside, a woman with grayish skin and strands of sweaty hair sat up, pulling a blanket up to her neck.

Calec genuflected. "My lady. I beg for your forgiveness at this intrusion and for what has befallen your late husband, Sir Jaremonde."

The woman coughed, a wet sort of sound, as if a marsh had settled in her lungs. "Jaremonde was a decent man, and I loved him at one time."

At one time? Calec nodded. "I will pray to the Mother and any others who may offer you aid."

"And now you understand," Desi said to Calec. "There is no reason for me to continue with my father's work. No need to keep trying to figure anything out about the curse. I've already lost everything. And Valtera cannot stop what is coming."

Calec's heart sank as he cleared his throat, hoping to reply with some deep counter that would bring Desi hope and strengthen her resolve.

"I'm dying," the mother said. "I know that now. Do not waste your breath on what must come. There is no getting over this. It is only the long slow decline into the grave."

Desi sobbed and took her mother's hand in hers.

"I wish things had been different between me and Jaremonde in the end," the mother said, "but I was sick for a long time, almost dead already. I do not blame him for what's become of us. I also found someone else to share my last weeks or months with."

Calec's ears itched. *More questions that will need to be answered.*

"Then I wish you any happiness this world can bring." Calec

rose from his knee. "And I apologize again, but if it is not too much trouble, and if you have the strength, would you consider answering a question or two? For Valtera."

The woman nodded. "I wish to help with anything I can. To serve some small purpose while I am bedridden might bring a bit of joy. Even the thought of being able to do something lightens my heart."

Calec smiled at her. "Please tell me how it is that you came to know of where Jaremonde and Rimmell were headed earlier today? While stuck here in bed?"

A weak grin lifted the woman's lips, but her eyes darkened. "From the one who loves me."

Ah, that is it, then. "And this person. They—"

Desi's mother fell into a fit of coughing, the result so loud it rattled her lungs.

A stack of books sitting on a chair caught Calec's eye. One of them he recognized. From the street along Branber's Hill. The book Lanigrad had been reading but gave to Desi.

As Desi comforted her mother and attempted to help ease her coughing, Calec took up the book and thumbed through the mass of pages, stopping at a spot approximately where Lanigrad had been reading. He flipped through more pages until his eyes settled on an entry. The entry where a witness claimed to give the account of a guard who'd entered the witch's manor and had seen sacrificed animals and blood markings and chained up skeletal women in the attic.

Calec's finger ran down the page and stopped abruptly. There at the bottom was a date and a scribe's name as well as the name of the witness—Lady Norella.

Calec's blood tingled with realization, an understanding, as he set the book aside.

The front door of the house burst open, and Aonor strode inside in his brilliant white and gold tunic.

"Desi! I've come for you. To warn you and"—Aonor glared at Calec from the open doorway before continuing—"let you know there's been much death in the past few hours. I came to offer you protection."

Calec set the book aside and strode toward Aonor ... but then darkness surrounded him again.

And veiled moonlight. The empty plains.

Ghost stood amidst swaying grasses approximately the distance of what would have been just beyond Desi's front door. His eyes were closed in sleep. He probably hadn't even realized that the city vanished.

Calec mounted Ghost and turned to ride him into the night. But as he looked skyward, he noticed the entire Demon's Coin moon was hidden in a cloudbank.

"Chasing after this city and its curse may kill us as well, my friend. If one of its people doesn't get us first."

46

"MY LEGS ARE OLD AND COLD AND STIFF, AND I CANNOT GALLOP the distance tonight," Ghost seemed to say as Calec rode him at a brisk walk along the snow-dusted plains.

"You've been trustworthy and have pushed yourself harder than I would have asked of most," Calec replied. "Tonight, I will not demand more from you."

The entire Demon's Coin moon remained concealed by clouds this night, and Calec could only guess in what direction the reflected markings might have pointed. Other clouds hurtled over the mountains and pushed against the dark sky and the moons. Only those clouds in the area around the Demon's Coin lingered.

Ghost walked on. The emerald city seemed to be roaming ever farther to the east, more distant from Calec's woods, as well as more northward toward the peaks that stabbed at the sky.

After many hours of traveling, Ghost began to move more and more slowly, and there was still no distant glimmer of the city. They continued until dawn was nearly upon them, stopping only when they arrived at a depression behind a hill. Here, Calec cleared an area in the grass and struck flint to make a fire. He rubbed Ghost down.

"We will camp here for the day," Calec said. "And we will

recover. There is no hope of reaching Valtera before daybreak. And there is nothing more I can ask of you, my friend. We will start fresh as soon as twilight falls."

Calec patted Ghost's neck and let him graze near the fire. Ghost didn't wander far either, as if he, too, required the warmth of the flames. Or maybe he feared what might lurk in the darkness.

Calec sat near the flickering fire, lost in thoughts of Desi and her mother and of Aonor and of the master of collection's claim that more deaths had recently occurred. As the minutes passed, Calec played with the yellow ribbon on his wrist while reminiscing about Serileen and imagining their future child, if the child could survive. He would be able to see them again when this was all over. He could be there to try to make sure his child survived until birth ... and then beyond.

The thought made him wish he were in Valtera now, but he would not sacrifice his steed for the destination. However, that did not stop guilt from weighing like a pile of stones on the twin scales in his heart.

Then images of the ancient tome he'd recently looked over rolled through his mind. The entry describing some guard's supposed claim of finding women chained up in the witch's attic was probably all a lie. The witness had been Lady Norella. And Ulma said that was the name of the discarded woman in her tale. It must have been the discarded woman's attempt to place suspicion upon the clanswoman.

Ghost slept, and Calec eventually lay down, curling toward the fire. His eyes closed, and he drifted off.

Dreams of dead men and women crawling through the grasses around him haunted his sleep. The blades rustled, forming a pathway, as if some giant mole used grass to burrow through instead of the deep earth. Then a head popped up from the foliage. A grinning man. Earth and soil dripped in clumps from his lips. A woman emerged beside him, and before long he was surrounded by many others. And the silhouette of the man with the flaming horns and black mask stood in the distance, outlined by moonlight, misty breath and smoke spewing from his mouth and nostrils. His arms were folded across his chest, and the ring with the golden skeleton and black heart flashed on his finger.

47

THE PLAINS SPRAWLED OUT AROUND CALEC AND GHOST AS THEY trotted on, but they headed closer and closer to the mountains. Calec kept an eye out for fires or mammoths or packs of predators. Ghost often sniffed at the wind, and his ears flicked about, listening for danger.

Intermittently, the nest of clouds around the Demon's Coin moon would ride south with the wolf wind. Then Calec would draw his blade and determine their course. But it had been several hours since he was last able to determine his bearings from that cursed moon. And there was no sign of Valtera in the distance.

"I can almost see the flat of the plains all the way to the mountains," Calec said, "and I do not see any city twinkling under moonlight."

"The moon dupes us again this night," Ghost said over the two-beat clomping of his hooves on frost and snow-covered grass.

They passed over several leagues of empty plains before the Demon's Coin moon again emerged from the clouds.

Calec tore his sword from its sheath and found the markings.

Almost due east now.

The last time he'd seen the markings, they pointed to the northeast.

Calec cursed and reined Ghost eastward. "We've veered far off course over the past hours when the Demon's Coin was hiding."

"Then we may not find Valtera again tonight," Ghost said. "Look to the horizon."

Far in the east, over the seemingly endless plains, the stars began to fade.

A sinking sensation tugged at Calec's gut.

"No," Calec muttered. "We cannot go another day and night without reaching the city. If what Aonor claimed about the increasing deaths was true, we could be too late to help anyone. Ride, Ghost!"

Calec pressed his heels into Ghost's flanks, and the horse bolted. They raced across flats and over small rises.

Minutes passed. No city appeared ahead, and the black sky in the east lightened to deep blues. The wolf wind blew off the mountains, its chill deepening, its gusts growing more powerful.

The sensation of hope began to crumble inside Calec as each star disappeared in the east and Ghost's hooves thundered over the plains.

The first rays of sunlight broke and painted the sky. And still, Calec let Ghost run.

"We cannot find the city in this light," Ghost said, and Calec cursed.

"Then I will dismount and run on foot the remainder of the day."

"It will not help, as the city will move again this coming night."

Calec yelled over the wind in frustration and pounded his thigh with a fist. There was nothing he could do. The Horseman and the ways of the world were far too powerful. No mortal could contend with them.

The dawn strengthened, and sunlight shone over the plains. No city stood out for as many leagues as Calec could see.

He slowly pulled Ghost to a trot and then a walk as the crushed hope inside him fell to pieces and seemed to die in the lowest parts of his abdomen.

We missed it. Because the moon was hidden too often.

"And so how can we even venture to hope to find the city tonight?" Calec asked, his voice ringing with desperation. "It could move another hundred leagues in the opposite direction. And we cannot get a head start by riding early. Its location will not be set until twilight."

Ghost remained silent as they walked without purpose, still heading east.

An hour passed before Calec's resolve waned.

"We should rest during these short days," Calec said as he pulled Ghost to a halt. "So we can start fresh and strong as soon as we can."

Then he saw something on the distant plains, a great fire and plumes of smoke. He scrutinized the area and searched all around for nomads before urging Ghost onward. When they drew nearer, he could make out a dark shape speeding across the plains. A lone horse and rider who carried a torch and circled an expanse in the distance. A cloak lifted behind the rider and streamed out in the wind like a banner of ill will.

Calec shuddered, and the cold wind slapped at his cheeks. His hand found his sword's hilt as they rode closer.

The thunder of hoofbeats sounded over the wind that now raged through the grasses and tore across the plains, wailing like a thousand spirits.

He watched as the horse and rider continued circling. And a distant shout carried to his ears, "Sir Calec!"

It was a woman's voice.

Calec's hackles bristled. But it was someone who knew him. He cupped his hands to his mouth and shouted into the wind, "I am here."

The rider continued in her circling path as Calec rode toward her.

"You must be prepared to flee for our lives," Calec said to Ghost as he patted his neck.

The other rider's torchlight flickered, and she wheeled about in a large circle before galloping back toward him.

As Calec and Ghost walked on, the rider approached but

stopped in the distance, her horse heaving for breath against frigid air.

"Sir Calec." Desi threw back her hood.

Calec's heart skittered in his chest.

"How did you find me amidst all these plains?" Calec motioned to the vastness around them.

"I assumed you'd be hunting for Valtera," she said. "And Valtera is right there." She pointed into the distance where Calec had been headed. "I lit a fire outside the city. So you would hopefully have an easier time finding us."

Besides the fire and smoke, the plains were empty save for grasses and rolling hills.

"I see no city," Calec said.

"That is because you're not a cursed citizen of the emerald city. And that is why I departed the gates. So you could find me out here this day."

Calec nodded in agreement, although the possibility of being able to see her but not the city did not meld with other ideas in his mind.

It could be a trick.

"Nine more of Valtera's people have died since you left the old woman's manor," Desi said. "Valtera needs you. And I have found that I've not quite given up. Not yet."

The deep fire in her ice-colored eyes, the one Calec had seen when she'd first pleaded to him about coming to Valtera, had returned. It raged somewhere deep in her soul.

Calec nodded. "Lady. Then if it is possible, lead us back into Valtera under the sun."

"I am not here to take you to Valtera this day. Not yet. Given where the city now lies, there is another place you must see first." She wheeled her horse around. "We ride for the site of the emerald city's origin. Today it is near."

48

THE DAY WAS STILL YOUNG WHEN CALEC RODE GHOST AND followed Desi and her palomino gelding to the base of the mountains. A river raged somewhere in the morning shadows amongst the crags, its headwaters pouring down the cliffs like silver lace in the early light.

And the towering mountains ahead seemed to bleed white. As if their peaks were wounded and white blood ran in rivulets through the ravines between skins of pine trees. Giants who bled snow and ice.

They crested a rise, a foothill, as sunlight broke full in the east and painted the sky over the mountains orange and red.

"Will we still be able to find the city later this day if we return to its current site?" Calec asked.

"You may not." Desi cast him a quick glance. "But do you assume the people of Valtera have not been venturing out beyond their walls during the day for the past century? I can lead you to it."

Calec nodded. The base of the nearer shorter mountains soared upward just beyond a few more foothills.

"We are on the hill now." Desi wheeled her horse around, her hair whipping in the wolf wind, whose breath came fresh off the mountains here, carrying the cold of the north. Her horse's pale mane and tail streaked around her.

"Branber's Hill?"

Desi shook her head. "Manor Hill."

Calec's heart jolted as he glanced around in the wind tearing at his hood and hair. He could picture it: the ridge along the rim of the hill, where Valtera's manors had resided. These foothills created part of the city. The expansive flats below had been filled with houses and churches and shops in some distant past. And the Rogue River still ran through a deep gorge in the middle of it all. Those waters still flowed here, although some kind of magic had also eternally bound them to the vanished city.

A sparkle on the distant edge of the hill caught Calec's eye, the raw sunlight leaning down over the area but also being thrown back up from one spot.

"What is that?" Calec asked.

Desi gripped her reins, clucked, and bounced her heels into her steed's flanks. The horse trotted off across the hilltop. Calec followed.

When he arrived at the area in question, he could see why it sparkled.

Ice.

A sheet of it but in the shape of a perfect rectangle. The size of a manor. The size of the clanswoman's manor. The burned witch. Lanigrad had mentioned there were patches of ice and snow noted in the records here, but he'd assumed they were not out of the ordinary.

Calec dismounted and walked about, his feet crunching along its brittle surface and punching holes through frost.

What madness or magic created this?

It was no mistake that the ice was only in the area of the witch's manor. Some dark dread swirled in his heart and spewed into his blood. The occult. This acknowledgment, and memories of Ulma's story, turned his stomach and chilled his marrow.

"What other than witchcraft could do this?" Desi asked.

"The Horseman." *If the Horseman is real.* Calec walked the area, searching for anything, his heart starting to jitter with fear.

"There's another one." Desi pointed into the distance.

Sure enough, another area glittered like a patch of diamonds in the sunlight. It was also in the former lands of the emerald city. Beside the river. Calec surveyed the area below them for any other similar regions, but he couldn't find any.

They returned to searching the area of the manor but found nothing other than the sheets of frost and ice.

"Shall we have a look at that other area?" Calec asked.

Desi looked up from where she knelt on the ice and was running a gloved hand over its surface. She nodded. They mounted and rode to the river. There were no longer any bridges to cross, but the second icy spot was on the same side of the river they were on. A pole protruded from the center of this area, and this sheet of ice was circular, as large as a—

"Stake Square." Desi dismounted and stepped onto the area, the frost cracking beneath her feet with a hollow sound, as if it covered some deep body of water.

She stepped more carefully.

"There's something here, Sir Calec."

Calec hurried across the ice, the cracking beneath him making him think he was walking across a field of dried bones.

A stake rising twice as tall as a man protruded from the ground. It had weather-worn surfaces. Cracks running along its length. And it was colonized by sheets of frost.

A blackened area around the base of the stake formed a ring in the ice. Soot or scorch marks. Not very large, and it didn't extend far. But there was something else. Something far more sinister.

The blackened boot prints of a man and four black horse-shoe prints were punched into the ice behind the stake. Spiked holes at the toes and heels of the horseshoes extended deeper.

The Horseman stood here.

That enigmatic being who supposedly made his home out of the sky sea *had* conversed with the clanswoman as they burned her. A dark pact was made and sealed right here.

Calec's heart rioted in his chest and drummed a deep percussion into his lungs. His palms grew slick, his mouth dry. A feeling of a growing presence, of the sky sea and its Horseman raging somewhere high above, washed over Calec.

Evil was real. Monsters or demons or beasts from some other world. Evil controlling more power than any man could ever dream.

Several silent minutes passed as the implications washed over and through him.

"What has struck you with such fear?" Desi asked.

Calec pointed to the black tracks of the Horseman and his red-eyed steed.

Desi's expression contorted into bewilderment. "That specific spot of ice?"

"No. The footprints."

"The what?" She stepped closer and knelt, scrutinizing the area. "Now it is I who doesn't see."

"You do not see the boot prints or the horseshoe prints marked in ice?"

Desi slowly shook her head and faced him. "You are not lying?"

The tracks seemed to bore holes in Calec's mind. Was she lying? "I would not have even thought to make up such a thing."

"Then we who are cursed do not see everything. Maybe some things are hidden from *us*."

Why? Calec brooded on this as he ran a finger over the ice and into the imprints. The ice inside felt colder than the rest. As cold as death.

Desi knelt beside him and did the same.

"Can you feel them?" Calec asked.

She shrugged. "Perhaps, if you tell me they are there. I feel indentations, but the ice is not disturbed in my eyes, and I do not feel a specific enough pattern to think of it as a print."

Calec's thoughts settled on one memory—Ulma had mentioned something.

"The Horseman's path," he said in a faraway voice.

"What does that mean?" Desi asked.

Calec shook his head. Ulma hadn't known what the path was, but her story claimed that if someone inherited the burning curse from the witch, they developed their power when they came of age and found the Horseman's path ...

But here at the site of origin or at the corresponding site in the vanished city?

"Then everything Ulma told us was true." Calec's voice faltered as he spoke more to himself than to Desi. "I only wish there were some way to know—somehow to watch—what'd happened all those years ago. I still don't understand the burning of the witch and how the event is linked to the punctures in the victims. Or even what could cause all those wounds. If the curse indeed burns a victim, there should be blisters along with the blackened skin. Flames should also not be able to burn holes in a victim's body without searing the skin around it. Even if the victims are burned or boiled from the inside, it still does not make sense. They bleed out because of those punctures."

"I recall one time when I believed I was actually viewing the scene." Desi's voice began low and fearful, but it turned high-pitched, as if she'd just remembered something as she spoke. "In Aonor's house. His paintings. He has so many of them."

Memories of the hundreds of paintings that adorned the master of collection's antechamber flooded Calec's mind. There were also many other works from a particular time period inside the bedchamber Calec had slept in.

"He has an entire chamber filled with paintings of the scene. Of the witch being burned." The cold had laid its red hand on Desi's nose and cheeks, and her teeth chattered. "He showed it to me once when he was trying to impress me by giving me a tour of his manor. I don't know if it'll help, but I do remember it now. A woman wreathed in flames. So many paintings of the event covered all the walls of one room, a room no visitor ever wanted to stay in."

Calec faced north toward the mountains and the area where the opening of the square would have stood between the church and houses. The wolf wind hit him like a cold fist on the nose and cheeks, flinging his hood back, stirring his hair and tearing at his cloak.

Calec's eyes were drawn upward to where the wind seemed to plummet down the mountain's face like a slide, gathering cold from the far north, gathering fury. Where clouds of snow crystals plumed from peaks and crags and dashed against the sky.

"She didn't burn," Calec said. "No one could burn here. Not in the midst of winter and with this wind. Not in the worst winter in Valtera's history. Not with all the oil Valtera had to spare. That part must be legend. Why the scorch marks are almost nonexistent."

"Then what happened to her? All the stories I've ever heard said she was burned. Didn't the old woman also confirm it?"

Calec nodded as his eyes watered under the shrill gale, and he squinted against its fury. "She did. But there is no pain like the cold burn of this wind on naked flesh."

49

Desi looked up and across the empty plains as if she saw something that wasn't there. Something immense. As if she were mad. She'd led Calec to a specific location on the plains, but only broken pockets of sunlight slipped their golden blades between the clouds and bathed the grasses around them. Nothing more. And the clouds were growing darker and grayer. Soon, there would be another storm of snow and ice.

"It's right here," Desi said as she trotted her palomino. The sound of its hoofbeats changed drastically from the rustle of punching through stiff grasses and the crunching of snow to the hollow clop of steel horseshoes on stone.

But there is no stone.

Ghost carried Calec onward, and out of the air around him, shapes materialized: a gateway with wooden planks and cross-beams, walls of black stone, towers, houses, a city extending as far as he could see.

A sucking sensation of fearful wonder formed in Calec's gut and pulled at his heart.

The occult magnified tenfold.

There was no dismissing this curse and the sheer power of it. Nor the abilities of some lost Horseman residing in the sky sea.

Calec's throat seemed to clamp shut as he rode in silence, watching people mill about the streets, moving carts full of tubers, conversing quietly. So normal and yet so unfathomable. Even now. Even after having seen this city at night.

Snow began to swirl in thin flakes as an icy rain dumped from the sky.

Time seemed to stand still as Ghost followed Desi's steed.

"Are you all right?" Desi asked.

Calec barely nodded as he swallowed and indicated the city around them. "Was all this only invisible to me? Or would any outsider have run into its walls if they'd blindly stumbled upon the place by sheer luck?"

Desi lifted an eyebrow. "The myths say only those who enter through the main gates can interact with us. So maybe the animals wandering the plains under the sun, as well as any people, pass right through us as if we are spirits."

"As I did that morning when I watched the sun rise and the city disappear before me. I ran all about but found nothing."

"Then you did not find the one gate."

They continued on their ride through the streets, Calec lost inside some world of his mind, attempting to comprehend mystical enchantments until Desi pounded on the door to Aonor's manor. Her gloved fist trembled, and she shivered with cold. Calec waited behind her and hitched their horses to a post as the sun's veiled light faded into late afternoon.

His mind continued to spin from shock. The emergence of an entire city that he couldn't see before he'd entered its gates seemed much different from having to ride to a new location each night.

The door before Desi cracked open, and a man Calec recognized—Aonor's guard with the pike—stared out at them.

"Ah, Lady Desi," the guard said. "Lord Aonor is not in at the moment. Would you like to step inside and wait for him? You are welcome here, as it may be yours someday. His lordship is always hopeful."

Lord? I thought Aonor was the master of collections and that there were no longer any lords in Valtera.

"Thank you," Desi said. "Yes, I'd like to wait inside, with my chaperone."

The guard glared at Calec for a moment but then nodded. He opened the door, and they stepped inside.

"I really can't wait long, however," Desi said. "Do you know when the master of collections will return?"

"No, lady. Not with all of these new deaths. He is helping investigate them."

"Then I wish for you to bring me to a room."

The guard's eyebrows rose.

"A certain room," Desi said. "One Aonor showed me before. The chamber with all the paintings of the witch who was burned in Stake Square."

The guard's face paled. "There are dozens of rooms in this manor, and I am not a servant. I don't know exactly where the one you speak of is located, but I see no harm in you viewing it."

The guard clapped, and two servants appeared from the antechamber behind him.

"Show Lady Desi and her chaperone to the chamber that displays the paintings of the burning witch," the guard said. "But do not leave the two of them alone in there." The guard glanced back at Desi. "My pardons, lady. If Aonor shows and allows you to do as you will, we will be more accommodating. But this is a strange request."

Desi nodded. "That is fair. Please, take us there."

A servant with a shaven head led them through the stark emerald antechamber that was littered with paintings and marble busts. They continued up a winding staircase with an ornate banister. All emerald. Then down a long hallway. The servant stopped at the last door on the left and propped the door open, standing and staring blankly as he folded his hands and bowed his head.

Calec studied him and waited, but it didn't appear that he was going to say anything.

Desi stepped into the room, and Calec followed.

Paintings hung haphazardly across the walls inside, similar to the rest of the manor, as if the master of collections had far too many works of art that needed to be displayed and not enough wall space.

Images of orange and red fire stood out on most paintings. Wings of flame wrapped around a body with pale limbs. A streak of black hair was evident in one. A pain-stricken face on another. There must have been a hundred paintings cluttering the room, flaunting their garish colors and scenes. The paint on many of the canvases was cracking, and on others it was peeling up, attributing to the age of these works.

Calec's mind wandered and returned only to marvel at the art and to again ponder the possibilities of the event.

Then Calec's eye settled on one painting. One work hidden amongst all the others. Muted and dark. Painted in tones that were inconspicuous to the eye amidst the masses.

Calec crept closer and stood on the bed. This painting hung near to where the wall joined the ceiling. He focused on the images buried inside a shadowy theme.

A black backdrop. A pale woman tied to a stake. Her dark eyes filled with shadow. Her black hair streaming in the wind. Naked. Her breasts bare and exposed to all as her hands were tied behind her back. Snow swirled in the wind around her. Ice lay on the ground and upon the stake. A dark silhouette of a man was barely discernable even now when Calec stood so close. A wisp of orange for a horn. The red eye of an indistinct horse beside him, its form extending to the margins of the painting. And the Horseman himself held an ethereal hand on the woman's shoulder, a hand as dark and intangible as shadow. The vivid expression on the woman's face made her appear tormented, as if she were burning, although there were hardly any flames. Only a tongue or two of yellow light extended from the piled kindling at her feet.

Calec's attention settled on the Horseman's hand on her shoulder. Then his gaze ran down the woman's arm to her fingers. Icicles had already formed on her fingertips and hung from them as if her hands were eaves.

A memory struck Calec like a jolt of lightning: him walking through the pines of the woods as spring had threatened to arrive before he left, the heated water in his skin that'd been boiled too hot, the skin bouncing against his leg and warming his hands, the ice forest melting around him. Frost catching the sunlight and sparkling. Water sliding down and then dripping from an icicle on the boughs as the sun lit up the crystal forest like fire.

Something unlocked in his mind. The holes. The punctures. He knew. He—

"That is one of my favorites." A voice came from the doorway. Aonor stepped inside and coughed softly into a closed fist. He smiled at Desi, and a scent of roses followed him and seeped into the room, flavoring the air as if it were tea. "Although the images in this chamber are too frightful to share with many. I merely harbor a love and taste for the arts. For the old masters."

Calec's hand surreptitiously slipped down to his knife's handle as he stepped off the bed. "Why is that painting the only one that doesn't show the witch burning?"

"That particular work was painted by the hand of a master of masters. Devoin the Scene Capturer, they called him. Unparalleled in ability with paint and marble. He had an eye for reality and could perfect dimensions and people's perception of a scene. You can see his name in the lower right corner." Aonor pointed to where a quick slash of a signature ran near the peeling golden frame. "But unfortunately, I cannot answer your question, witch hunter. I only know Devoin painted what he saw rather than what others commissioned him to paint, unlike many of the starving artists of old Valtera."

"Do you have more of his works?" Desi asked.

"Oh, yes, every known piece that still survives from the hundred or so years ago when he lived. But no others depict the scene of the burning witch."

"Could I trouble you for tea?" Calec asked Aonor.

Aonor studied him, a look of bemusement crossing his pale features. Then he clapped, and the servant outside poked his head in.

"Bring us tea," Aonor said. "It seems our guests would like to stay and discuss art for a spell."

The servant departed.

"And who painted these others with so much garish fire?" Calec motioned to the rest of the room.

"Many different artists of the time." Aonor studied a painting behind Calec. "Most of these works were commissioned long after the event. They represent the individual artist's take on the scene."

"Then how did they even know what it'd looked like?" Calec asked.

Aonor shrugged. "Perhaps they painted while they visited Stake Square. They were not so long removed from the event as we are now."

Calec attempted to keep one eye on the master of collections as he pretended to study other works, biding his time until the servant returned and handed out three mugs of tea before leaving again.

Calec blew on his tea to cool it and feigned sipping the liquid inside. "I think I've seen enough. If you will, would you please lead us back outside, Aonor?"

Aonor looked for a place to set his tea, as if he wished to clap for a servant, but instead, he nodded. He turned and led them down the hallway and staircase.

"You do realize that we found no one else inside the ancient woman's manor," Aonor said. "After you left us. It was *only* the old woman. The likely witch."

Calec nodded. "I didn't think you'd find anyone else."

"But what you also don't seem to realize is that after you departed and took days to return, there have been many more deaths. As if this witch believes she is now invincible and will never be caught. She is killing anyone and everyone she can. At first there were nine. And then during the past day in which you've been gone, there have been over ten more. I will say that again: over *nineteen* more people of Valtera have been cursed and burned with the witch's mark in less than a day."

Aonor stepped outside the front door of his manor into the roar of falling droplets of icy rain mixed with snow. Calec and Desi followed. Calec stooped and ran a gloved finger along the base of the stones of the manor, scooping together a handful of snow drift and frost. He then passed his mug to his hand holding the snow, and he coated the outside of the mug with it.

"You don't seem too concerned about all this death," Aonor said. "If you truly wished to help us, you would either have had us burn that witch or you'd be angry now and would be rushing about attempting to do something."

"Sir Calec has done more than anyone—" Desi started, but Calec cut her off.

"Please take this." Calec held out his mug until Aonor reached for it. "If you will."

Calec placed the mug in Aonor's grip and watched him closely. Aonor stared right back into Calec's eyes.

"What trick is this?" Aonor asked.

"Now, please dump out the contents of the mug," Calec said. "If you will."

Aonor glared at Calec, a small twinge of a scowl wrinkling his lips. He turned the mug upside down, and brown tea sluiced from it and splattered on the ground, sprinkling and staining the master of collection's white trousers up past his ankles.

"You are a strange man, witch hunter," Aonor said.

The tea didn't turn into a block of ice, but mayhap whoever uses the mark of the witch and grabs a victim can control when and if they will burn them.

Calec smiled and strode toward the horses. "It was too hot for my tastes, but only because I am not accustomed to Valtera's steaming drinks, nothing your servants did wrong. Will you accompany me, Desi? If you will?"

"It is Lanigrad, the scholar, who is deft with the javelin, not I," Aonor said. "And javelins make holes in their victims."

Calec studied the master of collections as he mounted Ghost and rode off, thoughts of the claim and why this man would say such a thing rattling around in his mind.

50

ONCE DESI HAD FOLLOWED CALEC A STREET AWAY FROM THE manor, Calec stopped and turned Ghost to face her. Snow and ice plummeted between them.

"What was the tea thing about?" Desi pulled her palomino to a stop.

"Just this. I ask you now to take a message to each person in question. If you will, please return to Aonor immediately and tell him I know what cold winter runs through his blood. Tell him he must meet me in the place where he found his power. I will be waiting. If he shows, we can talk and may be able to work something out. If he does not, I will tell all of Valtera his dark secret."

"What does this mean? And what do you intend to do?"

"I don't know for sure yet. But if he understands, he will realize this is his last chance for redemption or he will be given to the people. And it's his last chance to face me once and for all."

Desi's face paled. "Surely, Aonor isn't—"

"For Lanigrad, please tell him that I know ice runs through his veins and that I've been made aware of how accomplished he is with the javelin. Also tell him I know how he made the history of that era go missing from the texts. He's the only man in recent times who could have removed all the tomes' pages. The remainder of what you tell the scholar should be the same as for Aonor. For Rimmell, mention that I am now aware of what burns inside him and where that feeling began. Have him meet me at that location. For Olinia, tell her I am now keen on how the coldness of her ancestors has carried down to her, and also that I am aware of her ruse during the time between leaving the tavern and arriving at the manor."

Desi slowly nodded.

And you, Desi, now knowing all of this, it will have the same effect on you. "But whatever you do, please, do not accompany any one of them to the place in question."

"And what about Climson?" Desi asked.

"He *was* there at the time of the deadly javelin throw, but he was not present on Branber's Hill when the tea inside the mug was turned into a round of ice."

"But Olinia was never present during our long wait on Branber's Hill."

Calec nodded. *She is keeping track of things as well.* "But Olinia still lied to me about what she was doing before she arrived at Ulma's manor. Please hurry and find each of these people as quickly as possible. The sun descends into the west, and we are running out of time. I will be waiting for one or more of them before nightfall."

Calec wheeled Ghost around and trotted into the vanished city.

51

CALEC DISMOUNTED BESIDE THE STAKE LOOMING OVER THE circular area known as Stake Square. Kindling was now piled and packed against the base of the stake. As if someone expected something to happen here. It hadn't been there prior. But the people Calec wanted Desi to speak to shouldn't have arrived before him.

The wolf wind howled down from the mountains and blasted through the area, keening and skirling. Snow hurtled through the square, settling into a thick layer that already rose to Calec's ankles. He hid as best he could behind the stake and watched the wide bridge leading across the river as well as the gap in the buildings directly north of the square.

An hour wound away in a flurry of pelting ice and snow, and Calec's nose and fingers turned numb with cold. He flexed and worked his hands and arms, as he might need them soon.

Dark clouds strained the light from the sun and cast the city into a world of grays. Gray skies and clouds. Gray were the buildings around him now with the falling ice and snow landing on black stones. Ghost huddled against the back wall of the housing that ran along the western side of the square.

A figure drew Calec's attention. There on the bridge. Someone in a black cloak, their hood draping and acting as protection against the elements.

Calec's sword hand jerked, and his fingers wrapped around his sword's hilt. The figure dashed across the icy bridge, but they ducked and waited behind the only corner building blocking Calec's line of site between the bridge and the northern entrance to the square.

Ghost nickered and tossed his head.

The hair on Calec's arms and neck prickled like a thousand spikes.

He drew his sword in the whispered voice of steel sliding on wood and leather, a sound crushed by the howling of the wolf wind. After waiting another few minutes, he stepped from behind the stake and approached the building where the figure hid.

Calec crept to the corner of the building and peeked around before quickly pulling back. Someone stood there with their back against the wall, waiting.

After taking a few quick swipes with his sword to warm and loosen his muscles, he stepped boldly around the corner of the building with his blade raised.

"And what do *you* wait for, cursed one?" Calec asked.

The figure jolted and faced him. "I am not the cursed." The voice was feminine. "I am waiting with you."

Desi pushed back her hood. She gripped something in her other hand but kept it concealed beneath her cloak.

Calec's spine stiffened, but it was as he expected. "Then why have you come?"

"Did you believe that only *you* could figure out what is happening? Do you think I am thick?" Desi's young face wrinkled with anger. Her tone was darker and more menacing than anything he'd heard from her. "You behave just like my father."

"I know you saw and heard everything I did." Calec lowered his sword but did not sheathe it. "Or *almost* everything. I did not know how much you put together, but I did not doubt you. Why I am a little surprised you are here is because I asked you specifically *not* to come. So, there is only one acceptable reason then for you to now stand before me. The other reason is too dark. I wish for you to speak and answer why you've come. If you will."

Desi slowly advanced as her hands worked beneath her cloak.

"Why are *you* here?" Calec asked again, something inside him screaming for him to raise his sword in protection, some rational part of him telling him Desi couldn't possibly be linked with the curse.

"Because I do not follow what men tell me to do," she said. "You or anyone. I do not linger in my house when battles are waged for life and death. When the fate of *my* city balances on the edge of a blade. When some ancient curse stabs holes in the skin of my people and burns their arms. When friends and family die around me. I do not sit idle and pray that evil will not come knocking at my door. I go out looking for it with all the others who feel bound to pursue it."

Calec nodded and hesitantly sheathed his sword. "Simply stating you never listened to your father's commands about staying behind would have sufficed. But, please, then, lady, come and wait with me behind the stake. *After* telling me how you understood the meaning of the boot and hoofprints at the original location."

"Because you described the tracks to me."

"But you were not at Ulma's when she mentioned the Horseman's path."

"*You* mentioned it. When we were at the original location. And the same person who told my mother where the others were headed told me the tale when you were missing for so long."

This woman must pay very close attention to details. "We need …"

His blood chilled like the icy rain cascading around them. There on the closer edge of the bridge stood a figure, one who appeared to have just stopped rushing across it when the figure and Calec spotted each other.

A moment drew out as everything but the falling ice and snow seemed to pause and turn silent.

The figure glanced over their shoulder at the bridge, decided against that route, and then leapt over the edge. Deft and agile. Like the fit scholar.

Calec ran after them. When he reached the edge of the bridge, he peered down. A walk of blackened stone ran along the side of the river down there and led under the bridge. The cloaked figure had already disappeared.

After drawing his sword and knife, Calec stepped over the side of the bridge and landed on the lower walk in a crouch. He glanced around. The underside of the bridge loomed ahead, as dark as night. No more world of grays. Only black.

A silhouette appeared against the light at the far side of the bridge, which seemed as distant as the other side of a long cavern. Flames sprang to life upon a torch the silhouette was carrying. Firelight outlined Desi's brown hair and a small portion of her features. She slowly advanced under the bridge and motioned for Calec to come toward her. Whatever she'd carried under her cloak before was now visible in her hand. A long steel pole, sharpened—a javelin.

Calec's senses heightened: the air seemed to grow colder, slivers of light pierced the darkness, the confined area below the bridge smelled stagnant, as if wind hadn't blown through the area in years. The sound of Desi's faraway footsteps echoed like war drums.

A javelin? Is she taunting me? Or is it the only weapon she knows how to use?

Calec inched into the darkness in a crouch, holding his sword before him, his knife at his side. Each step he took, he placed carefully and quietly as he scanned as much of the vicinity as he could.

Desi started to hurry faster.

"Desi," Calec shouted, and his voice answered in a distorted echo from the walls around them. "Be careful! Someone else is in here."

She didn't seem to listen though as she rushed toward him.

Calec quickened his pace as well, keeping his left side against the wall. Now he could feel the cold sheeting off those blackened stones. Frost crystals scaled the height of the wall, clinging to its slick surface like white netting. The Rogue River rushed by in a dark and murmuring mass to his right just beyond the edge of the walk.

He advanced faster and faster until he approached the middle of the bridge along with Desi.

"I didn't see anyone," she said from not more than ten paces ahead.

Calec caught the reflection of firelight dancing on the stones around them and then noticed a gap in the wall ahead. "There's a passage or alcove there."

Desi eyed the area and advanced, her javelin poised to skewer anything that moved.

Calec eased his way up beside her as his eyes further adjusted to the dim lighting.

A dull thud sounded behind Calec, and then the quick patter of running feet.

Calec spun about, placing his back against the wall and trying to make sure he could also keep an eye on Desi and the entrance to the alcove.

Another man came running toward them.

"That's the same alcove where Jaremonde and I found a body," Rimmell said as he broke stride but kept walking toward them.

Calec's blood hammered and whooshed in his ears.

"And what brings you to this place, Sir Rimmell?" Calec asked.

Rimmell's face was pale. "I saw you leap over the bridge as if you were chasing someone. And Desi jumped over as well. I want to help you catch this witch."

Highly unlikely, unless you are not nearly as dense as Jaremonde believed. "Then do you mind peeking into that alcove? If you will?"

Rimmell shrugged. "I've done it before."

He hurried past Calec as he smiled at Desi.

"There's another body in there." Rimmell's eyes gaped like small moons.

Calec's thoughts tumbled over each other. He could be

wrong about so many things this time. Some of his suspicions were based on Ulma's stories and could not be verified.

He approached the entrance to the alcove, and he stole a glance down its length as he attempted to watch Desi and Rimmell at the same time. The alcove ran maybe twenty paces into the bank, and a heap of something, possibly a body, lay near its dead end.

"Here, take this." Desi held out her torch, but Calec shook his head as he showed her the knife and sword in his hands.

Instead, she stooped and rolled the torch along the walk toward the alcove. Its wooden shaft turned and spun as it neared Calec, but the tongues of flame burning on its end maintained their upward state, licking at the stagnant air, lashing at the darkness.

Calec glared at Rimmell and then at Desi before saying, "Keep your distance from me, and from each other."

They nodded, and Calec sidled into the alcove with his back against a wall. He glanced deeper into the darkness and then back at Desi and Rimmell.

They did not move. Neither did the heap.

Calec neared whatever lay on the floor and stuck his sword out to touch it. A cloak. Piled high. He stuck his sword tip under a fold and lifted the cloak away. No body lay beneath.

Desi yelled.

Calec spun back. She slipped and fell onto her back with a smack. Her javelin skittered across the stones and plunged into the river with a splash.

Rimmell pressed one palm against the frost-armored wall and another against the walkway.

Calec stood straighter now, his blood surging through his heart and vessels like the turbulent Rogue River.

"It seems I don't need to ask you to hold my knife," Calec said to Rimmell. "To see if its hilt turns to ice. To prove that you can pass the cold of the frost you touch into it."

Rimmell grinned, but then he lunged and grabbed Desi as she attempted to clamber to her feet, her hands and boots sliding around as if on the slickest sheet of ice. One Rimmell had probably just placed beneath her.

Desi screamed and kicked at Rimmell, but he yanked her backward and wrapped an arm around her neck, hoisting her off the ground. Her feet kicked frantically as her face reddened, and Rimmell backed up until he stood against the wall at the corner of the alcove.

He wants to keep in contact with the frost and ice.

"Drop your sword and knife and kick them over to me," Rimmell said. "Or, in another second, Desi will be full of gaping holes."

The sputtering torch on the ground drew Calec's attention and seemed to taunt him.

His touch is so vastly cold it will create a rash of frostbite—not a burn—and it can also extinguish nearby fire.

Images of ice and snow or burned-out torches or fires in the hearths at each scene of death, as well as with the frozen mug of tea, spiraled in Calec's mind.

"Do it!" Rimmell screamed, and his voice sounded like that of an enraged king of old.

The last time Calec threw down his sword for this young woman, he was struck over the head and abducted. Was he too gullible? Too bent on trying to save young women in distress? It would be his undoing. But then again, he would never have even known of the emerald city and its people if he'd resisted the temptation, the call. Something had been gained from his actions.

Desi squirmed, but her kicking slowed. Her lips started to turn blue.

Calec's sword clattered on the alcove floor. Then he quickly switched hands holding his knife and plunged its blade through his leathers and into the armpit of his off hand. The blade slipped into the wound already there from the javelin throw and bit deep into his flesh, cutting through the gut suture that hadn't yet been removed. Pain burned up his arm, and a rush of blood drained from the injury.

Then Calec dropped the knife and squeezed his arm against

his side to stem the loss of blood. He kicked his sword over as far as he could, then the knife, which settled a few steps from Rimmell.

Rimmell watched him with a bewildered expression. "You are a strange man, witch hunter. If you'd wanted to die from my javelin throw rather than what I've planned for you since, then you should have let the javelin skewer your heart."

Calec glared at him.

Desi's struggling stopped, and Rimmell dropped her like a sack of grain. Her head thumped against stone.

"I don't want to kill this one," Rimmell said. "I want her. To be my wife. To give me children who will also carry my magic."

Rimmell picked up Calec's knife, stepped over to his sword, eyed that blade for a moment, and then kicked it a bit farther, where it dropped over the edge of the walk and splashed into the river.

"A poor fate for such a finely crafted weapon," Rimmell said, "but I fear that I wouldn't have the appropriate skills to use it against you. I am much better with what I've been given."

Rimmell turned and scraped the hilt of Calec's knife against the wall, peeling up frost and rubbing it around the handle. Then Rimmell grasped the handle but held the knife behind his back as he approached Calec.

He still prefers to use the cold against me.

Calec glanced around. Only the dead end of the alcove and the heaped cloak lay in the darkness around him. There was no escape, and he was unarmed.

His armpit throbbed, and a pool of blood gathered and soaked his leathers. He lifted his wounded arm away from his body and let the blood run more freely, to drain in a rivulet. To drip and splatter on the stone. He tore off his left glove, dropped it, and rolled his sleeve up his forearm.

Calec steeled himself.

Rimmell advanced, Calec's knife held behind him, his clutching hand before him. The hand that created the marks of the witch's burn. Frostbite.

"You cannot evade me now, witch hunter. And then there

will be no one but the Horseman and Desi, my future obedient wife, to know what magic I carry. It will again be my secret to use as and when I wish." He paused for a moment. "Does the thought of cold writhing in your bones terrify you? More than a blade to the heart or throat?"

Rimmell seemed to ponder it, but Calec rushed a few steps toward him, making Rimmell raise his hand in defense.

"And so you deserve the winter death." Rimmell advanced. "I believe the cold is your weakness anyway."

Calec backed into the dead end, his hands working against the walls.

"It's an exquisite pain," Rimmell said. "Being frozen from the inside out. A burning like fire but with a different flavor. Nothing burns quite like the cold."

"So that is why you do it? To bring more pain to people's lives?"

"I do it for the fools of this city. For fools like Jaremonde who see nothing before them. Who show no respect and believe *I* am the dense one. At least he did right up until the moment he saw and experienced the pain of my magic. They all did. A mocking comment here. Laughter from a group of adolescents there. A constable who believed I was as inept as he was. But winter's fire burns deep inside me, witch hunter. I am blessed. It is a gift. A way to deal with them. A power over others that I can choose to use when they anger me. And so many have tossed insults my way. For years, I took all their comments in stride and could only smile them off. Then ... then there was the time I visited Stake Square and I felt it. My power. After that, it wasn't long before a young woman ridiculed me. I grabbed her. And *it* happened. I only wish you could feel the ecstasy of it once. You would understand. To hold someone and do that to them from the inside. I will just have to show you instead."

Rimmell stepped within three paces of Calec.

Calec's chest heaved. His armpit throbbed and dripped blood. Ideas and doubts continued to spin in his mind. Thoughts about the murders. Those who bled out from punctures all over their skin. He had no escape. No weapons.

Rimmell stepped closer, and Calec reached out with his wounded arm, almost an offer. But he did so subtly, as if attempting to shove Rimmell back.

Rimmell's icy grip wrapped around Calec's wrist, and Calec grimaced in pain. Burning like a red-hot lance being shoved through his skin rode up his arm. A gust of wind as chill and harsh as any he'd ever felt blasted around him. His skin turned blue, as if a wave washed through its length. His blood froze. At first in his hand. Water expanded as it became ice, and that ice tore through his jagged veins and cut and stuck out through his skin. Tiny little red icicles of blood.

When they thawed, he would bleed out. Or he would freeze to death first.

Calec attempted to jerk his arm back, but Rimmell's grip was like a vice, or their skin was now frozen together. The movement only caused Rimmell to stumble closer.

Calec howled in pain and dropped to his knees as he placed his free hand beside his bleeding armpit. He fought to maintain some shred of concentration as howling wind reminiscent of the worst of any winter's wolf wind berated him and pulled at his hair and beard, lashed at his cheeks.

Rimmell's ghastly grin broadened as he stooped but still loomed over Calec.

The same freezing of flesh and blood crept up Calec's arm as pain overrode all other thoughts. Shards of ice extruded from the skin of his forearm in larger holes than in his hand. These new shards were the size of their enlarging parent veins. The size of quill tips.

Calec grimaced, the seconds passing like minutes or hours.

Icy cold burned farther up his arm and into the larger arteries and veins. The blood draining from his armpit solidi-fied. And it was shoved outward as his more peripheral blood expanded and froze.

Calec's fist tightened about the area.

When a large icicle of blood formed between his fingers, an icicle about the size of a spike, he snapped his wrist, broke the icicle off at its base, and plunged it into Rimmell's looming eye.

The red icicle buried deep with a tear and a pop.

Rimmell shrieked and toppled over backward, releasing Calec's arm and using that hand to cover his wounded face. He hit the blackened stones with a smack. Blood poured in rivers around his fingers. He shrieked again and crawled away, flailing and slipping on the stones.

He continued to scamper away from Calec and slip as his limbs jerked erratically. Then his clawing and scraping arm found nothing but empty air.

He plunged over the walk and hit the dark mass of the Rogue River with a splash.

His body swirled in the water beyond, face up, staring at the underside of the bridge, one of his eyes viewing it all through an icicle of blood.

Then the snapping sound of ice forming followed.

And the river froze around Rimmell, encasing his floating body in a sphere of ice.

Rimmell, the icicle, and the sphere all bobbed as the current rushed them away.

52

Calec collapsed. Under the flickering torchlight, his arm appeared as blue as mountain water. No black rash yet, only a white ring where Rimmell had grabbed him. And shards of ice speckled his left hand and forearm. The bleeding from his armpit had ceased amidst the frozen blood there, but his head spun.

Cold climbed up into his shoulder and chest. His teeth chattered.

A chilling darkness swooped in and surrounded his vision. His insides burned like fire.

Then everything started to numb. First his left arm, then his chest. His extremities.

Hypothermia. That's what Father called it.

His teeth banged against each other, and he could not stop his jaw from quaking.

He lay there and attempted to wrap the other cloak on the ground around him, but that would only protect him from losing body heat and from the cold outside. More layers might only trap the cold inside him.

He curled into a ball, no longer able to control his body or limbs.

The last thing he saw was veiled sunlight fading beyond the burned-out torch.

Twilight was coming.
The vanished city would be leaving him soon.

53

THE CRACKLE OF A WARM FIRE CARRIED OVER THE WIND, THE sound seeming soft and inviting.

But the cold lingered, and he could not feel his limbs. He didn't even know *who* he was or where he was exactly. And his eyelids weighed as much as portcullis gates.

The wind blew over him.

Calec cracked an eye open as his brain recalled names and memories. The plains. The emerald city had vanished again. Surely he would freeze out here alone and injured and weak.

A fire burned low in the grass before him, a torch lying at its base, its handle touching his booted foot. He remembered a torch similar to or the same as this one. He remembered it rolling across the floor of the alcove under the bridge.

Calec groaned and sat up, his skin and muscles cold. The plains surrounded him, as well as a night with veiled moons. Snow drifted lightly in the air, although the wolf wind was merely a remnant of its typical winter self.

Throbbing rose along his left arm. A large bandage had been wadded up under his armpit and tied about his shoulder. His hand was gloved again, and his sleeve covered his arm. Fear of what the skin beneath his glove looked like swirled in his mind, and he tentatively peeled the glove off his hand. The skin of his left hand was pale, and circles filled with clotted blood dotted the back of it. But the skin was not blue, and no shards or lines of ice protruded through his skin. There was no black rash, only a ring of pale skin the color of a ghost. He flexed his fingers. They were stiff and resistant and a bit numb, but they bent to his will. His arm and hand seemed to have thawed during the time he was resting close to this fire. And he'd not been held long enough to develop the blackened and dead skin of severe frostbite. At least that was his hope. Sometimes it took longer for the evidence of frostbite to develop.

But how did he get here? And who lit the flames?

His mouth felt as dry as dusty old parchment, and a thirst called to him from deep inside. He found his waterskin lying in the grass by his feet, full of warm water, and he drank and drank.

Tea. With honey and grass flavors. It warmed his blood and quenched his deep thirst.

He felt around in his armpit. The bandage was dry, although spots of blood seeped through it. And a piece of parchment was held inside the outer wrap and tie.

Calec ripped the parchment free and unfolded it, turning it so that the firelight shone on its face.

Sir Calec,

The plains have remained a mystery to my people over the past century, as we rarely see the same place twice. I cannot find you like you can find me. So I will not be there if or when you wake, but if you do, please find us at least one last time. Otherwise, I will search all the plains for you for the rest of my life.

Desi

And please stop cutting your stitches out before your injury has healed. You tend to lose a lot of blood when you do that.

.   .   .

Calec almost laughed, but the sound came out as more of a croak. Tears crowded around his eyes. He was still alive, although he realized he had come too close to never seeing Serileen again and never laying eyes on his future son or daughter. One who would be strong enough to survive in this world. He looked for the yellow ribbon on his wrist. Still there.

The fire blazed on, and Calec noticed there was more than a torch burning. Kindling lay around the flames, feeding a fire that was protected from the wind by an incline and the taller grasses around him.

Kindling.

The only kindling he remembered had surrounded that stake in Stake Square. Kindling that hadn't been there before. Maybe Desi had even ventured out of the city, gathered more, and placed it around a torch so both would be left behind when the city vanished. But if she'd gotten a torch from outside Valtera ... who would it have been from? The nomads? Or if Calec was touching the objects or they were now considered his possessions, then maybe they stayed with him.

The finer points of the curse were still confusing. If anyone knew these answers, it would be the people of Valtera, although they probably never had to really worry about it, as they were always part of the city.

At least this kindling was used to save a life rather than to take it by burning flesh at the stake.

Something else lay in the grass beside Calec, the firelight reflecting off of it like a mirror. A polished blade. The intricate hilt of a longsword. *His* longsword. *And* his knife. Left behind in the wake of the city ... or Desi had somehow recovered them and placed them beside him.

That left only one other thing—Ghost.

Calec struggled to find his feet but stole a glance around the moonlit plains. A bay horse stood grazing just beyond a tussock of grass.

Calec's heart lifted free from some great weight, and a smile tugged at his lips.

"Now what stories do you have to tell?" Calec asked Ghost.

"The horse still does not belong to you," a voice said from across the fire.

Calec crouched and spun about. A face and white hair were partially visible through a distorted curtain of heat and flames. Calec had seen that face through fire before. Gomdon of the nomads.

"The young woman raced out from the walls on that steed, shouting for aid and for us," Gomdon said. "She wished to find something before night fell. We confronted her, but she claimed the horse was hers, as she and her people traded with us for the gelding *before* abducting you. She said they left the horse with you but that you did not trade them for it. So we let her go on her way after she traded with us for a torch and kindling. She pleaded with eyes so full of entreaty that I could not resist her spell. She asked that in the coming night, if we saw a fire burning in the area where the city had been, could we please ride to it. And if we found a man there, could we please make sure the man survives till morning. I promised her we would."

"Then you have almost succeeded," Calec said. "But I must depart before making sure you fulfill your promise. Before morning arrives, or I won't be able to find the city."

"You could stay through the following day," another man said. Runik stood from the grasses off to the side of the fire. "We could play the *gramdel* game again. I will not lose my temper to a novice of the plains, as you are no longer that. And I will best you."

Memories of that bizarre game hit Calec in a rush. "I'll only stay if I can play Mitag this time."

"I could find him," Runik said.

Calec shook his head. "As much fun as that sounds, I'd rather be off this night while the moonlight still shines."

"There is one thing you must see first." Gomdon stood and paced away to Calec's left while waving for Calec to follow.

Calec's knees wobbled, and his left arm burned, but he

managed to trail after the nomad leader for several strides. Gomdon stopped in the grass ahead and stared at the ground.

When Calec arrived, he saw what Gomdon was looking at, and it made his blood flush with cold. A swath of ice lay on the plains and formed a wavy appearance as if flowing water had frozen in place. There were no clear details in the ice, not like a sculpture, but there was the suggestion that two distorted ice hands emerged from the waves at the edge of its circular shape. And a face could be imagined between the hands at the surface of the ice waves. But the clearest aspect of the entire spectacle was a red spike of ice protruding from what could have been an eye socket in that face.

"This will become a sacred site," Gomdon said. "And a landmark of history for the people of the plains."

Calec's stomach rippled with nausea, and the pints of tea in those dark depths sloshed around. "Surely it will melt."

Gomdon shook his head. "Curses cannot be broken by natural or unintentional means. Have you not seen the frozen areas at the original site of the emerald city? Those areas linger, always."

These lands are cursed still. "Then how are curses broken?"

"Have you not heard the tales? There are rules and limits to any curse. No man or woman inside or outside the city can dispel the magic trapped in Valtera."

"I've heard that claim several times since coming here, but it doesn't leave many options."

Gomdon frowned. "Perhaps. Perhaps not. There may still be a way to rid the plains of the ice at the city's original location. And more importantly, those black prints."

Images of the Horseman's blackened boot prints and those spiked hoofprints formed in Calec's mind. The ones Desi could not see. It must only be the inhabitants of Valtera who could not see them. "And how do we rid the plains of those?"

Gomdon shrugged. "I am no expert in curses. If you wish, you may speak with our shaman man and woman. We've discussed many options, but we have never attempted them, as we feared retaliation by the ghosts of the plains or by this horse walker who left his dark prints. We fear what he may do to our people if his curse on the emerald city fails." Gomdon paced about for a moment. "But if *you* find a way to break the curse, it should not fall back on us. What both of our shamans seem to believe is that if the footprints of the evil horse walker are removed from the land, the curse will be broken. As long as the stake where the evil act took place is also destroyed. And no man or woman can remove the ice or the stake. Those are the laws and protective properties of this curse, according to all legend. Thus the shamans claim these laws are true."

"It is only the ice that doesn't melt that preserves the Horseman's prints," Calec said to himself.

Calec pondered ways to melt ice but couldn't think of how to do it without having a person involved. A mammoth would be large enough to do considerable damage, but how would he ever convince such a beast to tear up a specific area of ice? Even with food laid out over the spot, a mammoth would not spend time tearing up every last sheet of ice. And only a person would willingly carry water or fire to the area.

After a few minutes, Calec turned back for Ghost.

"I still wish to find the city one last time," Calec said. "Whether the curse can be broken or not is another matter."

"Ride the night plains well, Wolf Tongue." Gomdon raised a hand in a farewell salute. "There are greater dangers here than us."

Calec climbed onto Ghost's saddle and studied his sword. South. Away from the mountains.

"On second thought," Calec said. "I think I would like to stay. If you will. To rest and recover from my grievous injuries."

"For how long?" Gomdon asked, folding his arms over his chest and raising an eyebrow.

"For as long as it takes until the vanished city once again lies very near to this area or to the north of us."

54

Calec rode through the gates of Valtera one last time.

Nine days and nights of rest and eating and drinking with Gomdon and Runik and the nomads had passed. Ghost appeared well rested, and Calec felt stronger. He'd waited until the Demon's Coin moon finally showed the city lying to the north—this time to the northeast—of where he'd been with the nomads. With the mountains looming so close to where he'd been, he then knew that Valtera couldn't be too many leagues away. And that also meant the city would once again be near its original location.

People milled about the streets in the early morning before dawn, crying or hugging, drinking, and laughing. Some patted Calec's legs as he rode past, but most didn't seem to notice him.

News of their supposed witch's death must have only gotten around the city somewhat recently.

Calec arrived at Desi's house and knocked on her doorway.

The door swung inward.

"Sir Calec." Desi's eyes glowed with happiness.

Calec nodded. "I've come for one last request."

"Anything." She motioned for him to come inside.

"I wish to know—"

Muffled voices came from the back room, but the door to that chamber was again closed.

Desi glanced over her shoulder. "It's just Mother."

Talking to herself?

"I only wish Father were here to love her until she died," Desi said.

"But that love died some time ago." Calec strained to pick up more from the voices.

Desi's lips tightened and thinned. "How ... Yes, it's true. Father sought the company of other women before Mother even turned ill. They grew apart long before."

"But do not despair. She's found love again."

"What makes you say that?"

"Do I have to go and open the door?"

Desi studied him for the duration of a held breath. "No. I can. But only if you promise not to tell anyone in Valtera. Such ... ways are not tolerated or accepted here. I only wish to see her happy."

"I do not need to disturb—"

"No. She actually wants to see you. As long as you promise not to speak of it."

"I will not tell a soul what my eyes reveal."

Desi swallowed and shuffled to the door to the back chamber. She knocked lightly before opening it.

Inside, Desi's mother's gray face peered over a blanket as she sat up in bed. Another woman—Olinia the saddle maker—cradled Desi's mother's head and smoothed down her hair. A faint smile even lingered on the mother's lips, but it faded.

"Mother," Desi said. "Sir Calec has arrived."

"Yes, I see that." She eyed Calec. "You have done more than I can thank you for, man of the woods. I have wished for the deaths to stop before I left this world, and you have granted me this wish. You've also made my daughter very happy. You both have my blessing, if you seek it."

Calec's heart tumbled over in his chest. *Her blessing?*

He glanced at Desi as red swipes rose in her cheeks. "Mother, he is only here to say goodbye."

"I'm sorry," Calec said.

The mother waved off Calec's remark. "If only Valtera would

return to the base of the mountains and stop leaping about the plains like some giant jackrabbit. I'd love to see that as well. As well as all the buildings shining emerald under the sun. And I'd like to see my daughter wed. But I know not to rush her." She grinned at Desi.

"Mother!" Desi shook her head. "I will return shortly."

Desi motioned for Calec to step out of the room as she did so herself, closing the door to the bedchamber behind them.

"How did you know?" Desi asked.

"About Olinia?"

She nodded.

"Well, your mother knew the others were going to Ulma's manor, and the only one who would have told her besides you— *if* you were spying on them at the tavern—was Olinia."

A faraway look glazed Desi's eyes. "Olinia was there for her when she needed it, even before she'd fallen ill. They became great friends and even fell in love. Now Olinia helps care for her more than even I do, her own child."

"Nerves and distrust kept me wary of Olinia and *you* some of the time, but I wasn't too concerned about any carrier of the curse being a woman, because the parts of Ulma's tales that I could confirm proved true. So I had faith in most of the rest. And Ulma's story claimed that the curse would only be passed down to males. I fully believed it ... at least until I was under that dark bridge with you."

A moment of silence fell over them, and something rattled in a cage at the back of Calec's mind. Something Desi had just said. *Her own child.*

The yellow ribbon on his wrist seemed to grow light, to almost float and tug at his hand. The child's ribbon.

The children.

Desi studied Calec's expression, and she said, "Lanigrad and some others are looking into Rimmell's family and their history."

"Desi." Calec took her by the arms. "We need to gather the group of children who demanded the sweeties from Ulma. And we need to take them out to the original site of Valtera before the emerald city moves too far away."

Desi's expression lifted into one of surprise. "Why?"

"Because I have a hunch about this curse."

55

DESI LED A GROUP OF CHILDREN AWAY FROM THE ROGUE RIVER, the actual river flowing down from the northern mountains. Not the one that moved with their city. These children all carried buckets up to the area where Stake Square had originally resided. A fire burned there now, made and attended by more children. It'd taken several hours to gather the children of Valtera and get everything ready, and the sun was already well past midday.

Masses of men and women surrounded the area, watching the children work. These people spoke little, and when they did it was in hushed voices.

Calec waited for the children to arrive at the fire, and he absently ran a finger along the yellow ribbon tied to his wrist. The symbol of a child, his child.

Children are not yet men or women. The ancient curse may yet be broken. Its laws only claimed that no man or woman from inside or outside the city could break it.

He watched one boy with a circular scar on his hand dish heated water from a kettle into a bucket for Kirya. Calec imagined he could see those three marks on Kirya's arm, the marks not of a witch, but from an old woman she'd pushed too far.

Kirya's twin braids bounced as she turned with the bucket and came toward Calec.

"I'm sorry that message scared Father into making me give it to you," Kirya said to Calec, but Calec dismissed her worries with an amicable wave. "I knew it was bad."

Calec pointed to the black boot marks and hoofprints buried in the layers of ice. "Those are the deep-seated tracks of the Horseman."

"So I'm really breaking a curse now?" Kirya asked, grinning. "From a real witch? Even though I can't see the marks she made?"

"I hope the curse breaking will prove true. But I do not know for sure. The only thing I do know is that there was no real witch involved in this entire affair."

"You have a chance to become Valtera's hero," Desi said as she patted Kirya's head.

Kirya dumped steaming water onto the area of the boot prints. The ice around the prints hissed and sputtered as the liquid hit it, and steam boiled up and formed a dark cloud in the air. Kirya shouted and jumped back.

"It feels strange!" Kirya waved to dispel the cloud. "It's tingling my skin."

A gust of wolf wind howled down from the mountains and tore the cloud to tatters before driving its remnants away.

The little boy, with the help of a few others, followed Kirya's lead and dumped water around the ice in the area.

A distant echo, like a cry of warning or pain, carried over the plains, and everyone looked about for its source before eyeing each other warily.

More children arrived and poured water all around the circle of ice, starting at the base of the stake. Several others then used shovels to dig into the newly exposed earth around the stake.

Calec glanced northward to Manor Hill. Another group of children worked up there.

Hours passed slowly as all the adults of Valtera were forced to watch their youngest children work.

Late afternoon arrived before the children finally finished washing away the ice at both locations. Only dirt remained beneath those areas. A mass of children heaved at the stake, and it toppled over and clattered on the hard earth. Then it lay still as if dead. Nothing more than some long-forgotten post.

Calec and all the citizens of Valtera waited with bated breaths, watching the sites the children had worked on as well as all the previous lands of their city.

Minutes crawled along and died away. Another hour. Even more. One by one people—both men and women and children —muttered, turned, and began to leave the area and head in the direction of Valtera's most recent location.

"It was worth a try," Desi said as she patted Calec's arm. "Even I was hopeful there for a while."

"You mean it's not going to work?" Kirya whined and looked at her blistered hands. "I'm not going to be a hero? All that work for nothing?"

"I'm sorry, Kirya." Desi ruffled her hair. "It was fun to pretend, but the curse is not broken. At least not the less dangerous portion of the curse."

Kirya threw her bucket down and stomped away. The other children followed her. Desi trailed behind them, and Calec regretfully did as well. He'd allowed them all to get their hopes up with the thought of breaking a curse none of these people had ever lived without. And now he'd dashed those hopes upon the plains.

At least I helped rid them of a killer. Calec felt a bit better with that thought, but the ribbon on his wrist seemed to weigh a full stone now.

"I commend you for trying." Climson stepped forward from the masses and clutched Calec's wrist. "A damn sight that would have been. To see Valtera back in its rightful place against the mountains."

Climson turned with the others, and all the recently curious and hopeful of Valtera tromped back across the plains in one great pilgrimage. The last of the Valterians. The sun hovered just over the western horizon but threw long shadows across the plains, marking the people in shadow and light.

Calec took Ghost's reins and followed them, his head hanging as he went.

"Calec." Lanigrad emerged from a margin of the masses, hurrying away from them as he approached Calec and Desi. He nodded politely to Desi. "He had no living parents or siblings at all."

"Rimmell?" Desi asked.

Lanigrad nodded vigorously. "He was orphaned around five years of age and had no known brothers or sisters. The lineage on his end was sketchy, but it seemed his mother was probably the descendant of the clanswoman Ulma spoke of. The bloodline is broken."

A breath of relief escaped Desi's lips. "Then there are none we have to keep a close watch on."

"I am enormously relieved." Lanigrad unrolled a parchment. "Yet I still wonder why these types of murders occurred soon after the time of the witch's burning, or freezing rather, and then not again until recently."

"Maybe there were a lot of women in the bloodline," Desi said.

Lanigrad looked over his parchment and nodded. "From what I've been able to piece together in a short time, that appears to be true, but there were men as well."

"Maybe those were good men," Calec said. "Born with cursed blood, but they learned to control themselves and not use their magic to harm others. Maybe they learned to be content with themselves and their anger. Or maybe they didn't and each day was a battle, but they conquered their own silent demons anyway."

Memories of Calec's childhood and the hate he'd witnessed from those who knew of his witch mother and his cursed blood boiled up from the deep recesses of his mind.

"But we cannot know for sure," Desi said. "Rimmell's mother could have had brothers and sisters with children of their own."

"We don't know for sure," Lanigrad replied. "Not yet. But I'll be spending many months tracking down every bit of information I can on the matter."

They walked together, trailing behind the hundreds of Valterians, a sullen silence now cast across the plains with only the song of the wolf wind to ease whatever ache lay deep inside the chests of these people. A lone figure appeared on the plains to Calec's right, a stooped old woman in a black hat and dress.

She approached them, walking with a limp but moving as quickly as most of the departing crowd. When she stood ten paces away from Calec and Desi, she stopped.

"You give up too easily," Ulma said. "You will not make it to my age by doing that. I did not give up walking because of my ankle. I did not give up my stories just because there was no longer anyone who wanted to hear them."

She pointed to the mountains.

Calec glanced back. The bare site of Valtera's land and the rolling foothills were all that remained beside the river.

"There is no emerald city," Lanigrad said. "And there never will be again."

Ulma shook her head. "Not yet."

The last of the sunlight dipped below the horizon. Purple and pink streaks ran rampant through the clouds. Then stars began to speckle the sky in the far east.

Twilight.

Calec's blood tingled. He moved to stand beside Ulma. Desi joined them.

Minutes slipped by in silence, and the light of the plains dimmed. Twilight faded.

Then it happened.

The city appeared under moonlight at the base of the mountains. Its last vanishing and reappearance.

But this time it was so much easier to make out in the darkness even though there were no glimmering reflections of moonlight against black stone. Nothing shining like mirrors.

The city gleamed in the night like a forest full of bright green trees reclaiming its place at the foot of the mountains.

The emerald city had returned.

56

THE PEOPLE OF VALTERA HOLLERED AND CLAPPED AND CRIED AS they tore past Calec and Desi and Ulma, racing to their city.

None of them had vanished with Valtera's final leap. Ulma paced after them, but Desi remained behind with Calec.

It might have been easier if Desi had vanished. She glanced off into the moonlit plains.

"You can stay," she said. "If you wish."

Calec's insides cramped. Thoughts of his need to travel assaulted him and called to him. Not long ago, the woods had seemed to trap him in a world without change. He'd felt the urge to return to his ways and venture between different worlds. To seek new sights. Now that temptation called to him with its strongest voice. To live in Valtera ... His need to travel was real. But the city before him suddenly reminded him of his woods.

The yellow ribbon on his wrist caught his attention. It didn't feel as heavy as it had before.

And an overwhelming sensation of relief flooded him. As well as images of Serileen and the woods. Of their unborn child. Of friends he was making. Of the ways of the people of the woods, which he was learning. He'd chosen the woods before, after the winter plague. And his need to travel was more than satiated for the time being. It would likely rise again, but for now, all he wanted was home—the woods.

"I ... Desi," Calec said. "I wish I could. I really do ... if things were different."

"But?"

He chose to make his response light. "What if Valtera vanishes again? I would not follow it or you. I'd always be left behind."

Desi chuckled, but it sounded as if tears choked the sound. "Things will be different here now. More celebrations and happiness again. Less needing to hurry out to sow seeds we'll never see the rewards of. And if you wish to think about it, know that there have been a couple of others who have become part of or who have left Valtera. A person or two during the last century. A rare man or woman of Valtera who has gone out and fallen in love and married one of the clans people who keep their distance from us. And once that marriage was sealed, that person no longer vanished with Valtera. They broke away from it. The same is said to have happened with a clansperson who married a citizen of Valtera. They became part of Valtera and vanished with it. Or so the stories go."

Thoughts of the possibility made Calec's mind spin and ache. "I thought you never wanted to be forced to marry."

Desi tore her sky-sea blue eyes away from him and stared off into the distance. "That was before. When you first arrived. Things are ... different now."

Calec's heart pattered in his chest with the admission. It'd seemed more like a jest than an offer at first.

"It is not just that," Calec said. "I have a mate in the woods. And she carries my child."

Desi nodded. "Of course."

"But I can also offer you a chance to leave Valtera. If you've only ever sought to escape and find a life of your own. I can offer you a place in the woods. Our people will accept you."

Several long minutes of silence passed under moonlight, time drawing out and lasting much longer than it had when Calec considered her offer. Desi was smart and hardworking and would make a good addition to the people of the woods.

"I cannot." Desi faced away but then turned to him with

tears in her eyes. "All that I despised lived in Valtera, but all I love is there too. And I cannot abandon them to rebuild and find their heritage and their lands without me. I cannot leave my mother. Not now. The emerald city *is* my home."

She rushed up and hugged Calec, kissed his cheek, and hurried off toward the city and its gleaming walls of emerald.

Ghost's reins suddenly felt much heavier in Calec's hands.

"But this is your horse," Calec shouted after her.

She glanced back. "Consider him yours. The price for an abduction gone wrong. The best abduction I've ever been part of. Take him to his new home in the woods. And may he live out the rest of his days there."

She waved and ran to the city's gates, disappearing from Calec's sight for the last time.

Home. I want to stay there for a very long time.

Calec patted Ghost's neck and climbed into his saddle.

"Do we ride for Jaylen's Pass and the woods?" Ghost seemed to ask.

Calec untied the yellow ribbon from his wrist and wrapped it around his belt again. "For the woods, *and* for Serileen. I also have another horse there for you to meet. His name is Wyndstrom. He's my destrier from my days as a knight. He is much younger than you, and larger and thicker. But you can probably teach him a thing or two. You both should get along splendidly."

Calec kept his sword sheathed as they rode west into the moonlight, away from the light of the Demon's Coin moon.

~

Thank You! And for the good of the realm, Please Read!

I want to thank you, reader, for taking a chance on an unknown. For taking the time and risking your imagination on *Knights, Witches, and the Vanished City* and a book in the *Calec of the Woods Mystery Thriller* series. Without readers, books and most stories would be lost, and without your support, I could not continue to write and dream.

Please, if you enjoyed *Knights, Witches, and the Vanished City* or any of the *Calec of the Woods Mystery Thriller* series, consider rating or quickly reviewing them on **AMAZON**.

Every single review is important and aids me in practicing my art and standing out among millions of other books by encouraging other readers to take a chance while also showing Amazon the book is worth promoting. A review is the single most powerful thing a reader can do for an author. Reviews make all the difference in the digital book world where each year hundreds of thousands of authors spar for your attention and a place in your heart.

My vow and oath to you, reader, is that I will always continue to treat my skills like a blade and continue to sharpen them, and I will not stop looking for stories to bring into our world.

A fan of all those who still dare to read and tread the worlds of imagination,

Ryan

R.M. Schultz

Review and/or Rate Here: ***Knights, Witches, and the Vanished City***

~

Books in this Series - Calec of the Woods Mystery Thrillers

Knights, Witches, and Murder

Knights, Necromancers, and Murder

. . .

Knights, Witches, and the Missing

Knights, Witches, and the Vanished City

(The Missing and The Vanished City - Set)

Knights, Witches, and Sacrifice

Knights, Witches, and the Undead

Knights, Witches, and Those Who Walk in the Night

(Sacrifice, The Undead, and Those Who Walk in the Night - Set)

Knights, Witches, and the Afflicted

Knights, Witches, and the Dragon of the Lake

Knights, Witches, and the Final Death - to be released in mid to late 2024

(The Afflicted, the Dragon, and the Final Death - Set)

∼

YOUR FREE BOOK IS WAITING ... (for a limited time)

If you enjoyed Knights, Witches, and the Vanished City, you'll probably love Knights, Necromancers, and Murder:

Murders are occurring in a fantastical city by the sea.

For over a year these events have plagued Red Pike's Landing. And no one has been able to find the killer who takes all the fingernails of their victims and tucks them into bed.

Witnesses are unreliable ... but for good reason. Perhaps magic lies at the heart of these deeds and covers the Necromancer's tracks.

Get a FREE Full Copy of the book while it's still available

Knights, Necromancers, and Murder: A Calec of the Woods Mystery Thriller **here:**

https://rmschultzauthor.com/landing-page/

EXCERPT FROM KNIGHTS, WITCHES, AND SACRIFICE

The magical mysteries are growing, and the arcane is becoming more potent. Do you have the imagination to solve them?

With several unique ideas that haven't been seen before, a new book in the series is expected to be published every couple to few months in 2023.

Calec crept through the dark tunnel as he unsheathed his knife. This passage descended into the floor of the monastery, something none of the other hallways did.

His torchlight flickered off gray stone that seemed even older or longer forgotten than the stones above. And the air was heavier and more humid. It all smelled of something ancient. Scattered rocks rolled under his feet, or he kicked them, and they clattered on ahead in the darkness.

The walls around him narrowed, the ceiling lowering, so nothing of any substantial size could slip past him without him noticing.

Then light broke out ahead. An opening in the wall. He eased his way toward it, keeping an eye out for any traps or surprises as he went.

When he reached the opening, he peered out over the jungle

that sprawled to the horizon far below. It was merely an opening in the cliff face below the level of the monastery.

Sunlight poured in but didn't carry far into the passageway. There were no switchback stairs above or below the opening, and the exit appeared to face north. The opposite side of the mountain as the stairs he'd climbed.

The northern face.

He glanced straight down but stayed away from the edge. Somewhere far below, along that expanse at the foot of the mountain, he'd wandered about searching for flowers.

An old basket hung beside the exit on a system of pulleys, but this basket was more of a cage and was large enough to fit a person inside. Not like those baskets waiting below the stairway. Those baskets appeared only large enough to be able to haul goods up the cliff. But the rope holding this basket appeared aged, heavily frayed in several spots around the pulleys, as if it were very old or used far too much. Coils of rope lay on the floor just beside the opening, and these coils were stacked so high it was likely the basket could lower a person to the jungle below. However, it was questionable if the old rope would be strong enough to support any man or woman's weight.

Lin couldn't have traveled to the northern cliffs while we were in the jungle and then used this basket to come up to the monastery, cut Asu, and return to the jungle, could he?

Plants like those along the prayer walk grew in clumps and speckled the rock face of the mountain just outside the opening, but Calec was too afraid to stick his head out far and have a good look at the cliffs. He sheathed his knife and braced with one hand against the inner wall, found a good solid grip—tugged on it to make sure—and peered over the edge. Jagged stone cliffs plunged downward. Colorful birds swirled around areas of the mountain and landed in nests far below.

Something rustled in one of the plants growing along the cliff opposite the basket.

Calec set his torch down and leaned closer. It would be impossible for a man to hide in there. And the child he'd seen hiding in a plant before probably wouldn't be able to conceal herself either. Even if she were an expert climber.

He paused and let his senses reach out as he closed his eyes, fearing another small bird with a golden head.

Some presence lingered, something he'd never felt before, hiding in the brush, but he had the vague sensation that a snake lurked in those fronds. However, there should not be a snake on this steep of a cliff. Or could there be? There were plenty of birds to hunt, and a snake might be able to scale the jagged rock.

Calec considered ignoring it, but he didn't want to leave any stone unturned. He reached for the closest broad leaf of the plant, for an area he could see well and wouldn't have to worry about getting bitten by a venomous serpent lurking beneath.

He grabbed the leaf and shook it before quickly letting go and retracting his hand.

Something burst from the plant and scaled up the cliff away from him, moving as easily as a squirrel walking across a branch.

A lizard about as long as his forearm. But not orange and black. Spined down its back. And around the rear of its neck and elbows, more spikes as long as its body poked out. It was camouflaged in scales of silver and green but with a shimmery blue underside. It eyed Calec as it flicked a long tongue and came to a halt.

A shiver rippled down Calec's back.

Could this be the elusive mountain dragon?

It appeared similar to the tattoos he'd seen of the creature. A sense of awe settled over him.

Calec watched it closely. "Do you know where the demon who haunts the monastery has gone?"

The lizard flicked its tongue, and it pivoted about on the stones to face him. It didn't retreat or advance. "You have found my abode. My den and lair, Sir Calec," it seemed to say.

Calec suppressed a smile.

Then it ran at him, down the cliff like a sprinting serpent. It opened its mouth, and flame burst from the dark pit within, billowing toward Calec.

Calec jolted and heaved himself back inside the tunnel with his one gripping hand.

Fire flew over the opening. Not enough to engulf the area, but a cone of it large enough it would have hit Calec in the face and charred his hair and skin if not his eyes.

The god of fire.

Calec lurched away from the opening and backpedaled into the tunnel, afraid the creature might slip in after him. It moved *much* quicker than he did.

Knights, Witches, and Sacrifice

ACKNOWLEDGMENTS

Thank you to the following people for their insight into this mystery and into the mystery of writing.

To Matt Schultz for reading and editing the first sorry version of every book I write.

To Jason Weersma for cheering me on from the beginning.

To Laura Josephsen for the most detailed questions and concerns I'd ever consider.

ABOUT THE AUTHOR

After reading Tolkien, R.M. Schultz wrote his first 100,000-word fantasy novel as a freshman in high school. When he's not saving animals, he continues reading and writing fantasy and science fiction, and has done so for over two decades. R.M. founded and heads the North Seattle Science Fiction and Fantasy Writers' Group and has published over a dozen novels.

R.M.'s books have won multiple awards, including bronze and gold medals for fantasy. His latest series is being adapted into a video game! The game is slated to be released in the fall to winter of 2024. He has written and performed several songs—calling them dragon shanties—for the world that will be included with the music played for the game.

And more than anything, he wants to be knighted by George R.R. Martin.

www.rmschultzauthor.com

ISBN-13: 9798845619495

Published by Sky Sea and Sword Publishing

www.rmschultzauthor.com

Printed in Great Britain
by Amazon